AT THE END OF ALL THINGS

Terence West

AT THE END OF ALL THINGS

DOUBLE DRAGON

Dedication

To Lexi, who I am more and more proud of every
day, and
To Chere, who keeps me on the right path, and
To Duncan, Connor, and Barkley, who stand by me,
and make me smile, no matter what.
Thank you.

Chapter One

They started to awaken.

As they once again became cognizant, the chaos that engulfed this realm screamed in their minds with the voices of millions of anguished souls. It had been steadily growing over the eons, but now the roar was deafening and they could no longer turn a blind eye. The howl in their minds was pure torture, leaving them in shivering agony. It reverberated through flesh, bones, muscles, and feathers threatening to tear them down.

It had somehow completely fallen apart, and they had failed. Pride had been their undoing; pride in their flock, and pride in their abilities, but now they understood the true nature of this realm. They could no longer guide with a gentle hand or whispered persuasion, instead they would be forced to take an active role.

From thousands of places across the globe, buried in the sand, locked frozen in ice, under deep, vast oceans, and beneath mighty mountain ranges, they began to stir. Old flesh began to rejuvenate and take form, and bones began to solidify. Anger consumed their thoughts, directed at themselves and those they had vowed to protect. They had done so much for this place and people. Why had they been spurned?

For too long this realm had been without its shepherds, its guardians, but that oversight would now be corrected.

No matter the cost.

***

A hail of bullets exploded against the wall behind them, some ricocheting into the night with a shrill whine. Grabbing the pregnant woman at her side, Emily St. Louise, Saint, dove into the double doors of a grocery store and slid across the floor. Skittering over the floor like animals, they made it to the snack aisle before the next volley of bullets shattered the windows. Shards of potato chips, now unhappy campers, and jet-puffed corpses, rained haphazardly around them. After pausing for a moment to check on the pregnant woman, Saint whipped the tail of her leather jacket back and drew her scythe.

They were pinned down.

She could hear the clerk shouting somewhere in the background. He was alerting the authorities. Gritting her teeth, she shot an angry glance toward the man's voice. Police would only complicate matters.

It had been her idea to venture this deep into Prague. The need for food had outweighed the necessity to remain unnoticed. Saint knew there was a possibility they would run into trouble, but hadn't expected the Kryll to mobilize so quickly, if at all. One of the oldest demon clans still left in Europe, they had supposedly been here before Prague Castle was founded in 850 A.D. Once a very mystical and peaceful order, something had changed. In the past two decades, they had become militant and hostile toward other species. The overwhelming question wasn't why the Kryll had changed, but how Saint and the pregnant woman at her side had ended up

8

on their radar. More importantly, why did the Kryll want them dead?

Keeping low to the ground, Saint moved toward the mouth of the aisle. The sound of footfalls caught her ear. The troops were coming in after them. The sharp crack of breaking glass beneath heavy boots was growing louder. They were very near now. Controlling her breathing and heart rate just as she had been instructed, the Wraith peered through the bullet holes in the shelves and caught sight of the first Kryll. Clad in muddy brown, handmade leather, it was clutching a black semiautomatic weapon that seemed inappropriate for its garb. Its mottled, pale green skin seemed to shimmer as if wet, but Saint knew that was the Kryll's natural oils which could be poisonous if ingested. The noseless face had several long, squid-like tentacles stretching down from its upper lip and chin creating a slithering beard that stretched to the center of its chest. These tendrils were prehensile, but lacked the strength to do any serious damage. The Kryll's eyes were large and solid black like a shark's. It seemed like this demon would be more at home in the Black Lagoon than in the center of the Czech Republic.

The soldier sniffed the air and scanned for his target with his coal black eyes. The three, thick fingers of its hand wrapped tightly around its weapon. It was tall and imposing, but it was merely a soldier. It was born and bred for war, nothing more. It didn't think; it followed orders and killed. That was its only purpose; its only reason to exist.

And Saint could hear at least four more.

Glancing back over her shoulder, she looked at the pregnant vampire sitting uncomfortably on the hard floor. Saint could see the fear in Kat's eyes as she cradled her arms around her bulging belly. The fear was not for herself, but for her unborn child. Saint felt a sudden and deep sadness well up in her throat. She had promised to watch after Kat and the baby. This was her final gift to her friend, the baby's father. Saint turned her attention back to the Kryll. It would not end here. Kat and Thomas' baby would be born, even if she had to move Heaven and Hell to ensure it.

Activating her scythe, the weapon instantly quadrupled in length. Thumbing the activation stud a second time, a long, curved blade snapped open from the tip. The weapon hummed in her hands almost as if asking to be loosed on the Kryll. Saint rolled up onto the balls of her feet. Carefully taking a step forward, she inched closer to the soldier. She reached out with her senses locating the other four. If she misjudged her attack, the others could easily gun her down and then take Kat. She had only seconds, and one shot. It had to be a death strike.

She heard another crunch of glass.

Now.

Shooting up from her hiding place, Saint whipped her blade horizontally out and across in one smooth strike. Before the Kryll had a chance to react, she was gone.

The soldier felt his neck tingle. Dropping its weapon to its side, it lifted a clammy hand and quickly felt its throat. Pulling its stubby fingers away, it found them smeared with thick, black blood. Looking down, the Kryll watched its life ooze down its chest. As it tried to lift its head to report to the others, the tingle grew into searing pain. Dropping to its knees, the Kryll's head tumbled from its perch revealing Saint's perfect cut. The soldier's body quickly followed its head to the ground.

One down.

Saint pressed her back to the aisle. She placed her free hand on Kat's shoulder. She wouldn't let that happen.

"We only want the mother," a voice gurgled as if there was water in its lungs. "Release her and we'll let you live, Vampire Hunter," the Kryll added. "Defy us further," it paused letting the words drown in its throat, "and you will be destroyed."

Kat wrapped her fingers around Saint's hand. Lifting her face, she looked into Saint's icy blue eyes. Please, she said without saying a word, don't let it end this way.

The Wraith nodded and offered Kat a reassuring smile. Deactivating her scythe, Saint lifted her hands above her head and slowly stood. Kat's eyes were wide with fear and confusion. Reaching up, the vampire mother grabbed Saint's leather coat and tried to pull her back. The vampire hunter pushed Kat's hand away without looking at her face. Above the shoulder-high aisles Saint immediately felt eight coal black eyes settle on her. The click, snap of weapons ready to fire immediately accompanied her rise. Her expression was grim, yet stern.

"We want the vampire," one of the Kryll

gurgled.

Saint furrowed her brow. "Why?"

"That isn't your concern," another Kryll spat.

Saint flashed her fangs allowing the soldiers to see them. She felt a shimmer of confusion pass through them for a moment. Her eyes became a colder hue of blue as her stillness became unnatural, vampiric. Focusing her emotions, fear began to roll off her in waves. It was a trick she had honed over the past nine months on the run. She found she could broadcast fear, keeping most predators away. This, however, was her first attempt at close range. It was psychological warfare in its purest form.

The nearest Kryll ran his stubby fingers over his facial tentacles tentatively feeling the brunt of the pushed emotion. Cocking his head slightly, the demon blinked his lower eyelids unsure of what it was experiencing. "What are you?" it breathed.

Saint remained motionless, her icy eyes fixed on the soldiers. She refused to reply.

The Kryll closest to the window tightened the grip on his weapon. Uncertain as to exactly why, the Kryll became unsure of its actions. It took a step away, but forcefully stopped itself. It was one woman, it assured itself. The four of them could easily open fire and gun her down…yet, it couldn't. Fear began to collect in its throat like a thick, chewy ball of bile. It burned as it grew, threatening to choke the demon. Its muscles tensed and twitched threatening flight. It wanted to run.

Saint felt a twinge of pain behind her eyes. This was taking too long, expending too much energy. She couldn't keep this up for much longer, but she held her ground. Her gaze was unwavering. She had to protect Kat.

The furthest Kryll's eye twitched.

Then it snapped.

Clamping its clammy fingers around the weapon it mashed down on the trigger and fired wildly. The spray of bullets tore through another of the Kryll sending its body to the ground in a heap. The remaining two soldiers turned and fled, gurgling angrily.

Saint dove to her right and rolled past Kat. As she came to her feet, she activated her scythe and was on the attack. Her blade tore through the retreating Kryll sending halves of him in opposite directions.

Without hesitating, Saint cocked her weapon back and released it. The spinning scythe sang as it sliced through the air. Hitting the shooting Kryll in the side of the head, the blade dug deep into its skull and burst through the opposite side. The firing stopped. Before the Kryll could fully register that it was dead, Saint had pulled her blade free, knocked the demon to the ground, and was charging the final soldier.

Its black eyes widened. The fear it felt this time was its own.

With a quick swish snap, it was over. Saint stood calmly over the Kryll as it fell to the floor. Reaching out with her senses, she could detect no other threats. For now, anyway.

She thumbed the activation button on her scythe and carefully deposited it back into her pocket. Saint lifted her gaze to find both barrels of the shopkeeper's shotgun leveled directly at her head. She let out a long sigh. "Be calm," she advised him.

The shopkeeper shouted something unintelligible at her. She wasn't sure what language he was speaking, if any at all. Looking past the imposing black barrels, she locked eyes with the man behind them. He was quivering like a leaf, while his eyes were wide with anger and fear. She understood in that moment that he wasn't merely the shopkeeper, he was the owner and this was his entire life. His past, present, and future were entwined unchangeably to this store. If it went down, so did he.

"I'm sorry," Saint said slowly. She wasn't sure if he understood English, but it really didn't matter. Coming into the city was a bad idea in the first place, and it was quickly getting worse. She had had enough. Whipping her hand up, she snatched the shotgun easily from the owner. Thumbing the latch, the barrels dropped forward. After yanking the shells free, Saint dropped them into her jacket pocket and handed back the weapon. "I'm sorry this happened," she repeated, "but don't ever point a weapon at me."

She felt Kat's presence behind her. Reaching back, she took the vampire's hand. "We're leaving," Saint breathed. Glass crunched under her feet as she slid outside. Turning quickly the vampire and hunter turned and melted into the darkness.

They had to get out of Prague.

The owner slowly let the shotgun fall to his side. Leaning against the counter, more for support, he looked around his store. With a shake of his head, he dropped the gun on the counter and reached over the opposite side. Snatching a yellow handled broom, he stood staring at the destruction before him for a long time.

Finally looking away from the four dead Kryll on the floor, he sighed and started cleaning up. "Damned Wraith."

***

He was old. Not quite as old as the pyramids that loomed on the edge of this city, but he had seen more centuries come and go than he cared to admit. Yet he remained unchanged. Looking the same as he did roughly three hundred years ago when he held his wife's and daughter's dead bodies in his arms, he found the past difficult to escape. Their killer, an ancient vampiress named Caitlin, had finally been vanquished, but he felt no release; he still felt haunted by the savageness of the kill. The battle raged on in some form or another, never ending. He was a man haunted, by the past and his own emotions. He was old, unchanged...and tired.

Leaning back, he kicked his booted feet up on the balcony rails and slid a little further down in his chair. The sun rose above the western horizon casting orange and red hues off the land and sky. After pulling his pack of cigarettes from his pocket, he drew one and lit it. Taking a deep drag, he let it dangle from his fingertips as he stared out over the city. He hadn't left this place since Caitlin was destroyed almost four years ago; he hadn't taken up his scythe, and he hadn't wanted to fight. He wasn't sure what he wanted anymore. His life's goal, to destroy the vampire that killed his family, had been accomplished, yet he felt empty.

Marcus Specter had tried to live his life by the tenets of the Gwyliad Wriaeth, but knew now that revenge had consumed him. Every time he brought death to a vampire or demon, he saw Caitlin's sneering face. But when her end had finally come inside the Great Pyramid, something didn't feel right. The switch inside of Marcus' brain hadn't been shut off like he hoped, nor was there a deep sense of relief as he watched her burn. For three hundred years he wanted her dead...now that she was, he didn't know what to do. She had risen from the depths of Hell before, and he knew it was possible again, so he stayed and watched this place. He lurked like a ghost in the background waiting for any sign or hint that Caitlin had been resurrected. Even though he knew that was a flimsy excuse to hold on to. He had destroyed her once before, or so he thought, and somehow found a way to go on and continue with his work. Why is this time different? Where is the sense of finality? Where is the resolution?

The months following his battle with Caitlin and her vampire minions had been hard on Specter, mentally and physically. The vampiress had taken great pleasure in torturing him, reviving him with her vampiric blood, and repeating the process. His body was scarred, his mind broken, yet he had escaped her clutches. The Wraith outpost here in Egypt had taken him in, and tried to heal his wounds. They had been successful in repairing his flesh, but his spirit, his soul, refused to mend.

16

Drawing another mouthful of smoke from the cigarette, he took a breath and pulled it into his lungs. The sunrise was casting long shadows off the pyramids in the Valley of the Kings deep into Cairo making them somehow seem all the more mysterious and awe-inspiring. Still Specter hated it here. It was hot, dusty, and generally miserable. He longed for the cool, damp weather of England, but wasn't sure he could return home. It had been so long…

Brushing errant ashes off his stained, white, sleeveless shirt, he took another drag off the cigarette then flicked it off the balcony. He watched the glowing red cherry spin in the predawn sky until it was swallowed by darkness. Standing, he lifted his arms over his head and stretched his body. Specter turned and faced the small, studio apartment. It wasn't his, but last night, it was home. He had been moving from place to place, sometimes sleeping in the streets like a common vagrant. He was the proverbial man in a suitcase, if he actually had one. The entirety of his belongings consisted of the clothes on his back, the brown knee-length leather jacket slung over the edge of the bed, and the scythe he wore on his belt. It wasn't much, but it was his. The order had taught him to live without and not be concerned with worldly possessions. In the old days, he would have been more akin to a Knight of the Holy Order, but now he was just a shell of a man.

Snatching his jacket off the bed, he slipped his arms into the sleeves and stared at the battered skin. Light brown patches showed through where the leather had cracked and peeled away. It's what he should look like, but instead he was perpetually twenty-five. He caught a glimpse of himself in a mirror that hung opposite the bed. His once short, dark hair hung past his shoulders, and a beard was quickly getting thicker on his face. Two dull, blue eyes stared out of the sockets, a painful reminder of who he used to be.

Lost in his own despair, he barely registered the click of the door handle.

Spinning on his toes, he sprinted to the balcony and dove over without a moment's hesitation. As his preternatural skill spun him in the air, he heard the door open and a man's voice shout angrily. Before he could fully register what had been said, Specter hit the concrete and rolled. He was back on his feet and sprinting away before the apartment's true owner even reached the balcony railing.

Chapter Two

He paced uneasily, the sound of his footfalls shivering off the tall buildings that rose on all sides. This place was quiet, empty, almost devoid of humanity. He could feel that peculiar buzz in the back of his head that life created, but it was far too faint to concern him. It was the reason the location was chosen. The Supreme Chancellor could not learn of it. No one could. Under the Order's new laws, this could be considered treason.

He gritted his teeth and tried to suppress his anger.

Tucking his hands behind his back, he glanced up at the full moon above. He worried silently. This was not a good idea. Already notoriously unstable, the sway of the moon seemed to bring out the madness in those he waited for. He was not defenseless, to be certain, but not many Wraiths had ever survived an encounter with multiple werewolves. He was a skilled warrior, but they were pure engines of destruction.

This decision hadn't been made lightly, but he knew they couldn't run forever. Something had to be done.

"Master Verge," a guttural voice rumbled from the darkness.

Conrad Verge fought the urge to activate his weapon, spin and attack. He was a leader now, but first and foremost a skilled warrior. To walk into a situation with open hands didn't feel right, yet he remained calm. Turning slowly, he kept his hands visible and motionless.

A hulking figure loomed in the darkness, its dark flesh fighting the moon's gaze. He was massive, probably nearing seven feet tall in Conrad's estimate, and his wide chest looked more like the grill of a Mack truck than flesh and muscle. The black leather coat that covered his arms and shoulders had the same sheen as his cleanly shaven head. His eyes, however, revealed his preternatural secret. Hard and cold, they were the eyes of a predator, not of a human being. The figure made no attempt to disguise them, or the moon's sway on him. Barely holding himself together, the beast was clawing inside to be free, and Conrad knew it.

"Stark," Conrad greeted, yet he held his position. Every muscle in the High Wraith's body was tensed. "Thank you for agreeing to meet with me."

Stark stomped out of the darkness and pointed an accusing finger at Conrad. "Despite what you may think, I do not owe the Wraith any favors."

"Oh?" Conrad asked. "So saving the life of your chieftain means nothing to your honor?"

"Ben was foolishly risking his life protecting one of your Wraith," Stark snarled. "Honor does not dictate debt in such a situation. You should be glad I agreed to meet with you at all."

Conrad laughed politely in that quintessential British way. "Have more important things to do like chase cars and dig up bones? I'm sorry to have taken up your time then."

"How dare you mock me?" Stark was right on top of Conrad now, his scleras showing the first

20

signs of transformation as they were ringed with red. "I could gut you where you stand, vampire hunter."

It wasn't an idle threat, and Conrad knew Stark was more than capable of carrying it out. He had to be careful of his tongue. "We are here as friends," Conrad reminded him. "I need your help, Stark."

Stark was breathing heavily, his grasp on humanity slipping by the second. "And why should my clan help you, Wraith?"

"Because I saved your chieftain's life, returned your clan's sacred axe, and helped bring justice to Talon Creed," Conrad said evenly. "I am not asking for any debt to be repaid, but I need your help. I scratch your back, you scratch..." Conrad let the old adage die in his mouth. He certainly didn't want Stark scratching any part of him. "I would ask Ben personally, but I haven't heard from him in months."

"I may be Ben's second-in-command," Stark said, "but in his absence, I am chieftain, and I think it's best if my clan has no ties to the Wraith."

Conrad wanted to reach out and shake the werewolf, but that probably would do more damage than good. "Why? Have not the wolves and Wraith fought side by side many times?"

"The Wraith have brought war and death!" Stark yelled, his voice echoing angrily off the pavement. "Bane continues to march undeterred across all lands, wiping out anything preternatural in his path on his quest to eliminate all Wraith. Many, many wolves have died because of this."

Conrad couldn't hide his shock at the pure

venom that spilled from Stark's mouth. "How can you blame Bane on the Wraith?"

"If there were no Wraith," Stark breathed, "there would be no Bane."

Conrad felt his heart sink. Technically, the statement was true.

We are those who are to blame…

Vampires and Wraith were yin and yang. One could not exist without the other, and neither would be as they were today. Through centuries of battle and bloodshed, the two sides had created and recreated each other. They were the light and dark side of the same force. Their existences were so tightly bound, it was hard to imagine a world without vampires and Wraiths. And Conrad knew they had brought about their own destruction.

The High Wraith lifted his face to Stark. His conviction was unwavering. It had to be, for her sake.

The werewolf's angry visage softened somewhat as though taking pity on a disobedient child. "What is it that you want from my clan?"

"Sanctuary," Conrad answered calmly. There was a time when the Wraith didn't have to seek safety outside the Order, but that was prior to Vampire Lord Bane, and before he brought sweeping darkness to all the continents of the world.

"Sanctuary?" Stark laughed. "For you?"

"No." Conrad smiled. "For Saint and Kat. They can't run forever."

"Absolutely not," Stark barked without hesitation. "You will bring Bane down on us like a guillotine. We will not harbor the Wraith woman and the pregnant half-breed. That would be suicide."

The two fell into an uncomfortable silence. Each was sizing the other up. Conrad wanted to call the wolf a coward, but he held his words. There would be a time and a place.

"My clan will have no part in this madness of yours," Stark said finally.

"Ben would do it," Conrad reminded Stark calmly.

"He's not here," Stark growled, his eyes shifting to werewolf red. The wolf's lips peeled back allowing the Wraith to see the razor-sharp fangs growing in his mouth. He was on the verge of transformation, but somehow holding it back.

"And that is a shame," Conrad concluded. This meeting had come to an end. "Thank you for your time. I leave in peace."

Taking one last look at the powerful werewolf, the High Wraith turned and started slowly away. Conrad was done.

To turn his back on a werewolf was never a good idea, but this wasn't a tactical retreat, it was an overt slap to Stark's face. Conrad's actions proved he had no respect for the wolf's strength or authority. It was an outright insult, and one he hoped to survive, but he had enough of this cowardly lion, as it were. There was no help to be found here, and Conrad wouldn't waste any more of his time.

Anger blossomed in Stark's brain like a nuclear blast. In that moment he wanted to tear the Wraith limb from limb and feast on his flesh...he took a breath, but he knew that would bring more trouble than it was worth. To kill the head of the Wraith's Council of Seven would bring too much attention to the clan, not only from the Wraith, but from other wolf and demon clans that wanted to usurp his power. It simply wasn't worth it. Spinning away from Conrad, the werewolf skulked angrily into the night.

***

"I have to stop," Kat cried. Crashing to her knees, the vampire clutched her chest trying to catch her breath.

Saint skidded to a stop and turned back. Squatting down, she placed her hand tenderly on the other woman's shoulder. "We have to keep going."

"I can't." Kat tumbled onto her back and stared up at the blanket of stars. She secretly hoped one of the brilliant points of light was Thomas watching over her. She needed him now. Slowing her breathing, she started to gain control.

The same Troika Serum that had given her the ability to become pregnant had changed her body in other ways as well. Hovering somewhere between humanity and vampirism, Kat had traits of both species, but belonged to neither. Her lungs had begun to atrophy from disuse. She was like a newborn learning how her body worked again. The Wraith physician who examined Kat told her if she were merely human, she probably would have died, but somehow her vampire side was keeping her alive. It was a delicate balance. The Troika, a triad of Russian vampires that fell at the hands of Bane, had developed the serum as a weapon, and she

24

understood why now. It would strip away a vampire's preternatural gifts then leave them to die in the most horrible of ways.

"I'm nine months pregnant," Kat reminded Saint. "I can't do this, Saint. Please...?"

"I know," Saint replied softly. "We'll rest for a moment."

Sitting down on the cold ground, she surveyed the golden lights of Prague in the distance. They were well out of the city now, but not safe yet...not ever safe. Reaching into her coat, she pulled a small leather bound journal and began to scratch words onto the pages with a half used pencil she kept within. It was her intention to record every moment of her journey with Kat, so others may someday understand. Hell, so maybe she could understand herself.

Saint had given her word that she would watch over the unborn Wraith's baby, no matter the cost. Thomas had been like her brother, but he had fallen. There was more in Kat's womb than just his genetic material, it was his salvation, perhaps the salvation of them all. Saint let her eyes fall away from the city lights. Or perhaps it was their damnation. No one knew. That worried her more than she cared to admit. She had once called this pregnancy a "miracle," but time had allowed doubts to seed in her brain and they slowly began to blossom.

She had been with Kat through all nine months, protecting her and the baby. And Saint was tired. The future looked bleak. What kind of world would Thomas' child be born into? Humans fought needless, prideful wars over resources and land, but the Inhumans were no better.

And what of this half-breed vampire that lay beside her? Saint had vowed to dedicate her life to the eradication of vampires. They had taken almost everything from her—her home at the Wraith Academy, her Master Ben Quinn, her lover Miller Barnes, and her best friend Thomas Cross—and yet now she gave up everything to protect one. The irony tasted bitter in her mouth. This vampire, this mongrel of species, had danced naked through Thomas' dreams every night of his life, yet had been the very reason he fell and lost his life to Master Verge's scythe. Saint was understandably confused and angry. She would have had a seat on the newly reformed Council of Seven, but instead she was an outcast. Seemed the vampires weren't finished taking from her yet after all.

As she finished recording the night's events, and the encounter with the Kryll in her journal, Saint slipped the pencil inside and bound it closed with a thick rubber band. Depositing it back into her leather jacket, she leaned back on her hands and eyed Kat.

"What?" Kat asked nervously.

"Nothing," Saint replied as she exhaled.

"No, really," Kat pressed. She felt Saint's eyes boring into her flesh. "What?"

"I was just thinking," the Wraith remarked, "how odd it is that a Wraith is protecting a vampire and her unborn child."

Kat pulled herself up into a sitting position, and rubbed her bulbous belly gently. "That is sort of odd now that you mention it. Thank you for helping me," she looked down at her stomach, "for helping us."

Saint dismissed the gratitude with a quick flick of her wrist. It was nice to hear, but she didn't want to talk about it anymore. It was just making her angry.

"What do we do now?" Kat asked after a moment.

Saint wasn't sure. She took a long, deep breath and stared up into the stars hoping vainly to find her answer there. "We keep running," she said finally.

"But to where?"

"I don't know," Saint barked. "Anywhere!"

Kat shrank back from the Wraith's anger. She wasn't a warrior, or even a fighter; Kat was a novelist in the wrong place at the wrong time. She didn't have Saint's killer instincts, despite being a vampire. She had hoped to be sitting behind a desk, tapping away on her computer writing novels by this point in her life, but, as always, fate had a different plan for her. Now she was alive but shouldn't be; a vampire-human hybrid that shouldn't be, and carrying a child that shouldn't have been possible. She had wished many times that she had just stayed dead.

And Saint knew that. "I'm sorry." She placed her hand on Kat's shoulder. "I didn't mean to yell. I'm just..." She exhaled and her icy blue eyes seemed to dull. "I'm just so tired."

Kat nodded. "I know. I'm frustrated too. Will I ever be able to stop running, or is this the only life my baby and I will know?"

"I wish I knew," Saint said in a much softer

tone. "We can't run forever. Something's got to give."

Kat didn't like the Wraith's ominous statement, but she knew it to be true.

Saint stood up and brushed a bit of dirt from her pant leg. Extending her hand to Kat, she helped the pregnant vampire to her feet and waited while she steadied herself. "Are you okay?"

Kat nodded. "We just need to take it slow. Please?"

"All right." Saint nodded. "Let's go."

Reaching down, the Wraith took the vampire by the hand and continued into the darkness.

Chapter Three

Chancellor Ramius Alexander stood with his hands on his hips, the red robe of his position bunched behind his back. He stared out the window of his newly renovated office onto the churning ocean beyond. Much like the waters he watched, this was a tumultuous time for the Wraith. Bane and his vampire army had killed the ruling Council of Seven, and the original academy was nearly leveled. He had argued that the old ways had failed by letting this vampire raise an army, and that new ideas and leadership was needed to salvage the Gwyliad Wriaeth. For the first time since the Order's inception, a single man instead of a council governed it. Alexander had been swept into office quickly on the strength of his convictions, and a hasty election. Now, almost a year later, he was still rebuilding and reorganizing.

Of Russian decent, Alexander had been in the motherland when Bane had struck. A Wraith his entire adult life, he had found he was much better at battling with words than his scythe, yet there didn't seem to be a place in the old Order for a skilled politician. They were trained soldiers, fighting and dying on the front lines, but that wasn't his calling. Ancillary positions, still vital to the war but far from conflict, were discovered to occupy his focus, but it was this moment, this cataclysm that threatened to engulf the Wraith and tear them apart, that his true talents surfaced. He would forge the aging, dulling Gwyliad Wriaeth into a powerful instrument of good again. He had become the savior of the Wraith, and to speak anything contrary was blasphemy.

As he caught his ghostly reflection in the window, Alexander slicked his dark hair back with his hand. Tracing the crow's feet that stretched away from his eyes with his fingertips, he realized he was probably closer to ninety than the thirty years his face displayed. Wraiths aged, but at a dramatically slower rate than average humans. The same virus that created vampirism had mutated and created the Wraith. They were inexorably bound to the vampires they hunted, as if charged with tracking and killing their own kin, yet they couldn't do it without the gifts and benefits the mutated vampire virus gave them.

This section of the Wraith Academy had survived Bane's bomb blast, though it had been badly damaged. On the south side of the compound looking over the Atlantic Ocean, it was the first to be completed in Alexander's proposed rebuild. He wanted this place to stand tall again, to say that the Wraith could be bloodied, but not broken. It had to be a shining beacon that lit the darkness and boldly proclaimed the Wraith would not stand down. Alexander knew that this place, more than any of the lives lost here, was a monument to what the Wraith were, and could be again.

Before this had merely been a classroom, but under Alexander's direct supervision, it had been transformed into an office befitting the Chancellor of the Gwyliad Wriaeth. His desk sat in the center, elevated slightly from the main entrance with huge windows stretching behind it and making up the entire wall. A row of three flat panel computer monitors occupied the side of the desk, but the room was minimally decorated. A tall, black statue one of the students had created hundreds of years ago, depicting a Wraith in battle, stood in the back corner of the office, watching over the proceedings.

Alexander felt the High Wraith's presence before seeing him. He slowly turned.

Conrad stood quietly in the door of the Chancellor's office waiting to be acknowledged. His arms were crossed and his posture was rigid.

"Master Verge," the Chancellor greeted the other man. He could already sense there was something on the old warrior's mind. He decided to broach it carefully. "Please," he gestured to the chairs that sat empty in front of his desk, "sit down. Thank you for coming."

Conrad relaxed his posture somewhat and complied. Sliding into the nearest chair, he watched Alexander circle around his desk and lean against the front. He tried to hide the worry in his stomach. Having been summoned to the Chancellor's office shortly after his return from London, he wondered if Alexander had somehow learned of his meeting with Stark. He waited for the Chancellor to make the first move.

"It's strange," Alexander said slowly, "that we are both in the Academy, but I haven't spoken with you in some time. Don't you think?"

"You're a busy man, Chancellor," Conrad said diplomatically, "as am I."

"Yes, yes," Alexander agreed, "which is

precisely why I asked you here, Master Verge."

Conrad waited.

Alexander decided to launch straight in. "Has the search for Emily St. Louise yielded any results? I haven't received an update from you in some time."

"I'm afraid not, Chancellor," Conrad answered as evenly as possible. "The trail ran cold somewhere outside of Berlin."

Alexander's face darkened. "You assured me that by leaving this in your hands, you would find and deal with this rogue Wraith. Did you not?"

Conrad started to argue but Alexander cut him off and continued.

"And yet almost a year has passed and we have nothing," Alexander added. "I find this almost unimaginable."

"There's a war on, Chancellor," Conrad spat. His anger flared, but he quickly reeled in his emotions. "What resources we have left are consumed by fighting Bane on all fronts. We lost another Academy last week in China."

"I'm well aware of our losses," the Chancellor hissed. "And I'm also aware of our tactical situation. Still, it doesn't seem possible that one girl would be so difficult to track and recover."

Unsure why Alexander was so bent on the capture of Saint, it unsettled the High Wraith. Shortly after returning to England from America, Conrad had been tasked with this mission. The Chancellor claimed it had the highest priority, yet Conrad couldn't fully understand why. It seemed there were greater things at stake than the apprehension of a rogue.

Conrad needed to know. He set his jaw. "Why is this so important, Chancellor? Shouldn't all of our efforts be on the war and rebuilding the Wraith?"

"That is at the very heart of the matter," Alexander urged. He walked slowly to the chair next to Conrad's and sat down. "I have uncovered information," he lowered his voice, "that is vital to our future."

Conrad cocked a wary eyebrow. "And that would be?"

"Before Bane's attack, the Council discovered that Saint was," Alexander paused, "let's say unique. I hesitate to use the term, but she could very well be the Chosen One spoke of in Wraith prophecy."

Conrad wasn't sure how to respond. He had held that very belief since the former student completed the graduation ritual from this very Academy, yet it was not something he openly discussed.

"Tests were run on her," Alexander continued, "that proves her body accepted and mutated the Wraith Virus. She is the first of a new breed of Wraith."

She was indeed the first, but not the only. Conrad knew the truth about Thomas and his baby, but had revealed it to no one. He couldn't tell if the Chancellor knew or not.

"If we can harness this gift of hers, it could turn the tide of the war," the Chancellor explained.

He wasn't worried about the capture of a rogue,

Alexander only wanted a new weapon in his arsenal. The idea infuriated him, but Conrad chewed it back and did his best to bury it. Conrad lowered his gaze, trying to play it up. "I had no idea."

"It is imperative you find Emily St. Louise and bring her to me," the Chancellor said finally.

"I understand now," Conrad admitted.

"Very good." Alexander clapped his hands together in delight. "Then you will double your efforts?"

"Of course," Conrad added with a nod.

"If you should require any assistance…" the Chancellor offered.

"I will most certainly contact you," Conrad finished.

Alexander stood, walked to Conrad's side, and placed his hand on the High Wraith's shoulder. "I knew I made the right choice appointing you as the head of the Council of Seven. You do the Order proud."

Conrad felt the Chancellor's words hit and slide down his face as though he had been spat upon. He gritted his teeth and tried to hide his growing abhorrence for Alexander. The Chancellor wasn't what he first appeared.

"If you'll excuse me," Conrad tried to be a tactful as possible, "I think I should like to get right on this."

"Very good," Alexander purred. "Thank you, Master Verge. Your assistance has been a great help to both myself and the Order."

Conrad slipped away from the Chancellor's grip and stood up. With a respectful nod, the High

Wraith quickly exited the office and walked briskly out into the corridor. Wraiths buzzed frenetically around the Academy, working hard to restore it to its former glory. While Conrad did feel this was a necessary step in rebuilding the Wraith, he felt to pull this many of them away from battle was foolish and arrogant on the part of the Chancellor.

Coming around a corner, he spotted one of his fellow seven on the Council speaking with several Wraiths. Stepping around the young men and women, Conrad slipped his hand around the High Wraith's upper arm.

Xavier turned and looked at Conrad, and found nothing but concern and worry on Conrad's face. Excusing himself from the young Wraith, the two old friends walked away from the workers, and hopefully out of earshot.

Xavier glanced nervously over his shoulder then returned his attention to Conrad. "What is it?"

Conrad frowned deeply. "We have a problem. Gather the others as soon as possible."

***

Night settled like a blanket over the ancient city, enveloping and holding it captive. Most of the citizens had retreated into their homes as betrayed by the light, some vestige of their primordial ancestry compelling them, leaving only those who didn't want to be seen. Darkness hid a multitude of sins, and those who remained out counted on that. It's when the monsters came out, both human and inhuman.

And it was where he belonged.

Stumbling forward, Specter fell to his knees.

Shaking hard, almost uncontrollably, he wrapped his arms around his stomach and rested his forehead on the still warm concrete. Every drink he had taken wanted back out, and it was clawing at his stomach and throat. Rolling back onto his knees, he placed his arm against the wall of the building for support. He stared at the passing traffic on the street. The cars appeared as blurs in his inebriated state, and were only causing his world to spin faster.

He just wanted to go home.

But he didn't know where that was anymore. With a moan of pain, he fell back against the alley wall and closed his eyes. His hand slid up to his inside coat pocket and felt the familiar bulge that had been there for as long as he could remember. Reaching in, he pulled a stack of letters free and held them in his hands as he had done so many times. Dog-eared, creased, and worn, the letters were hundreds of years old. They were from his wife, sent while he was on assignment for the Gwyliad Wriaeth. They were all he had left of her and his home. Holding them close to his heart, Specter felt his ancient wound, still open, still hurting.

His eyes fell on the envelopes. He thought for a moment about opening them, but he knew every stroke of ink, every loop, every word she had created had been already committed to memory. He could smell her perfume, feel the softness of her flesh, and still see the depth of her eyes. Specter had loved her from the first moment they met and hadn't ever stopped. She was his everything. She fell around him like rain, elusive and random. And his

36

daughter... She had been the sun in his sky. They were all he had.

With their killer dead, his heart was an empty room. Revenge had been the singular motive that had kept him going. He was lost, within and without. Specter had become his namesake, and like a ghost, he hovered somewhere between life and death, but belonged to neither. Yet he felt somehow betrayed by them. They had left him on this road alone, and despite whether it was their fault or not, they were gone and he was alone. Did he partially blame them? How could he? The thoughts, the feelings, the anger didn't make sense to the Wraith. He was a wreck lashing out at anyone and everyone, even those he loved.

He felt abandoned, haunted.

Stuffing the letters back into his pocket, Specter tried to stand but was far too drunk. He spilled back to the ground with a thud. Immediately his digestive system threatened to switch into reverse, but he took a slow breath and fought it. He let his head fall back against the alley wall and he stared at the stars above.

One seemed to move. Cocking an eyebrow, he stared at the moving light but his world continued to spin. He couldn't seem to lock onto it. Not a star, and certainly not a satellite, Specter rubbed his eyes with the heels of his palms and tried to shake a bit of the inebriation off. Looking back up, he watched the light grow in size.

The Master Wraith felt suddenly weak and weary, but it wasn't the alcohol, at least not entirely. As though he had become Atlas and the weight of the world rested solely on his shoulders, Specter felt compressed, and in danger of being crushed. His insides ached as pain and anger coursed through his veins and invaded every fiber of his being. He felt empty, lost, and again saw the faces of his wife and daughter. Their pain was his pain. Slumping down the wall, he watched the light becoming brighter and brighter as it neared. Despair gripped him like a fist, unwilling to let go.

The light was getting closer.

Sinking down between the two buildings, it illuminated the fading graffiti in the alley and washed over Specter. As the light touched him, he felt a strange wave of respite. He rolled onto his knees and lifted more fully into the light. As he did so, his pain and anger seemed to somehow fade. As quickly as it had gripped him, it receded leaving the Wraith with a strange, but welcome, peacefulness. In his mind he could hear what sounded very much like music, but of a type and rhythm he had never heard before. It was beautiful, chaotic, and somewhat frightening. He sank back, unsure what to do.

The light hovered above the Wraith, then receded slightly as if it were equally unsure. Specter felt the peacefulness fade like the tide, leaving only the beach and rocks that were the pain and anguish he was so familiar with. He hurt; he ached. There was no fear, no more uncertainty. He lifted his hands toward the light, longing for release.

Suddenly the light exploded knocking Specter to the ground. He smacked the concrete hard but quickly pushed away the pain. He felt a pulsing

38

breeze push down on him, and a sound he had never heard before. Returning his gaze upwards, Specter watched the being unfurl its beautiful, feathered wings.

It was everything he wanted.

And it wanted Specter too.

Chapter Four

They stood on the banks of the Danube River, admiring Bratislava as it seemed to sprawl endlessly on both sides. The golden-hued lights reflected off the still, deep water creating a ghostly haze that crept along the ground. In the distance, they could see Bratislava Castle rising above the city, looming like a persistent specter that would not allow time to forget. Its four towers jutted into the night air atop one of the Little Carpathians offering an unmatched view of Austria, Vienna, and on clear nights, even Hungary. It seemed to be watching the two even now, a silent bastion aware of their intent.

Creeping quickly and quietly like shadows, both moved with preternatural speed and agility. Their footfalls hushed, only the barely detectable swish of fabric and leather betrayed their presence. Careful to avoid all prying eyes, the two made their way toward the seedier side of the city. Undetected, they scaled a fire escape and perched on top of a small building. Silently, they watched and waited.

"I don't like this."

Kat wanted to place her hand on Saint's shoulder to comfort the Wraith, but could not bring herself to complete the act. She stepped back from her companion and rubbed her growing belly with a worried look on her face. "I can't do it by myself anymore."

Saint trudged to the edge of the roof and brought her foot up on the ledge. Leaning over, she rested her arm on her knee. She watched the smattering of souls below in the street moving about their lives. Did they have any idea what hovered above them? Despite the stories, legends, and tales, humans didn't accept the possibility of the supernatural, yet here it was perched mere feet away.

She tossed her long black trench back and straightened her posture. The wind came up around Saint and whipped her midnight-black hair around her face. "I can't do this."

"Please," Kat begged, stepping forward.

Saint shook her head, stepped off the ledge then turned to face the vampire she had sworn to protect. "There has to be another way. This isn't right, Kat. I'm sworn to protect these people," she paused, "from things like you."

"I know." Kat let her gaze fall away, ashamed of what she was, and what she was asking Saint to do. She gasped as she felt the baby kick in her womb.

Saint rushed maternally to Kat's side and placed her hand on the vampire's belly. "Are you okay?"

Kat paused, then nodded. "The baby just kicked me really hard. I'm okay."

Saint watched Kat's face, then let her eyes fall to the vampire's belly. It was easy to forget there was a living, growing being in there, and no matter what it was, it was her job to protect it. Taking a step back from Kat, Saint's blue eyes seemed to dim somewhat. She let her head fall and turned back to the ledge.

"Saint," Kat said almost pleadingly, "Emily—"

Without looking back, Saint held up her hand to silence her companion. Her decision had already been made.

Her gaze again fell on the people below. These were the Lost Souls, as Saint had come to call them. They were humans with no direction, no family, no friends, and no life to speak of. That didn't make what she was about to do any easier, or any more right, but there was less chance one of the lost souls would be missed. Her eyes danced over them one by one trying somehow to make a choice. But how could she put one over the other when she had no idea who they really were? She was letting her conscience get the better of her, and with good reason. She was betraying everything she believed in, and everything she stood for.

Yet she had made a promise, and that bound her to this fate.

Reaching out with her mind, she scanned the crowd. Selecting one of the Lost Souls below, Saint stepped fully onto the ledge and jumped.

Sailing through the air like the angel of death, she landed on her toes without a sound. Stepping back to the wall of the building, she watched carefully for any signs that her descent had been detected, but the crowd went about their business. Saint's gaze locked on her target: a dark-haired man who looked more like a walking skeleton than a human. His withered skin was stretched tight over his bones, with faded blue reminders of his past etched into it. He staggered drunkenly along the sidewalk; his eyes hollow and his face bereft of expression. He looked as though he were already dead.

This man was a killer, and it had happened recently as the memories were still fresh on the surface of his mind. Saint could see his victim's screaming face as he tortured her. It had been a game to him, and Saint couldn't understand why. His motives were buried too deeply in his subconscious. Still, she knew this man had done it at least once and was capable of doing it again. Saint had picked him specifically for this reason. It was the only way she could justify the act to her conscience.

The Wraith waited as he approached, muscles tensed and ready and she knew in that moment what it must feel like to be a vampire. It sickened her, and made her hate them even more.

The man stumbled and almost fell, but somehow kept his balance. Digging a pack of cigarettes out of his pocket, he tried to pull one free with wildly shaking hands but only succeeded in spilling most of them on the sidewalk. As he bent down to retrieve them, others walked nervously away hoping to avoid the black pit of despair that obviously engulfed him.

This was her chance.

Maneuvering into the crowd, she easily bypassed oncoming people and headed straight for her target. He rolled onto his toes and started to collapse onto the wet concrete. With one swift motion too fast for human eyes to follow, Saint scooped up the man, pinned her hand over his mouth, and pulled him into a nearby alley.

"Don't scream," Saint warned the man,

slamming him against the wall. She grabbed his wrist with her free hand and pinned it hard behind his back. Feeling his muscles pop and crack in protest, she eased off slightly. She stared into his terror-stricken eyes as he tried to struggle against her, and felt her heart sink. "I'm sorry. I'm so sorry. Please," she breathed out, "please forgive me for this."

Saint heard Kat move out of the shadows behind her.

"Do this quick before I change my mind," Saint growled. She shifted to the left and bent the man's head over exposing his throat.

Kat's eyes were luminous gold in the low light. Opening her mouth, she bared her fangs. The pregnant vampire moved in quickly and stood at the Wraith's side. Running her fingers over the man's neck, she spotted a vein barely hidden beneath his paper-thin flesh.

Saint felt the hairs on the back of her neck stand up...but it wasn't from what she was doing. She saw a glimmer of light out the corner of her eye. Slowly turning to her left, she gasped and fell back from the man and Kat. He was free to run away, but didn't.

None of them did.

"Oh my God," Saint breathed.

It descended slowly bathed in a soft, ethereal glow. Its features were perfect and delicate, but neither masculine nor feminine. As it neared the ground, the breeze it created kicked up trash from the alley and tossed it away as if clearing the perfect spot to land. Its body was lithe and elegant, wrapped

44

in loose-fitting white and gray clothes that billowed majestically. The hood of its robe was pulled over its head, shadowing its facial features. Beneath the hood, there was only darkness, a void of unimaginable depths. As it touched down gently, it spread its perfect, white feathered wings then folded them neatly behind its back.

The man fell to his knees next to Saint and quickly muttered a prayer in his native tongue. His words sounded hasty and rushed, ramming into each other as they spilled off his tongue. He seemed both frightened and relieved to see the being.

Kat, her eyes still vampiric gold, wrapped her arms protectively around her belly and shrank back into the darkness.

The being took a step toward Saint. Saint straightened her spine as though it was suddenly inside her mind. Its melodious presence sounded like a choir in her brain. Her head throbbed as though the sound was too much to contain within her skull. She felt warmth on her upper lip. Lifting her hand to her nose, she found a thick streak of crimson across her fingers. Clamping her hand to her nose, she tried to stem the bleeding. Returning her gaze the being, Saint couldn't hide her confusion.

The being gracefully offered its hand, not to Saint, but to the man.

Saint watched the man's face veer wildly from relief to fear. Standing, he took a tentative step toward the being, but stopped. Drawing a breath into his skeletal frame, he finally summoned all of his courage and opened his arms. Moving forward, he tenderly took the offered hand.

Pulling him in and wrapping its slender arms around the man, the being stroked the man's dark hair gently in a very loving way.

Saint felt the sting of jealousy.

Lifting its head, the being seemed to gaze at Saint from the darkness of its hood. She could once again feel the depth of its existence in her mind. As the sides of her head throbbed, her vision angered to red. Slamming her hands to her head, Saint tried to stifle the pain, but was unable to tear her eyes away from the angelic being. Her legs quivered, but she somehow fought against her muscles and gravity to remain standing.

Unfurling its wings, the being snapped the man's neck with one quick twist. Dropping the corpse to the ground in a broken heap, it started toward Saint.

Every muscle, every nerve, and every fiber of Saint's being screamed for her to flee yet she couldn't. The pounding in her brain and terror in her blood froze her in place. It meant not only to kill her but teach her a lesson through pain. The being's chorus in Saint's mind turned shrill and horrible like a million voices crying out in a tortured scream. The pressure in her mind felt as though it doubled, threatening to burst her skull from the inside. In complete agony, Saint started to crumble toward the concrete.

She felt a hand wrap around her neck. But it wasn't the being's.

Yanked back, Saint's world became a blur as she felt herself flung into the air. Spinning and twisting, the Wraith tried to right herself but had no sense of up or down. She spotted the ground rushing toward her. Throwing out her arms to brace her fall, it was too little too late. They crumpled under the force of her descent and she hit hard. Stars sparkled before her eyes as her head cracked against the ground. Before she had even a chance to recover, she saw a pair of golden eyes materialize out of the darkness and lunge at her. She was lifted off the ground and slung like a sack over the vampire's shoulder. The vampire took off like a shot, sailing from rooftop to rooftop. Amidst a rush of pain, Saint lifted her head to see the ethereal light of the angelic being rising into the sky behind her. As she was jostled and bumped, Saint watched it fade into the distance. It wasn't following.

Saint closed her eyes and felt her body become limp.

**

The mighty clock tower tolled eleven times as they gathered. As each moved inside the agreed upon location amidst the fog that had rolled in off the Thames, no words were spoken, and barely an upward glance was shared. These were men and women of honor and tradition. They knew what it meant to keep a secret, and the price they paid to do so. Right and wrong weighed heavily on their consciences, and motivated their actions this night. They had once been called traditionalists, but under Alexander's regime, they were considered traitors. It was salt in an ever-deepening wound.

One they hoped to heal…through whatever means necessary.

Conrad circled slowly around the flat—watching, observing. Drawing his battered leather trench coat tightly around his chest, the High Wraith crossed his arms and backed into a corner. His body language was anxious, angry. He lowered his gaze and let a dark shadow fall over his face. His thoughts were elsewhere. They were with Saint. He hadn't heard from Saint in almost a year, not since Thomas' death. She was in trouble, and his options were limited. His hands were bound by circumstance, but by staying here, he had protected her. Now, however, things had changed.

There was little furniture here as most preferred to stand. The flat was nothing more than a studio apartment they had secured well away from prying eyes, no matter whom they might belong to. It was a place to talk, to plot, and to ready their plans. The group had grown from the original two—Conrad and Xavier—to more than twelve like-minded members. Conrad had warned Xavier on many occasions that to continually bring in new faces threatened their existence, but Xavier knew that to truly bring their plans to fruition, they needed more resources. It was risky, but in his opinion, necessary.

Xavier, the only other High Wraith here, had formerly been charged with protecting the original Council of Seven. During Bane's attack, he had fought and nearly died at the hands of the Vampire Lord. His left hand had been severed in the battle; an injury he wore now like a medal of honor. A jagged scar sliced down his forehead from his short, messy hair—a result of Bane's bomb that nearly destroyed the Academy. He had proven that he was a patriot through sacrifice of flesh, and had been one of the main detractors of changing the Order and electing Alexander Chancellor. Shortly after Alexander was rushed into office during the Wraith's first ever election, he joined with Conrad on the reformed Council of Seven and helped organize what he referred to as an "underground resistance." It was dangerous business, but Xavier was a good man, and Conrad knew it.

As the last Wraith shuffled into the flat, Xavier brought the emergency meeting to order. "I'm sorry we had to call you here on such short notice," he opened apologetically. "Some of you have traveled far. Thank you."

Xavier was much more the diplomat than Conrad, but each had their part to play. Pushing off the wall, Conrad circled slowly around the group, eying each warily. Trust was earned, not given, and though Xavier vouched for each new member, Conrad was still unsure. His life, and Saint's, was in the hands of each of these Wraith, whether they were aware of it or not. Lurking in the background, the High Wraith waited.

"We have come into possession of some dangerous information," Xavier informed them. "Alexander has tasked the Council with personally tracking and recovering Emily St. Louise."

A murmur of disapproval washed over the group.

"Why do we hide in the shadows and do nothing?"

It was a valid question. Conrad's eyes jumped

over the twelve and settled on Garrett Nacamora. One of the inner sanctum, he had been assigned to protect the Council of Seven. Since Thomas' death, he was considered one of the most promising and skilled Wraith in the Order. He had lived in Thomas Cross' shadow for his entire career, but he had somehow managed not to become bitter and angry, at least not outwardly.

"We have to bide our time, Master Nacamora," Xavier chided. "We are few, but Alexander has many, many Wraith at his disposal. If we were declared rogue..."

"Our insurrection would be crushed pretty quickly," Conrad finished pessimistically from the back of the room. His expression was stern, yet worried.

The assembled few murmured in displeasure again.

Garrett turned and addressed his question directly to Conrad. "Why is he so interested in this one rogue Wraith?"

Conrad shifted his weight from foot to foot uneasily. Saint's history, condition, and current situation were secrets he guarded with his life. Of the people in this room, only him and Xavier knew the whole truth and he wanted to keep it that way, at least for the time being. "We don't know why Alexander is so suddenly interested in Saint," he lied. He had to redirect. "This is just another example of the Chancellor abusing the power of his office. There's a war on, gentleman." He started to pace. Folding his hands behind his back, he imagined a giant, waving flag behind him and almost felt like Patton. "And it's a war we're clearly losing. Another Academy fell in China, yet the Chancellor has tasked the Council of Seven with locating a Rogue. This is gross misconduct."

"So the question remains," Garrett interjected, "why are we sitting here doing nothing? We should remove Alexander and install a strong Chancellor who will return the Wraith to their former glory."

Conrad was horrified at the thought. "You can't be serious."

"To hell I'm not," Garrett added forcefully.

"Assassination?" Conrad felt corrupt for even speaking the word. "Is that your solution?"

Garrett nodded and folded his arms. His expression was deadly serious.

"Two wrongs don't equal a right," Xavier chided. "And despite what he's done, Alexander is still a Wraith."

"We need action!" Garrett shouted.

Disagreements and shouts broke out among the others like a tide that threatened to drown them all. The volume in the small flat suddenly skyrocketed. The meeting disintegrated into a shouting match as tempers flared.

Conrad shouted for order, but his voice was easily lost in the noise. He looked across the room to Xavier and the two High Wraiths locked eyes. Xavier's gaze was apologetic and confused. This wasn't what they wanted.

With a heavy heart, Conrad waded through the angry mob, pushing Wraiths out of the way, and headed for the door. It was obvious no solution was to be found here tonight. The other Wraith, though holding the same beliefs as himself and Xavier, were too young and volatile. They couldn't see the forest for the trees, and it was his generation that was to blame. It was a failure in their training, Conrad surmised. They hadn't been taught to see the larger picture, and instead opted for violence when the situation didn't call for it. They had bred a generation of warriors who knew nothing but battle. They had failed.

Pushing through the door, Conrad slammed it and grabbed onto the iron railing that ran the length of the level. The metal guard was cold against his flesh, but it felt refreshing. He had hoped to stare into the stars, but only found a thick blanket of fog locking the city in. He was alone.

His thoughts turned to Thomas, as they often did. He knew his failure, of all the Masters, had been the most complete. Thomas Cross was one of the best and brightest the Order had ever seen, and yet he met his end on Conrad's scythe. He had truly gone rogue and fallen from grace, and Conrad had let him. There was nothing to be done now but mourn his fallen student, his friend, and his brother. Conrad's failure was complete.

"It wasn't your fault."

Lost in thought, Conrad hadn't noticed when Xavier joined him. He considered the High Wraith's words for a moment. Had he become that transparent?

"Thomas was a good man, but he was arrogant," Xavier said. "You taught him right from wrong. It was his choice. You can't blame yourself for that."

52

"To hell I can't," Conrad grumbled. "I wasn't there for him when he needed me. I was here taking this bullshit assignment from the Chancellor. I was too busy getting promoted to notice that Thomas needed me." He turned to his friend. "I was the arrogant one."

"Like hell." Xavier frowned. "You are the most selfless man I have ever known, and one of the best teachers the Academy has ever turned out. Yes, you took the assignment from Alexander, but only to protect those you love."

That much was true. Conrad had accepted the appointment to the Council of Seven to protect Thomas and Saint, but the opposite had happened. He had been forced to kill Thomas, and send Saint away. His plans had turned against him, and now he was useless. He turned and looked at his old friend. "I need to do something."

"I know," Xavier said with a smile. "You told the Chancellor that you would see to this assignment personally, did you not?"

Conrad nodded.

"Then see to it personally," Xavier finished.

It was as if a light bulb went off in Conrad's brain. He suddenly straightened and understood what Xavier meant. It was the perfect solution, and he wondered why he hadn't thought of it. Conrad considered the idea for a moment. "Alexander won't like this." He laughed.

"Screw 'im." Xavier patted Conrad on the shoulder. "I'll manage things here in your stead, and keep the Chancellor off your back. Go take care of Saint and Kat."

Chapter Five

He walked carefully, but with purpose. It had been quite some time since he strode unescorted anywhere. A cadre of High Wraith was always at his side, especially in this time of war, but his errand had to be completed away from their watchful eyes. They were the most loyal the Order had, and he had handpicked all of them, but he knew the only way to ensure a secret was to keep as few people in the loop as possible. And tonight, it was just him.

Dressed in black with a heavy pea coat wrapped tightly around his chest, Ramius Alexander weaved through back alleys toward his destination. The collar of his jacket was hiked high on his neck, and his hands were stuffed deep in his pockets. His scythe, mostly worn for ceremony now, was nevertheless slung on his belt. He didn't think there would be trouble, but knew a wise man always expected the unexpected. Before becoming the Chancellor, he was a Wraith after all. And despite the fact he didn't enjoy fighting, he was very good at it.

Exiting an alley, Alexander stopped. The street was empty and the streetlights looked distant in the thick London fog. The opposite wall was bare of windows, doors, and even the spray-painted graffiti that seemed to occupy every other blank surface. It was nothing more than a gray, brick wall, yet it was his destination. Stepping through the fog, he stopped before the wall and lifted his arm.

Spreading his fingers, he pressed his palm to the smooth surface, but watched it slip through. The wall rippled out from his hand, as though water. He hadn't been here in a long, long time and hoped it hadn't moved. This was a good sign.

Stepping completely though the wall into a recessed stairwell, the Wraith Chancellor stared at a hidden blue neon sign that read "Boda's." This was a supernatural bar, a haven for inhumans, and also home to London's preternatural bounty hunters guild. No mortals allowed. Walking down the dank staircase, Alexander stared at the heavy steel door at the bottom. There were no doormen or bouncers. There wasn't a need for them here as most things in Boda's could take care of themselves. It was more often the case that those who stepped beyond the steel door needed protection from what they found inside.

Pushing open the heavy door, he was assaulted by a puff of smoke and a sickly sweet smell. He recognized it as some sort of opiate, but couldn't be more specific than that. Unbuttoning his jacket, Alexander kept his hands at his sides with his scythe within reach. He scanned over the dank bar, and the villainy contained within. They made their living off the pain and suffering of others. In Alexander's opinion, there were none lower on the food chain, but, for the moment at least, he needed them.

After pulling a rolled sheet of paper from his inside pocket, he stared at it. Little more than a sheet of A4 with a red ribbon tied in a bow, he wished it were an actual scroll made of parchment or lambskin. The modern version had somehow stripped the magic and mysticism away. Slipping off the ribbon, Alexander stowed it back in his pocket and held the scroll tightly.

Few lights hung from the ceiling of the establishment. Instead, candles in tall glass cylinders occupied the center of most of the tables. A bar ran the length of the room on the right, while thirteen tables occupied the remaining floorspace. An odd number of columns were placed in a seemingly random design, but Alexander knew they, along with the tables and candles, were placed specifically to defuse spells and magical attacks. Beings in shades of gray, green, red, blue, black, and orange littered the tables and bar, the din of their combined conversations barely rising above hushed levels.

A massive gray creature, Boda stood behind the bar observing his patrons. Spikes and heavy plates covered his entire body, only revealing his glowing, blood-red eyes, and jagged teeth. He stood nearly nine feet tall, so he had to stoop to serve beverages on the bar. His face was pure evil, his mouth pulled into a perpetual sneer. He was the stuff of nightmares, except for the long white apron that hung from his neck and was strapped tightly around his waist. Wrapping his oddly shaped clawed hands around a bottle, he poured a drink and set it in front of a vampire seated at the bar. Boda looked up and acknowledged Alexander with a scowl then returned to his work. No one knew what Boda was, and he liked it that way.

The Chancellor scanned the bar and spotted what he came for. Adjusting his jacket nervously,

Alexander walked straight to the back of the place. Shuffling around an empty table Alexander stood in awe before a huge board with hundreds of pages tacked to it. These were beings with bounties on their head. It didn't matter who they were, or what they had done, someone, or something, wanted these people dead or alive. This was "Boda's Wanted Board." To make it on the board was bad news as this was also the hub for London's Preternatural Bounty Hunter's Guild. Anyone and everyone looking to make a name for themselves used this board to start, and even seasoned professionals were known to pick through it from time to time to score what they thought was "easy money."

Unrolling the paper, Alexander stared at it. It wasn't that he was having an internal conflict, he simply wanted to make sure all the information was exactly as he wanted it. He had poured over this document for hours, making sure it contained everything a potential bounty hunter would need, but keeping it vague enough that he could ensure plausible denial if this somehow made it back to him.

He simply didn't trust Conrad anymore.

Grabbing two thumbtacks from the board, he pressed the paper flat and tacked it in an empty spot. Stepping back, he stared at the image of Saint printed near the center of the page. He needed this Wraith, preferably alive, but dead would work just fine. She was the future of the Order, and he would let no one, not even the man he appointed as head of the Council of Seven, stand in his way. This was too important. Alexander considered the seven digit bounty printed on the bottom of the page in bold font. He hoped it was enough to draw out the rookies, but all the veterans as well. Alexander wanted every bounty hunter in Europe to be looking for Saint. This would ensure he attained his prize.

Turning away from the board, Alexander nodded to the hulking Boda and made his way toward the door. His business was concluded, and the less time he spent here the better. Buttoning his heavy coat, the Chancellor pulled open the heavy door and left without speaking a single word.

A figure, swathed in black, materialized from the shadows. He had been watching Alexander's every move with keen interest. He wondered for a moment if the newly elected Chancellor was losing his edge, as he hadn't been detected. He could have killed the Wraiths' leader with little resistance, yet the old man hadn't even twitched. Gliding like a ghost across the bar, the figure hovered in front of the board. Lifting his gloved hand, he ran his fingers tenderly over the printed image of Saint. His temper flared for a moment and he wanted to rip the paper from the wall, but he fought to control it. She was his to capture and end, not some two-bit bounty hunter's. But his rational mind won over the anger as he came to a realization. This way would be much more fun.

Turning, his golden eyes flashed in the low light, as did the silver and black scythe hilt on his belt.

***

Saint felt nauseous. Her eyes ached as they

slowly opened and her brain throbbed dully behind her skull. Smacking her lips, the Wraith tried to work some saliva over her parched mouth. Her limbs felt heavy and useless as she tried to roll onto her side. Instinctively pulling her knees up to her chest, she wrapped her arms around them and buried her face. She felt as though she was coming off a three-day bender then rode hard and put away wet, with one hell of a hangover. She hadn't felt this way in a while. Not since the week with Miller in Barcelona...but that was a long time ago.

Saint's thoughts snapped back to the angel and she sat straight up.

Remembering its beautiful, light features, her memories nevertheless focused on its remarkable feathered wings. It looked as though it had stepped right out of Christian scriptures and into her nightmares. She remembered the man's expression of peacefulness then utter horror as the angel snapped his neck. He wasn't there to save the man, but to bring swift vengeance from God. And Saint was next. What would it be like to be an angel, one hand always raised toward Heaven with wingtips dipped in blood? To be the right hand of God...the thought was staggering. How does one kill in the name of the Lord? Efficiently, she supposed.

But there was another, more pressing question that plagued her mind. Where was she, and how had she come here?

Saint's eyes wandered around the meager room she occupied. The walls were a sickly green, and the once lush, matching carpet was hammered down by years and years of overuse. A television, probably older than her, occupied the far corner and the bolts that held it to the stand and floor were readily evident. Her clothes were laid neatly over the back of a dull orange chair opposite the bed, and only then did she realize her nakedness. Wandering past the dresser and broken mirror with copious amounts of tape used to fix several cracks, Saint's eyes settled on what was surely the bathroom door. Closed tightly, bright, yellow light spilled out from beneath.

She spotted her scythe sitting quietly on the chair's cushion. Not out of her reach, but damned inconvenient.

The Wraith reached out with her evolved senses and found a familiar sensation behind the door. With a sigh of relief, Saint recognized Kat, just getting out of the shower. She couldn't detect any other presences nearby, save for the bugs and rodents that constantly cluttered her preternatural awareness.

Falling back in bed, Saint pulled the covers over her breasts and laced her hands behind her head. The ceiling was a mottled collection of stains that seemed to defy the laws of physics. And if they were bodily fluids, she really didn't want to know how they had come to stain the ceiling. Disgusted, Saint rolled onto her side and stared vacantly out the only window in the room. Pea colored curtains rustled softly on both sides as the faraway sound of traffic wafted in on the breeze. The city's light pollution drowned out the stars, but the moon hung low in the sky surrounded by a hazy halo. Buildings reached into the night sky vainly, hoping to capture some piece of Heaven. If they only knew what they would find when they got there…

Saint knew, and it frightened her.

"How are you feeling?"

Saint almost jumped. She hadn't heard Kat open the bathroom door. "Okay," the vampire hunter breathed. "A little shaky."

"You were in bad shape," Kat admitted, leaning against the bathroom doorframe. She had a large, white towel wrapped around her naked body, but it was barely enough to cover her due to her belly. "You've been out for quite a while, since last night. I wasn't sure you were going to wake up. I had to strip you down and dump you in the shower to get all the blood off."

"All the blood?" Saint echoed worriedly.

"You were bleeding from your nose, ears," Kat paused, "and your eyes."

Lifting her hand, Saint ran her fingers gently over her eyes. That would explain the pain when she awoke, although the why was still a mystery. She remembered the angel's voice in her mind and the pain she felt.

Kat walked in slowly and sat on the edge of the bed. "The angel was about to touch you when I pulled you out."

Saint shook her head. "It couldn't have been an actual angel. There is simply no way."

"Why?" Kat asked.

"Because they don't exist," Saint answered.

"Neither do vampires," the vampire replied.

Saint scowled.

Kat adjusted her grip on the towel. "If monsters

exist, why can't angels?"

"Because they can't," Saint said again, this time more forcefully.

"Ah." Kat smiled. "I get it."

Saint smiled politely as though she were missing the joke. "Care to share?"

"You strike me as a very no-nonsense kind of person, Saint," Kat answered. "Despite your particular line of work, you like to keep your beliefs rooted in the scientific."

"So was this a mail in course you took? Because I don't recall you having a psychology degree," Saint growled. "So spare me your analysis, Sigmund."

"For you to believe in angels," Kat continued unabated, "you would have to therefore believe in God, something you can neither prove, nor disprove. Something you aren't prepared to do."

"I don't really have the strength, or patience, for a philosophical debate right now." Saint stared at the vampire, but let her gaze fall away. Sliding out of bed, the moonlight silhouetted her beautiful frame as she walked slowly across the room and grabbed her clothes. "Where are we?"

"Motel on the outskirts of the city," Kat answered. "I needed to get us out of the open."

Saint pulled on her tight black shirt. "Unpaid?"

"Paid," the vampire corrected.

Saint looked at Kat curiously.

Kat shook her head. "Don't ask. Vampire," she reminded Saint, pointing to herself.

Saint sighed. "You can't go around killing people. Not under Wraith protection."

"My apologies." Kat stood up in a huff. "But my Wraith protector was a bit incapacitated at the time. I had to do something."

"So while I was out," Saint said angrily as she pulled on her pants, "you whacked somebody, sucked his blood, and robbed him. Nice."

Kat pointed at herself with her thumb and shrugged. "Vampire."

"Not a good excuse," Saint spun and barked. Grabbing Kat by the throat, she lifted the pregnant vampire off the bed and slammed her against the wall in a flash of motion. "I don't care who you fucked," Saint's eyes flashed gold, "I will not hesitate to destroy you if you do that again."

Kat struggled but couldn't break the Wraith's grip.

"And I will not help you feed," Saint felt dirty even saying the word. "You have to find another way. I can't stand by and watch you hurt those I've vowed to protect, nor will I help you. Do you understand?"

Kat's eyes changed to solid gold and she bared her fangs, but she was still unable to break the Wraith's grip around her throat. Fortunately, there were other vulnerable areas Saint had exposed in her anger. Kicking forward, the vampire brought her knee solidly into the Wraith's pelvis.

Saint coughed and doubled over involuntarily as her diaphragm was compressed.

Bringing her palm straight up, Kat forcefully bent the Wraith's elbow in the wrong direction. Saint released her grip quickly enough to avoid a broken arm and knocked Kat to the floor. Without hesitating, the vampiress charged the Wraith. Stumbling back, Saint sized up the naked, pregnant vampire rushing toward her. Kat had only succeeded in pissing her off. Dodging the vampire's first swing, Saint knocked away the second and retaliated. Punching Kat solidly in the bridge of the nose, Saint watched the vampiress' head snap back before she crumbled to the floor.

Kat's mental projection faltered revealing the pale, decaying corpse that was her true form. Grasping at her nose, the vampire tried to stop the blood that was gushing down her mouth and chin. Saint had cleanly broken her nose with one punch. Her blonde hair was actually gray and hung in filthy clumps from her scalp, while the original vampire bite on her neck was a massive wound that revealed veins, tendons, and muscles beneath the flesh. She looked more like a zombie than a powerful vampire. It was only the false image she psychically forced on others that looked human. She was truly a monster.

And Saint had never seen her this way before.

It was a stark and forceful reminder of what Kat truly was. She may be the most human vampire that had ever existed, but she was still a vampire. Saint fell back into the orange chair and looked at her own hands. She, by comparison, was the most vampiric Wraith to exist, but she was still a Wraith and not human. Her eyes fell on Kat again. Somewhere between them humanity existed, yet both were something that should not exist. They were both monsters, and they belonged together.

"That really hurt," Kat said, finally restoring

her mental projection. It wasn't an automatic function for most vampires, like their lack of reflection, it took concentration and skill. Kat was still learning to control hers.

"You kicked me in the gut," Saint countered.

"After you went psycho and pinned me to the wall," Kat finished.

Saint wasn't sure how to reply. Kat had her there, but she damned sure wasn't going to apologize. "Look," she said slowly as she regained her composure, "we can't keep on like this. We need ground rules."

"Fine." Kat frowned. "Rule number one: no punching me in the nose."

"Okay." Saint shook her head. "That's not exactly what I meant. I was thinking more along the lines of no killing humans, and I won't kill you."

Kat knew she was no match for the Wraith, even on a good day, and Saint could dispatch her with little trouble. "I'm stuck in the middle," she admitted. "I can go out in the light of day, but I still need blood. I need to eat," she shrugged, "and so does the baby. What am I supposed to do?"

Leaning back in the ugly chair, Saint ran her fingers through her hair. "I don't know," she admitted, "but I won't let you, or the baby, starve. I'll think of something. I made a promise." She wasn't sure if she was reminding the vampire, or herself. "In the meantime," Saint continued, "we have to get a message to Conrad at the Wraith Academy in England about this angel sighting. He needs to know what's going on."

"And how do you propose we do that?" Kat

asked, still massaging her nose.

Saint took a breath. "I wish I—"

The exterior exploded in before the Wraith could finish her statement. Shards of wood, glass, and metal rocketed into the room like missiles creating a gaping hole facing out onto the balcony. Rolling over the armrest, Saint felt multiple splinters bite into her flesh before she could clear the chair. Hitting the floor she heard Kat scream as her mind was again flooded with the angel's terrible, but beautiful song.

Pain throbbed in her temples and eyes, but she forced herself off the carpeting. "Let her go," Saint growled. What felt like a tear ran down her cheek, but she knew it was blood. The Wraith refused to wipe it away.

The angel stood motionless with Kat pinned to its chest, its arms and feathered wings wrapped around the pregnant vampire. As Kat struggled helplessly, the angel regarded Saint unemotionally. It seemed the perfect pillar of patience and calm. Saint tensed and readied herself. Fairly certain she would be dead before she even had a chance to lay a finger on the angel, she still had to do something. Her knees started to buckle as the angel's song grew louder in her mind.

Saint gritted her teeth.

The angel refused to act.

Springing forward, the angel's song instantly intensified. Falling short of her target, she spilled to the carpet but tried to fight back to her feet. She could feel her blood flowing freely from her eyes, nose, and down her neck from her ears as the chorus reverberated in her mind. She fell again. Her sense of balance was gone as the world spun wildly around her. The sides of her head felt as though they were about to split open from the pain. Bringing her fists up, Saint pressed her knuckles hard against her skull hoping for some relief.

Then it was gone.

Gasping then drawing in a slow breath, Saint rolled onto her stomach. Drawing up onto her knees, she felt a wave of relief as the song stopped. She lifted her eyes, but already knew what she would find. The angel, and Kat, were gone. She was alone. Her head throbbed.

Saint crumbled to the floor.

***

Conrad stood beneath the large, silver moon enjoying the cold, crisp English night. Born and raised in London, he took every opportunity he could to get back. It held some sort of sway over his soul, some sort of siren's song that always called to him no matter where he was. He had traveled all over the world and back again, but had found no place like London. It was a hub of humanity, culture, and a world entirely unto itself. He couldn't exactly explain why, other than this was his home.

Walking slowly with his hands in his pockets, the High Wraith watched people moving about Trafalgar Square. This place had almost a magical quality at night as the moon shone down through the fountains surrounding Nelson's Column, and glinted off the backs of the four massive bronze lions that guarded it. Admiral Horatio Nelson, sculpted in granite, looked south toward

67

Westminster from his perch on the column, a still vigilant sentry for the country he died protecting. A red double-decker bus, which had become a London icon, roared past on the far side, bored faces framed in the windows. Several couples walked hand in hand through the square while a family let their children climb on Admiral Nelson's lions. It was a perfect night.

This is how it was at the end of all things.

Slipping his backpack off and setting it on the ground at his feet, Conrad slowly sat down on a metal bench and simply watched. This had become a tradition of sorts. Like a soldier kissing his girl goodbye before shipping out to war, he took in London's atmosphere, and breathed the air one more time...maybe one last time. Conrad frowned and mentally scolded himself. He couldn't think like that. Pessimism and self-doubt were a Wraith's worst enemy.

Reaching into his backpack, he wrapped his fingers around several metal cylinders. Drawing them out, he considered the amber fluid held within the transparent vials. Created to be a chemical weapon by the Russian Vampire Triad known as the Troika, this serum attached to the vampire virus, and stripped it from a body. The Troika planned to use it on rival clans, but their plans had never come to fruition. Instead, the Wraith had seized, studied, and refined the chemical. It was now the only known cure, besides death, for vampirism. And they had found a way to make it equally effective on Wraith. It was a weapon of last resort, and Conrad had only four of the precious vials. He didn't like it, but it was better to have it and not need it. Attaching an auto injector to one of the vials, he slipped it into his inside pocket, and returned the others to his pack.

Letting his head fall back, he took a breath in through his nose as his eyes wandered across the barely visible blanket of stars above despite London's light pollution making them difficult to see. Focusing on the moon, his attention was captured by two bright lights. They looked like stars, but were too bright. Not twinkling, they looked more like planets. Conrad let his mind wander playfully trying to guess which two celestial bodies they could be.

Two more appeared.

Curiously, Conrad held his breath and became very still as he watched. He overheard a woman's voice across the park exclaim about the lights, but kept his focus trained. As he watched, four became six, and then eight. He felt dread slide down his spine and land with a plop in his stomach like a rock as he lost count of the rapidly appearing lights. Standing, he spun slowly and saw that they were everywhere. They had to number in the hundreds as the night sky was being blotted out behind them.

The High Wraith's mind reeled with possibilities. Was this some sort of natural event, perhaps a meteor shower? No, the lights appeared stationary...at least for the moment anyway. Having seen his share of movies, Conrad wondered if this was the alien invasion Hollywood had been preparing the world for since the 1950's. His rational mind wanted to crush the idea almost immediately, but he forcefully reminded himself that rationality and reason didn't often play a major role in his life. He was a vampire hunter, after all. Would an alien invasion really be that implausible?

A child shrieked.

Conrad had drawn his scythe, activated it, and hit a dead run before his eyes fully registered what he was charging toward. Every fiber of his being told him to stop running as his brain tried to process the scene before him, but he didn't. It had a child. That was all that mattered. Conrad was about to attack what looked very much like an angel.

Wings spread majestically, the being hovered above the ground with the child cradled in its arms. Conrad recognized the boy as the one who had been climbing on Admiral Nelson's lions. Clad in white and gray, the being glowed with a light that seemed to somehow warm and purify the night around it. The child cried and writhed trying to free himself, while his parents stood dumbfounded.

Bringing his weapon to bear, Conrad initiated his attack.

But he was blindsided. Snapping into existence as the High Wraith was starting his swing, another being knocked Conrad off his feet. Hitting the concrete and skidding, he heard his scythe skitter away. Rolling onto his back, the Wraith pushed off the ground and jumped back onto his feet. Facing the second being, he stared into the void that existed beneath its hood. He could detect no face, no head...only infinite darkness.

Conrad scanned quickly for his weapon, but found it well out of reach on the other side of a fountain.

Another voice cried out.

Conrad spotted two more of the beings lifting the couple he had glimpsed earlier off the ground. Even though they struggled vainly to hold onto each other, they were ripped apart and lifted higher into the sky.

The High Wraith felt his heart break, but couldn't deal with that right now. He had his own problems. Bringing his attention back to the angelic being before him, Conrad gritted his teeth and charged. He was going down fighting, that much he knew. Dropping his shoulder, he barreled in and connected solidly. Throwing his arms out, Conrad tackled the being and slammed it hard to the ground. Drawing up on his knees, the Wraith threw three quick punches into the being's midsection. He felt an immediate pang of guilt as he felt something in the being's chest, it could have been ribs, crack under the force of his blows.

With a shriek, the being lashed out but Conrad was able to dodge the clumsy attack.

While rolling forward, Conrad pinned its arms and wings to the ground with his knees. He had to make this quick and dirty. There were far too many of them to waste time. Guilt gripped him again, as if he were about to destroy an innocent.

"Father, please forgive me," Conrad whispered.

He drew a quick breath then slammed his fist down. Breaking through its flesh and bones, Conrad wrapped his hand around what he hoped was the heart and ripped it free. Holding the disgusting, discolored organ in his hand, Conrad stared at the black ooze that covered his hand. It must have been blood.

As the being fell back dead, the others in the square shrieked in horror and agony. Dozens more appeared, and their focus was squarely on the High Wraith.

At least he knew he could kill them.

"Well," Conrad said, stumbling to his feet, "that did it." He looked down at the black blood on his knuckles and felt sick. As he slowly lifted his face he looked upon the beings with regret as they converged on him.

He swung his arm and knocked the first one out of the air, but was broadsided by a second. Stumbling and spinning, the Wraith gained control and retaliated. Grabbing a third's outstretched arm, he swung the being full force into three more that were almost upon him. He felt claws tear down his back. His flesh sizzled as he fell forward. Grunting, the warrior was hit a second and third time. Swinging wildly, he felt his fists connect with an angel, but it was too little, too late. There were too many. Conrad felt claws rake the side of his face then stars sparkled in front of his eyes as he was hit hard in the back of the head.

Conrad fell.

Chapter Six

They were awake.

Angry, enraged, and hurt, their Eden had somehow sunk into Hell. The tenets set forth had been widely disregarded and repeatedly broken, leaving nearly every man, woman, and child washed in sin. Even those who spread their word had fallen. This was not the world as they intended it. It had become sick and perverse. What they had worked so hard to create and cultivate, humanity had tossed aside with little indifference. But they would remedy this iniquity. Their final crusade, their holy jihad, would wipe away strife and sin. They would convert the nonbelievers and spread the word of God, by force if necessary.

"We must hold the Basilicas!"

The cry was barely heard above the clamor of battle. Beneath the cold, silvery moon, throngs of orange-clad warriors did their best to follow the orders against wave after wave of opposition. The crack of gunfire echoed off the granite walls, while the clang of melee weapons created an almost musical cacophony. Snipers on the roofs of Saint Peter's and Lateran's Basilicas tried to pick off both ground and airborne targets, but were easily snatched from their perches. The chug of a diesel engine and the familiar rhythmic jingle of churning treads filled the square as a tank maneuvered against the superior force. The main gun fired with a thud destroying both attackers and priceless architectural treasures. Granite crashed into Saint

Peter's Square, already littered with the dead of both sides.

It was full-scale war, man versus angel. As one angel fell, ten more appeared to take its place. The winged beings swooped down and through Saint Peter's Square snatching the orange-robed warriors with ease then killing them in the air. Tossing the bodies to the ground like rag dolls, the angels crushed anyone who wasn't lucky enough to get out of the way. It was just a matter of time now. The angels had already won, but this wasn't a siege, rather total annihilation of the Catholic Church.

The Second War of Heaven had begun.

***

Seemingly organic in nature, tubes and tendon-like columns weaved through the strange environment at odd angles leaving no flat surfaces. It looked as though this place was alive as fluid could be seen moving through the veins, and the floors, walls, and ceilings somehow shifted and contracted. Light filtered in through the fleshy areas between, silhouetting a network of what looked like veins, and casting everything in an ominous blue glow.

Looking down, he realized he was somehow cocooned in the wall. Tubes and a skin-like substance stretched over his body, suspending him off the floor. Seeing that his hands were free, Marcus Specter ran his fingertips lightly over the surface. It was moist with a glittering sheen, and produced a rubbery tactile sensation. Pushing out, the cocoon stretched, but refused to give. Marcus was trapped.

74

With each breath, he became more aware of the heat and humidity in this place. He felt wet, sluggish, but oddly relaxed. His body tingled as though pulses of electricity skittered across his nerves, but it wasn't painful or unpleasant. He had never seen anything like this before. It was stunningly horrific, yet intriguingly beautiful. He felt lost, but at the same time safely encapsulated as though tucked neatly in a womb.

Lifting his head, he scanned the cavernous chamber. Two tunnels led off in opposite directions as far as he could see, while a third exited vertically. Somehow, he knew that human hands did not create this place. Across the way, Marcus spied several concave depressions in the wall that appeared very similar to the one he was in. They were empty, save for a lone female on the far side. Her head was limp letting her blond hair fall down over the cocoon. He didn't recognize her, nor did he see any movement from her. She looked as though she were dead.

Marcus lifted his gaze to see a beautiful being descending from the upper tunnel. As it emerged into the chamber, it opened its wings majestically and touched down lightly. Feathered like those on the other angel Marcus had seen, these wings were not white. Instead, they looked more like a crow's, jet black with just a touch of brown in the coverts. The being wore a lavish blue robe with intricate designs embroidered in golden thread. Its hood was up like the others completely hiding any existence of its face. Still, it was the most beautiful thing Marcus had ever seen.

Marcus wanted to speak, but found the words

dying in his throat. Swallowing hard, he tried again. "Who are you?"

"I have had so many names," it replied in a voice that seemed to be accompanied by a heavenly choir. The angel folded its wings back and adjusted its robe. "Once I was simply named Enoch. I lived for three hundred and forty-five years."

That admission may have shocked a normal mortal, but not Marcus as he had already existed for three hundred years as well. Still, this was an amazing, beautiful creature, and it put Marcus completely at ease. He could sense no malice, no hatred, and no ill intent.

"You may have heard of my great-grandson," the being offered. "He is known for saving the human race, and much of the animal kingdom from the great flood."

Marcus cocked an eyebrow. "Noah? I thought that was just a story, a myth."

"Like vampires?" the being asked slyly.

"Point taken," Marcus acknowledged.

The being circled around Marcus slowly. "I walked with God, but did not die," the being continued. "Through the pain of flame, I was transformed into what you see before you, and given the name Metatron."

"Metatron?" Marcus mouthed the name.

It stood before Marcus. "I am the messenger, the communicator," Metatron paused, "The Voice of God."

Marcus knew it wasn't lying. He wasn't sure how, or why, but he could feel it in his gut. The being that stood before him, Metatron, was indeed an angel, and the most vaunted of their kind. It seemed all of his questions about existence and religion had been answered. He felt suddenly insignificant and confused. "Why am I here?"

The angel waved its hand before the cocoon.

Marcus felt a powerful surge of electricity shoot through his body and was gripped by paralysis. As his muscles twitched uncontrollably, he felt the cocoon weaken, then give way. Crumbling forward, Marcus fell hard unable to bring his hands and arms up to brace against the fall. As the Wraith hit, searing pain exploded across his back. Feeling as though his insides were being torn apart and rearranged, two sharp spikes erupted from his flesh. Marcus shivered as his warm blood splattered across his skin. It was overwhelming, but he refused to cry out.

Metatron knelt down and ran its slender, perfect fingers down Marcus' cheek. "God has a plan for us all, even for you, my wayward hunter."

Chapter Seven

Her black hair spilled messily down around her face and shoulders, while her knees were tucked tightly to her chest. A vicious migraine ran rampant through her brain, pounding angrily behind her temples. Her eyes ached, and her mouth felt as though it was stuffed with cotton. No matter what she tried, or what she took, the symptoms refused to abate. Leaning over slowly, Saint wrapped her arms around her knees and rested her head on the carpeted floor.

"You gonna live?"

Saint's icy blue eyes settled on the source of the question. She licked her lips to try and generate some moisture. "That's the plan," she croaked meekly.

Her eyes wandered over the four walls. It was a room very similar to the one Kat had rented, minus the gaping hole in the wall the angel had created. Glancing at a small wooden table in the far corner, Saint saw her dinner. Certain that some pimple-faced teen had slaved over a hot microwave to warm the soggy burger and fries, her appetite hadn't quite been whetted by it. It had been sitting there for hours, and would most likely remain there. Saint had no desire to eat it, or anything for that matter. Still, it was nice of him to make the attempt.

She looked at the hulking form seated in front of the window. He had been there for most of the day, and so far well into the evening. Drowned in shadows, he had the edge of the heavy curtain pulled back letting a splinter of moonlight slice across his face. He was exactly as she remembered. He had twice put his life on the line to protect her, and he had done it yet again. Saint didn't even know why. There were rumors that he was fulfilling his role in the prophecy regarding the Chosen One, while others claimed it was more of a life debt. That made sense though.

Honor was everything to a werewolf.

Letting the curtain slowly down so as not to cause it to wave and draw attention, he leaned back in his chair and rested his hands on the arms. Glancing over his shoulder, he watched Saint worriedly. Standing, he stepped closer, but remained in the shadows. "You okay, Emily?"

He was the only one who could get away with calling her that. His voice was deep and creamy, and very soothing to her ears. "I don't know, Ben."

"What does that mean?" Ben watched her for a moment longer.

She couldn't find an explanation that even came close to summing up how she felt. Anger, pain, frustration, angst, sadness, and loneliness swirled in her heart. Saint wanted to rage and destroy every angel she could find, but she couldn't bring herself to even get off the floor to eat. How could she answer Ben's question, when she didn't even know herself? "How did you even find me?" she asked as though she didn't want to be found.

"I'd been tracking you since Prague," Ben admitted and pointed to his nose. "Werewolf, remember?" He smiled, but quickly let it fade. "You left without saying goodbye."

79

Even though she wanted to say she was sorry, she couldn't form the words. She wanted so bad to stay with him, and to take care of him, but fate had a different plan for her.

Emerging from the shadows, Ben sat down on the edge of the bed causing it to creak in agony and sighed deeply. "Are you ever going to let me in?"

She let her gaze fall silently away from his, knowing she had let him down.

Running his hand through his short, messy, dark hair, Ben let his eyes fall as well. With a midnight blue hoodie draped over his shoulders and a pair of tattered jeans clinging to his legs, the werewolf looked fashionable, despite not trying to. The white Henley he wore was completely unbuttoned allowing a glimpse of several deep red scars across his chest that had almost claimed his life. If Saint had been unable to get him back to his clan after his battle with the bounty hunter Talon Creed, they very well may have. He owed her his life.

But she owed him her life too.

Saint pulled her hand down her face. She had to change the subject. "Any sign of Kat?"

Ben shook his head.

She hadn't seen or heard anything from Kat in two days, and had no idea if the vampire was even still alive. Saint had failed not only Kat, but her unborn child, and Thomas. So much for the great and powerful Chosen One... She couldn't even protect a single, pregnant vampire.

Saint sighed. "Every time I get close to one of those damned angels, my brain feels like it's melting and I can't do anything." She pulled her fingers through her hair, yanking a knot free. "I don't know what to do."

"We'll find Kat," Ben assured her. He knew how important this woman was, not only to the Wraith, but to every preternatural being. There was no precedent for a pregnant vampire. This could mean an evolutionary shift was occurring...or possibly something much more sinister. The werewolf's feelings were mixed. Still, he felt obligated to see it through. "I have several clan mates scouring Slovakia, but we're being hunted by the angels as well. It's slow going."

"What do these creatures want?" Saint posed to Ben. "There doesn't seem to be any logic to their attacks."

"I wish I knew," Ben answered stoically. "They're attacking everything randomly." He shrugged. "No pattern. It doesn't make any sense."

Saint knew one thing for certain: "We need to mobilize."

Ben turned to the Wraith and cocked an eyebrow. "Pardon?"

"Werewolves, Wraith, humans, hell," Saint paused, "even vampires. We're all targets. We need to stop these creatures and find Kat, and we're going to need an army to do it."

Ben continued to stare at Saint in disbelief. "You can't be serious."

Saint slowly stood up and straightened her shirt. "We need to get to Conrad."

Ben stood to meet her. "Saint, maybe the angel did more damage to your brain than we realized."

He smiled slyly. "That isn't going to happen."

"Then we're all dead," Saint answered unemotionally.

The two stood staring at each other in silence. Dropping her head, Saint stepped around Ben, grabbed her leather trench and pulled it on.

The werewolf held his position.

Moving to the door, Saint stopped, spun and faced Ben. "You coming?"

Ben let his head fall back, as if looking to the heavens for answers. He drew a quick breath and held it. He could argue, but he knew it would be fruitless. Saint had already made up her mind. His choice, it seemed, had already been made.

"Yeah," Ben finally exhaled.

***

"Wake up!"

Conrad's eyes snapped open as he was slapped hard across the face. Reeling back into a defensive posture, Conrad's back slammed against a wall. His hand snapped to his belt, but found his scythe missing. Knowing he was pinned and weaponless, he slowly stared up at the hulking form that loomed over him. As the fog started to clear from his mind, Conrad's senses reached out and he started to ease.

"I should have left you with the winged monsters," the beast growled and took a step back into the shadows.

Conrad lifted his hand, felt the deep scratch marks on his face, and winced. He remembered being overwhelmed by angels in Trafalgar Square, but couldn't remember anything after that. He turned his attention back to the beast. "What happened, Stark?"

Nearly ten feet tall, Stark's werewolf form was impressive, and utterly threatening. His long, slender muzzle hid the rows of perfect, razor-sharp teeth, but his vibrant yellow eyes told the tale of his power. Curved claws jutted from each fingertip at the ends of both of his long, muscled arms. His fur was as black as midnight, but had an undeniable sheen beneath the moonlight. His ears were perked straight up, constantly listening for any hint that he had been detected. He was a tank created of flesh and bone.

Stark's eyes settled on Conrad. "I just happened to be in the neighborhood," his voice was deep, jagged, and sounded painful, "when I found you."

Conrad couldn't hide his surprise. "You saved me?"

Stark snarled. That was probably as close as Conrad was going to get to an acknowledgement.

After their last meeting, that came as quite a shock to Conrad. His eyes wandered over the werewolf, but stopped on a glistening patch the size of a small melon on the left of Stark's abdomen. A chunk of fur was missing revealing the deeply damaged flesh beneath. "You're hurt."

Stark clamped a massive paw over the wound. "Only a flesh wound." He downplayed it, but his body posture exposed his pain. "An angel got lucky."

Straightening his back, Conrad felt pain shoot through his body. He wasn't in much better shape than Stark. The angels had torn him up.

The two were in an empty flat overlooking

Trafalgar Square. The pungent reek of death was strong here, but the High Wraith couldn't tell if it was emanating from inside the building, or from the street below. The square was empty now, free of the chaos Conrad had witnessed earlier. An eerie orange glow rose behind the buildings, fighting against the subdued hues of the sunrise. London was burning, yet the city was strangely quiet. There were no sounds of automobiles, emergency vehicles, or people. The sky was choked with smoke, creating a terrible blanket that threatened to smother everything beneath it. It unnerved Conrad. He had never seen his beloved city this way.

"What the hell is going on?" Conrad asked, turning back to Stark.

Kneeling down, the final vestiges of his werewolf form were shed as Stark regressed. His eyes were weary and tired, while his huge, naked, muscular form seemed somehow fragile now. He turned and stared out the window. "I wish I knew."

Pulling off his battered, brown, leather trench, Conrad tossed it to Stark.

Snatching the coat out of the air, Stark tried to slip it over his huge arms. After several failures, he slung it over his back and grunted somewhat appreciatively.

Conrad sat in silence for a moment, sizing up the wolf. "Why are you alone? You never go anywhere without your entourage."

Stark lifted his head, but couldn't bring himself to look Conrad in the eye. "They're dead."

"Who?" Conrad asked.

"All of them!" Stark roared. He fell back

against the wall and slid down to the floor. Stark ran his meaty paw over his smooth, bald, head and hid his eyes. "The angels killed all of them." The wolf lowered his voice. "My clan is gone."

Conrad understood where the pain in Stark's voice was coming from. A wolf's clan was his family. It was something thicker than blood, and deeper than genetics. It was a sacred bond that most would never understand. There were no words that Conrad could utter to ease the situation. Stark needed action. It was the one thing a werewolf understood.

"We need to get to the Wraith Academy," Conrad said after a moment. "We need to mobilize to combat this threat."

Stark lifted his head. The whites of his sclera stood out ominously against his dark flesh. "I watched twenty werewolves, at total strength under the full moon, die at the hands of these winged monsters." He gritted his teeth. "They swarmed like flying insects and picked us off one by one. I watched my clansmen ripped in two in midair!" He ran his fingers over his bare scalp again, nervously. "What chance do you think a band of vampire hunters have against them?"

Conrad shot off the floor and charged toward Stark. "They're good men and women, and they're all we have!"

Stark refused to budge or blink. "Then we're dead."

Conrad balled his fists. He wanted to fire back, but realized it would fall on deaf ears. The High Wraith took a step back. "I don't need this, and I don't need you." Snatching his coat off Stark's back, he turned and marched toward the door.

"Wait."

Conrad stopped, but didn't turn.

Silence.

"I don't want to die," Stark whispered.

Taking a slow breath in through his nose, Conrad considered the wolf. He had wanted to call Stark a sniveling coward during their first meeting, but now he saw something different. The wolf was scared.

"Come on," Conrad said finally. "We need to get to the Academy."

Stark slowly stood and started toward Conrad, his head down like a dog that had been punished. His movements were slow and deliberate, yet he wasn't fully able to hide the pain that chewed up his side from the angel's attack.

"First order of business," Conrad sized up the wolf then smirked, "you need some clothes."

Cocking an eyebrow, Stark raised his right hand and extended his middle finger.

Chapter Eight

"We are dying, Chancellor!"

"I am very aware of the tactical situation, Master Xavier." Chancellor Alexander rubbed his fingertips lightly over his forehead, barely able to contain his disdain. His eyes wandered over the gathered group in his office before settling on the source of the outburst. "There's no need to keep restating the obvious."

"I'm sorry," Xavier breathed, "but I don't think you do, Chancellor. Not only are Bane's armies wiping out Wraith, but now we have these 'angels' annihilating anything in their path." The High Wraith adjusted his robe. "And no one's heard from Master Verge."

Xavier stood with the remaining five members of the Council of Seven, and several Master Wraith designated for protection. They had marched unannounced into the Chancellor's office demanding an explanation, or any assurance that something was being done to combat this new threat. The meeting was, so far, not going as they had hoped.

"And what would you have me do?" Alexander shot up from his desk and slammed his fist down. "We're already fighting a war with Bane, and losing! We don't have the manpower to effectively combat this new threat."

The Chancellor's stark comments stole the wind from Xavier's sails. More accustomed to hearing the Chancellor sugarcoat his statements,

Xavier didn't know how to respond to the truth. "We need to do something."

"But my question remains, Master Xavier," Alexander calmly reiterated. "If we use Wraiths to combat these—quote, unquote—angels, then we will be spread too thin and Bane will wipe us out. If we continue to focus on Bane's attacks, the angels will continue to destroy humanity. This is the proverbial rock and a hard place, no? Suggestions?"

"We are Wraith! We are warriors!" Garrett Nacamora shouted from the back of the room.

"Thank you." Alexander sighed. "That's very helpful."

Garrett pushed past the Council of Seven and stood before the Chancellor. As the Council's security, he was to be seen and not heard. "You don't understand," the young Wraith argued. "We are warriors. If we are to die, let us die fighting. Enough of this pointless debate!"

Xavier tried to hide the smirk on his face. He remembered another strong, powerful, young warrior who had told Alexander nearly the same thing. Thomas and Garrett were very similar indeed, but he had to act on this breach of protocol. "Garrett," he scolded, "restrain yourself or you will be removed."

Garrett balled his fists and glared at Xavier. The two Wraiths stared at each other for a long moment, trying to discern what the other was going to do. They both held their ground.

Finally Garrett acquiesced. "My apologies, Master." Like a scolded dog, he lowered his head, tucked his tail between his legs, and marched back to his place behind the Council. And it was killing him. He made a vow that it wouldn't be this way forever. Garrett would make sure of that.

Xavier watched Garrett a bit longer to ensure there would be no further outbursts then returned his attention to Chancellor Alexander. "It's obvious there's no solution to be found here. I'm sorry to have taken your time, Chancellor," Xavier spat and turned away. Facing the other members of the Council, he paused to see their response. He hoped someone would keep him there, would tell him to fight, but nothing was forthcoming. He frowned. Cowards.

Without another word, Xavier tossed back his robe and marched out of the Chancellor's office. The remainder of the Council followed quickly behind like sheep.

Alexander waited until the office door closed and sank back into his chair with a sigh. Lowering his elbows to the desk, the Chancellor cupped his face in his hands. He was facing an insurrection, and only an idiot wouldn't see it coming. Everything was quickly spiraling out of control. Something had to be done.

Immediately.

***

The destruction was almost unimaginable.

Entire buildings were torn open and left like rotting carcasses, and bloody corpses littered the streets like trash. Men, women, and children, it made no difference. They were all dead. Street lamps were uprooted entirely, and shards of glass glittered under the morning sun. Vehicles were overturned and piled like discarded toys beneath traffic signals that flashed pointlessly. War machines were scattered about, waiting helplessly without their human commanders. A lone tank occupied an intersection, its heavy barrel silent. Jagged hunks of thick armor jutted skyward as the metal beast had been utterly eviscerated. Craters were gouged into the streets, creating gaping chasms nearly impossible to navigate, while smoke rose into the sky from fires that seemed to burn everywhere. With each breath, they felt the smoke chew like battery acid into their throats and lungs, yet Ben and Saint pressed on.

No words had to be spoken. Each was lost in their own thoughts, trying, somehow, to get a handle on the moment. They were soldiers in their own way, and had been taught to block out pain, yet this atrocity was of such a magnitude that it was nearly impossible. Everywhere they looked there was more destruction. The city was in ruins.

They were marching through a war zone.

Saint couldn't help remembering walking through this ancient, magnificent city with Kat a few nights before. She recalled standing on the bank of the Danube, watching the lights reflect against the surface, facing the grisly task of feeding a pregnant vampire, and seeing an angel for the first time. She scanned the devastation. Had an angel done all of this?

Moving ahead, Saint felt a soggy crunch. Glancing down, she found the smashed, orange shell of a jack-o'-lantern beneath her foot, the chunks scattered with remnants of cardboard and tissue paper that were previously Halloween decorations. The pumpkin's forced grin was still partially visible, locked permanently in death. Saddened, Saint stepped back and tried to wipe orange goo from the sole of her boot. This should have been a time of celebration, instead it was more like the ancient pagans intended it to be—a time of mourning the dead.

The werewolf stopped and perked up his head. Taking a deep whiff of the air, he arched his back in a very animalistic way.

Saint knew he had caught a scent. She waited.

Taking a step, Ben turned to Saint. "Survivor."

Her eyes widened. "Go."

Ben launched away faster than a mortal could follow, but Saint pursued closely behind. She marveled at the wolf's agility as he bounded over debris, and cars that stood in his path. He moved more like an acrobat than a tanklike werewolf. Hard pressed to keep up, Saint pushed her body to its limits. Controlling her heart rate and breathing, the Wraith pumped her arms and legs fiercely. His pace was brutal. She felt more like she was chasing a missile than a man.

Without stopping, the wolf pointed at his destination. "Meet me downstairs."

"Hurry!" Saint shouted urgently.

Flames licked at Ben's feet as he leapt onto an overturned car and vaulted toward the side of a building. Snatching the fire escape railing with his hand, he planted both feet on the wall and pushed out hard. Swinging up backwards, he planted his other hand on the railing and stopped in a handstand like an Olympic gymnast. Using his immense arm strength, he vaulted into a somersault and landed on the balls of his feet on the fire escape. Without hesitation, he shot up the escape.

Smiling, Saint watched from the ground below. He was showing off, and she knew it.

She watched Ben smash through a fifth floor window and vanish inside. Tossing her leather jacket back, she called her scythe to her hand, leveled her gaze at the building, and walked inside. Moving easily though the apartment's lobby, the powerful Wraith kicked open the security doors and marched inside. Spotting the elevators beyond a bank of mailboxes, Saint moved in and found a defensive position. Her thumb hovered over the activation stud on her weapon. Looking up, she saw the floor indicator above the elevator blink on and begin to descend.

Saint twisted her head to the right and popped her neck nervously. With four loud cracks, she felt a momentary numbness in her fingertips. It was a bad habit she had picked up a long time ago that drove people crazy. Still, it had become a ritual for her.

As the indicator reached one, the doors slid open. Ben stepped out with a thin, young girl lying limp in his arms. She couldn't have been much more than sixteen, and from the lacerations and bruises that covered her skin, it didn't look like she was going to see seventeen. What was once a light, white and yellow sundress was matted to her slender frame by sweat and blood. Her short blonde hair was a mass of knots, and ground-in dirt. She had taken a severe beating…and somehow survived…but it didn't appear that she had much time left.

Spotting an overturned couch on the far side of the lobby, Saint rushed over and righted it with the heel of her boot. "Put her here."

Dropping carefully to his knees, Ben laid the girl gently on the cushions. Holding his breath, he pulled a bit of her dirty, matted hair away from her face with the tips of his fingers. The wolf stared at the girl, yet somehow was very far away. The image of another young girl appeared in his mind. The blood, the bruises, and the cuts…it was all so similar. Knots formed in his stomach.

Saint sank down next to her werewolf protector and gripped his hand tightly for reassurance. Holstering her scythe, she pressed her fingertips to the girl's throat. Tucking her hair behind her ear, Saint leaned over the girl's mouth and listened for breathing. "Her pulse is very, very weak," Saint whispered, "and her breathing shallow."

"We're going to lose her," Ben said, a hint of agony and remorse floating just beneath his words.

The young girl opened her eyes painfully. Her irises dilated as she tried to focus. It seemed as though the communication between her eyes and brain was getting lost somewhere.

Saint pulled her head back quickly and caressed the girl's face, careful not to hit a cut or bruise. "My name is Emily, and this is Ben."

Ben waved silently.

Pursing her lips, the girl tried to speak but couldn't.

"It's okay," Saint said. "We're going to get you

out of here and find help. You're safe with us now."

As the last word passed Saint's lips, a rain of bullets exploded into the wall just missing them.

Without pausing, Saint wrapped her arms around the girl, threw herself over the back of the couch, and had drawn and activated her scythe. Landing hard on her back, the Wraith rolled onto her knees and gently set the girl down. She watched Ben come over the couch the same way she had. As he started pulling off his clothes, another round of bullets chewed into the back of the couch sending chunks of fabric and stuffing into the air like snow.

Ben tasted the air with a frown. "Gun powder." He licked his lips and sneezed trying to clear his sinuses. "Two distinct scents, both male." He sniffed the air again. "Demons."

"With automatic weapons." Saint mirrored Ben's frown. "That's so cheating."

Ben nodded with an evil grin as his eyes shifted to blood-red. Wrapping his arms around his chest, he growled painfully as his flesh began to rip apart revealing thick hair beneath. Blood spurted from his mouth and nose as his facial bones were broken and instantly reconfigured into a long, vicious muzzle. The sound of cracking bones echoed off the walls as Ben's legs broke, lengthened, and transformed into the triple-jointed limbs that added almost four feet to his height. The transformation was utterly horrific, and immensely painful. As the last of his flesh fell away, the wolf inside was freed. He became a true engine of destruction. Lifting his hands, he extended his fingers and snapped out a long, curved claw from each tip. Perking the ears on the top of his head, he turned and glared toward Saint.

She felt a shudder run down her spine. No matter how many times she had seen Ben in wolf form, she was never comfortable with it. Somewhere deep in the back of her brain, she had a fear that he was sizing her up for a quick snack. She had to hope that beneath the wolf, there was enough of Ben left to prevent it.

"We'll do this on three," Saint started. "I'll charge, draw their fire, and then you—"

The werewolf threw his head back and howled at the top of his lungs. Grabbing the couch, he ripped it cleanly in two and charged without hesitation.

"Or, you just go berserk and kill everything," Saint finished with a sigh. Scooting the girl behind what was left of the couch, the Wraith pressed her hand gently to the girl's face. "That's the problem with werewolves. When you're built like a tank, there's really no need to plan. I'll be right back, okay?"

Snapping her hand up, the girl grabbed Saint's wrist and shook her head as another volley of bullets pounded the wall behind them.

Saint paused. "You don't want me to go?"

The girl shook her head again, this time more emphatically. She raised her arm and pointed over Saint's shoulder. Her eyes were wide with terror.

"Damn," Saint breathed as a familiar sound began to emerge in her mind.

A long, black shadow ran up the wall before her. She watched in horror as it spread its massive wings.

The Wraith tightened her grip on her scythe. Action was required before the angel's song overtook her. Pulling the girl's hand free of her wrist, Saint tensed. She could feel the angel looming ever closer.

Springing up and spinning, Saint brought her scythe up and across in one quick snap. Dropping into a defensive pose, the Wraith held her blade ready for the second strike.

The angel cocked its head slightly, sizing up the Wraith. It suddenly furrowed its brow and looked down at its outstretched hands. A thin line of blood crossed both arms just below its elbows. Suddenly both hands slid down under the force of gravity and fell to the ground from Saint's perfect cuts. As the angel's arms landed with a wet thump on the floor, it lifted its head and focused angrily on Saint.

The angel's song tore across Saint's brain like fire. She felt her temples throb, and the familiar tingle of her nose starting to bleed.

Saint hardened her gaze. "Not this time."

Lunging forward, the Wraith snapped her scythe out laterally in one powerful motion. Spinning it with a flourish, she brought the weapon back across her body then planted the end on the floor with a snap. Like the image of the Grim Reaper with his scythe at the ready, Saint stood tall and watched patiently.

The angel's eyes softened and its mouth fell open as a trickle of blood spilled down its throat. As its wings folded to its sides, the angel's knees buckled and it collapsed. As it tumbled, its head came free and the torso separated cleanly just above the waist. The many pieces of the angel crumbled to the ground, dead.

The angel's song completely gone from Saint's mind, she returned her attention to the girl on the floor. Her eyes widened.

Her scythe clattered to the ground.

Dropping to her knees, Saint gently pressed her hand to the girl's face. Trying to rub a bit of the crusted blood away, she felt a trickle of blood run down her lips. Staring at the girl, she saw the trickle drip away from her lips and land on the once yellow sundress.

Ben, back in human form, walked up behind Saint and stopped. He started to speak, but stopped as the gravity of the moment overtook him. Quietly, he hung back and let Saint grieve.

"I'm sorry," Saint breathed finally. She slowly closed the girl's eyes, and bowed her head. "I'm so sorry." Brushing her hair away from her face, Saint stood.

"We have to go," Ben said, scooping his clothes up while trying to avoid the angel parts.

Saint tried to compose herself. The death of the girl had rattled Saint more than she realized. Perhaps it was the girl's age, but more likely it was her blond hair.

The girl looked like Kat.

"Kryll bounty hunters," the werewolf said, pulling on his pants.

She lifted her eyes to Ben, barely registering the words. "What?"

"Two Kryll bounty hunters," Ben said again as

he buckled his belt. "That's who was shooting at us." He looked down at the angel's body. "But I see you had problems of your own."

"It appeared out of nowhere," Saint said vacantly as if she were a million miles away. Which, in truth, she was. Her eyes fell on her hands. A fine spray of the angel's blood had landed there. It immediately disgusted and enthralled her.

Pulling on his boots, Ben snatched a crumpled piece of paper from the floor and handed it to Saint. "I found this on one of the bounty hunters."

Wrapping her fingers around the paper, Saint carefully unfolded it to find her picture with the headline, Wanted, dead or alive.

"I don't think you're worth seven figures," Ben said then laughed, trying to inject a bit of levity.

Saint's eyes rolled down to the bottom of the page and stared at the number printed in a heavy, black font. It unnerved her to say the least. To see her life reduced to a figure, even one this size, was disheartening. Someone wanted her badly. She let the paper fall from her hand and gritted her teeth. Without a word, Saint called her scythe to her hand and marched out of the lobby.

Ben shook his head.

"What do you think we should do, Ben?" the werewolf mockingly asked himself. "I don't know, Saint, but thank you for asking." Running his hand over his face, he sighed and started after her. "Why do I even try?"

Outside, it started to rain.

Chapter Nine

"Wake up, my friend."

Specter opened his eyes without hesitation. Holding out his arms, he stretched and sat up. He felt as though he had just awoken from the most restful sleep of his entire life. His body felt powerful, and his mind was clear and sharp. He felt absolutely amazing. Turning, he dropped his legs over the edge of the bed and stood.

Alarms suddenly blared in his brain.

Immediately his eyes focused on a dark figure standing in the corner, and Specter became aware of the alien surroundings again. Blue light filtered in from the walls and washed over him. He shivered involuntarily, and fell back into a defensive posture.

"There's no need for that, my friend," Metatron said, stepping forward. "I apologize. Frightening you was not my intent."

Specter didn't relax.

Metatron's wings flapped once then folded back. "I trust you rested well?"

"I did," Specter answered.

The Voice paused, "How do they feel?"

Specter couldn't help the confused look he gave the angel. "Pardon me?"

Metatron opened his wings and held out his arms suggestively.

A wave of panic gripped Specter as he became aware of the new sensation on his back for the first time. Glancing over his shoulder, he saw white feathers. "What did you do to me?"

"What you wanted," Metatron answered.

Specter's shoulders tingled as he unfurled his wings for the first time. He could feel new muscles and bones attached to his shoulder blades working in tandem and the movement seemed perfectly natural. The wings felt light, but powerful. Stretching them wide, he stared at the perfectly white feathers. Flapping them, he could feel the immense lift they created. "I didn't want this," he folded the wings back.

"Perhaps you are right," Metatron offered. "Perhaps 'wanted' is the wrong word." He considered his word choice. "You did not want this, you craved it." He stepped toward Specter. "You were lost, but wanted so much to find your way again, to once more find the path of righteousness. I plucked you from your misery, and have given you the means. I have even gifted you with that which you need to complete your journey."

Specter couldn't find the words.

"You have ascended, my friend," the voice admitted. "No longer will you take your name and strength from the physical realm. Before, you called the shadows and darkness home, but you are the light now."

"Do you always talk in cryptic riddles and rhymes?" Specter asked. "You sound like you've had a stroke. I don't understand."

"You will," Metatron promised. "We can discuss this later." He held out his open hand. "Please, I have something you need to see."

Specter hesitated. He wanted to stomp his foot like an angry child and demand answers, but felt guilty for even considering it. Wary of Metatron, but at the same time, completely taken by him, Specter wanted to sit at the angel's feet and be regaled with stories of the ages, hopefully unlocking the mysteries of fate, time, and space, yet there was an undeniable separation between the two. It wasn't merely the biological differences, after all he had spent lifetimes around various Inhumans, he felt somehow inferior to the angel. He had been born and raised in a vastly different age, one where science was barely beginning to develop and religion ruled supreme. This was God's servant, the very voice of the Lord. The Wraith was unworthy of Metatron's presence.

And yet, here he was. Specter couldn't find a way to rationalize this in his mind.

Long ago he had abandoned his tenuous grip on religion. Christianity had failed him. Its God had allowed a vampire to kill his beloved wife and daughter. He had often been told that God had a plan, but how could three centuries of torment be permitted and how could good people be allowed to die? The Wraith felt the same cold bitterness that had long ago swallowed his soul gurgle in his guts and claw at his brain. All of his awe and glory drained away leaving the same shell of the man he had always been. He denied the alpha and omega— no beginning and end. He simply was, and this was all he would ever be. He felt utterly empty again.

Specter lifted his eyes to The Voice. Metatron was patient and understanding, waiting for the Wraith to work through it, yet offered no guidance. This was something Specter needed to deal with on his own, and the angel knew that. There was no amount of proselytizing that would sway him. Specter had to find his own answers. And that only frustrated him more. He was alone in the dark, with no light to guide his way.

Metatron offered his hand again. "Please."

He hesitated again, but realized he had fallen apart long ago. He had nothing left to lose.

Specter took Metatron's hand.

***

In the distance behind the Wraith Academy, waves rose and fell endlessly under blackened skies. The Atlantic Ocean seemed somehow angry with its stewards, and was threatening to wipe all traces of them away. With one mighty swat, the water could wipe all traces of them from the planet and return everything to an easier time. Undoubtedly, as had been demonstrated six times already, a new species would take hold after their extinction and rise to dominance. The Earth would continue on, in one form or another, until that fateful day, billions and billions of years in the distant future, when the sun expanded and engulfed it. That is the very nature of things, the way of the world. Yet knowing everything was predestined to end, didn't make it any easier to accept.

Marching toward the Academy's gates, Conrad pulled his eyes away from the churning waters beyond and slowly scanned. After what had felt like an eternity of night, day had finally broken, but there was little light to ease the Wraith. It looked like a traditional, stormy, English morning, but felt harder, more bereft of life. Conrad knew why.

London was dead, and he felt a small part of him had died with it.

Conrad and Stark had been forced to bear witness to the death and destruction that was once London. Nothing had survived the angels' onslaught. It was all gone. Everything. Yet, it had become apparent that the attacks were sporadic at best. Well into Wales, the two had taken a route that led through the coastal city of Cardiff, and amazingly, found it completely intact. The citizens were of course aware of the attacks, and the scale of the disaster, but somehow had been spared. It didn't make any sense.

Still, Conrad was thankful that the Academy had thus far been spared, unsure he had the stomach to witness its total annihilation a second time.

After they passed through the front gates, Conrad and Stark walked up the path that led to the Academy's entrance. Feeling the first tiny raindrops on their flesh, the two quickened their pace as they both knew how fast a light sprinkle could turn into a full-blown English storm. Conrad glimpsed the ever-present guards making their rounds. Two stood watch at the door, while several more patrolled the compound. More than usual, the Chancellor must've thought the extra protection was necessary. Although Conrad wasn't sure how much good it would do against this new foe.

"Hold there!"

Conrad didn't stop because he had been commanded to, but because of sheer confusion. He stared at the two guards with their scythes crossed in front of the door. Was he, the head of the Council of Seven, actually being barred entrance? "What is the meaning of this?"

"The Academy has been locked down," a guard answered without addressing Conrad. "No entrance is permitted."

Conrad knew this Wraith, and had seen him grow up inside the Academy's walls. One of the few survivors of Vampire Lord Bane's attack on the Academy, he had been chosen by the Chancellor to be among his personal guard. Conrad had even shaken his hand and congratulated him on the posting. This didn't make sense. "Alan," Conrad breathed the young Wraith's name, "what is going on here? You can't deny access to the head of the Council."

"I have very specific orders," Alan answered unemotionally, staring into the distance like the Queen's Royal Guard. "No entrance is permitted."

"This is outrageous," Conrad barked. "I sit on the Council of Seven! On whose authority was this done?"

"Chancellor Alexander's."

Conrad gritted his teeth, but remained composed. "I demand access immediately. You have no right to bar me."

"Seems like they do." Stark laughed.

"I'm sorry, but I have my orders," Alan answered again. "No entrance is permitted."

"I will speak to the Chancellor now!" Conrad commanded. "Send for him!"

Alan refused to look at Conrad or Stark. "I'm sorry—"

Conrad moved before either guard could react.

Knocking away their scythes, he tossed the second guard back to Stark's waiting arms and slammed Alan to the wall. Spinning the young Wraith, Conrad pinned Alan's arms behind his back, and smashed the young Wraith's face into the wall.

"I'm sorry," Conrad said apologetically, "but you left me no choice." He looked over his shoulder to see the other guard struggling against Stark's steely grip. He wasn't going anywhere. Lifting his eyes above the werewolf, he saw the other guards react and begin to converge. He didn't have much time.

"Stark," Conrad barked, "we're going. Now!"

"I'm not running into a compound filled with pissed off Wraith," Stark protested.

"Fine," Conrad tossed Alan away and pulled open the front doors, "stay here and play with your new friends." The High Wraith disappeared inside without another word.

Stark turned to see at least five guards rushing toward him, their scythes drawn. "Crap."

Tossing the guard down next to Alan, Stark shot off like a bullet. Inside the Academy, he immediately found another Wraith lying unconscious on the floor. More of Conrad's handiwork, no doubt. The sharp metallic clang of weapon on weapon met his hypersensitive ears. The soles of his boots squeaked on the tiled floors as he skittered around the corner toward the source of the sound. Ahead, he spotted Conrad engaged in a duel with two Wraith. The High Wraith was holding his own, blow for blow, but wasn't making any headway. Further down the hall Stark could smell several more Wraiths, and their heightened adrenaline. The scent was growing more powerful. They were coming.

"This isn't a good idea," Stark said as he threw off the leather jacket he had scavenged in London. He tightened his jaw. Kicking off his boots, he charged into the fray.

With each step he took, he became less human and more animal. Tearing free of his skin, Stark snapped open his midnight black claws like switchblade knives and leapt. Bringing his legs up, he hit one of the two Wraith attacking Conrad with full force. Unaware the attack was coming, the Wraith had no chance to counter. Smashing down onto the tiled floor, the Wraith's body hit with a sickening crunch. He wasn't dead, but Stark knew the Wraith wouldn't get up. Pulling his claws free of the Wraith's torso, Stark turned and growled at the second Wraith. The wolf's lips peeled back revealing its massive, daggerlike teeth.

Snapping the Wraith's scythe down with his own, Conrad used Stark's distraction to his advantage. Spinning into the Wraith, Conrad threw his elbow up and connected with the Wraith's jaw. He heard a snap, crack and the Wraith's head was thrown back. Twisting, Conrad completed the attack with a vicious backhand that dropped the Wraith to the floor like a sack of potatoes.

Conrad brought his scythe up defensively. "Bad doggie." He stared at Stark warily. "Good bad doggie."

Stark woofed in approval and licked his chops.

"What is the meaning of this?"

Conrad spun and found the focus of his anger. He thought for a moment about unleashing Stark, but his overriding sense of duty got the better of him. Still, he refused to lower his scythe. "Ah, Chancellor Alexander," Conrad greeted mockingly. "Just the man we were looking for."

The Chancellor stood behind two Wraith with their weapons at the ready. "You will lower your weapon and surrender for arrest," Alexander growled. "Immediately!"

Reinforcements arrived behind the Chancellor, activated their weapons, and dropped into defensive postures. Another Wraith stood back with a high-powered rifle aimed at Stark.

The wolf could smell the silver bullets down the barrel of the weapon. He glared straight at the Wraith and bared his teeth.

"I don't think so." Conrad smiled. "I think it's you who will be placed under arrest. As the head of the Council of Seven, I have the power to declare no confidence in your leadership, and assume control of the Gwyliad Wriaeth until a new leader can be elected."

"Really?" Alexander returned the High Wraith's smile. "In your absence, changes were required." His face suddenly hardened as though a dark shadow enveloped him. "I have disbanded the Council, and declared martial law. You have no power anymore."

Conrad felt his heart sink as he knew the Chancellor—now dictator—wasn't lying.

Alexander stepped forward, leering at the High Wraith. "We are at war," he savored the words deliciously, "and emergency measures had to be taken." He paused. "It was at the urging of Master Xavier and the Council that I took this course of action. We are mankind's protectors, but time after time, we have seen man demonstrate his ignorance. The old ways are gone, my friend. It is time the Order truly begins to safeguard mankind," he wrung his hands, "even from itself."

Conrad felt his grip loosen on his scythe. The Order that once vowed to protect mankind would now be perverted to control it.

"You will surrender right now," Alexander sneered, "or I will order you killed right now."

The High Wraith glanced to his werewolf companion. Stark's expression seemed to say, let's go out fighting. Conrad could certainly understand the wolf's sentiment, but he knew the cunning warrior fights not with his heart, but with his head. Saint and Kat were still out there, somewhere, and they needed him alive. He could not die foolishly. He would not go out in a blaze of glory like Stark wanted.

He would live to fight another day.

Standing tall, Conrad tugged on his leather trench to straighten it. Deactivating his scythe, he dropped the hilt and stared at Alexander as it clattered noisily to the floor.

There was a sharp whistle, then several wet thumps. Conrad snapped his head around to see multiple tranquilizer darts lodged in Stark's dark hide.

Looking down angrily at the silver tubes with a red nap on their ends, the wolf immediately started yanking them free. Tossing his head back as he removed the final dart, the werewolf roared in rage. He lunged toward the Chancellor, but the high-powered sedative was already working in his system. Stumbling over his own paws, the werewolf fell helplessly to the floor. He clawed and tried to right himself, but couldn't manage it. Arms and legs shaking, Stark summoned every scrap of his remaining strength, but it wasn't enough. Stark collapsed, and his muzzle smacked the floor with an angry crack. With a whimper, the werewolf closed its eyes.

Conrad watched helplessly as several Wraith moved in and quickly scooped up the wolf. Large clumps of hair flitted to the ground as Stark was already reverting to human form. He returned his attention to Alexander. "What is to be done with Stark and I?"

"You have voluntarily attacked another Wraith." The Chancellor-turned-dictator took a step back. "You know the law, Master Verge. You must be judged." Alexander turned and started away. "Place him under arrest."

Conrad set his jaw and felt bile churn up the back of his throat. Alexander was going to make an example of him in the Tribunal. It would most certainly be a mock trial, performed only to cement the Chancellor in his new role as dictator. The thought sickened Conrad. The so-called angels were leveling entire cities, and instead of trying to unite the Order and combat them, Alexander was using this emergency to gather more power.

Conrad dropped his head as two of Alexander's

men took him into custody.

Chapter Ten

The sky opened up, dropping its watery cargo as thunder rumbled ominously in the distance. Massive drops spilled down from charcoal gray skies, pounding the Earth as they hit. Huge chunks of soil were dislodged and washed away in what was quickly becoming a flash flood. Blue electricity skittered along the clouds, gathered, and struck the ground with all the force and raw fury Mother Nature was capable of.

Stumbling through mud and water, Saint was soaked to her core. So cold that each raindrop felt like a hammer strike, her flesh twitched as though a colony of ants worked beneath it. Saint was doing her best to look strong and in control, but inside she was utterly and completely lost. She searched a continent vainly for any signs of the woman she had vowed to protect, but there was nothing. She had no leads, no clues, and no idea of where to look, yet she refused to stop. The Wraith would peer in every darkened crevice and kick over every stone until she found Kat. Of that, at least, she was certain.

Pressing her hands to her temples, she could hear the angel's song in the distance, almost as if calling to her. Closing her eyes, she focused her thoughts on a breathing technique that Master Quinn had taught her. In through her nose, and out through her mouth, she breathed methodically and began to take control of her body. But the angel's song flared in her brain, and a white-hot surge of pain assaulted her.

She opened her eyes and was instantly gripped by panic.

It stepped forward and spread its wings majestically. Draped in beautiful white garments, an angel stood on the shore of a large lake, watching.

Saint was separated from the being simply observing. Its song was gone, as was Ben and the rain. This wasn't real. It couldn't be. She was seeing another place, and another time. In the distance, she could see a small gathering of thatched huts, and humans who barely deserved the name. Hunched around a fire, they knelt on their knees and bowed before another angel. The sun shone brightly overhead but was nearly blotted by the dark forms of angels. Everywhere she looked, Saint saw more angels. They were guiding the early humans, teaching them basic skills, and giving them the word of the Lord.

This was the beginning of religion.

No, it was more than that. This was the beginning of understanding, and of spirituality. The angels were once mankind's benevolent benefactors, starting them on the path that led out of the dark times, and into the future.

But where did they come from? Were these beings truly God's first creation as the scriptures claimed, or something else entirely?

Saint tried to let go of her religious-based prejudices and misconceptions to understand. It was more than a student/teacher relationship, the angels were behaving in an almost parental fashion. There seemed to be no malice toward the angels. They were worshipped like the God they supposedly represented. They moved freely among the early humans, living among them, yet none spoke. They existed in a strange vacuum, these angels of the silence.

Saint began to walk about the lush, green land she guessed was prehistoric Europe. She watched men gathering to hunt, farm, and tend to the needs of their families and villages, all under the careful, watchful tutelage of the angels. Amidst the thick foliage, the angels played with children, and were teaching some a very basic writing and numbering system that Saint knew would evolve into cuneiform.

Everything was perfect.

This was Eden.

Stopping at the bank of a river, Saint took a deep breath of the air and enjoyed the sunlight beating down on her back. She listened to the water, and the distant chirp of songbirds. Looking down, she watched the water lap over her feet. Taking a step back, she saw the river begin to swell.

It was flooding—

Saint shook her head as she was snapped back to reality, but couldn't escape the vision.

It all seemed so real.

The angel's song appeared in her mind again, and her brain throbbed. She didn't feel well. She didn't feel like herself.

In the distance, amidst the rain, Saint witnessed an old oak tree erupt in sparks and flame as lightning struck. The fire burned despite the downpour, leaving the once mighty tree decimated. The pair, against Ben's protests, had abandoned well traveled roads and set off cross country. Tracing the curves of the slithering Danube River, they trekked over farmlands, which had already seen their crops reaped, and through patches of wilderness that seemed somehow dark and foreboding. Neither Ben nor Saint had ever traveled this part of Europe before. They had crossed into Austria some time ago, and the terrain was becoming more rugged the further they went. It looked undeniably foreign, and as though it was at least a century behind the rest of the Union. This was a place of superstition. Wreathes of garlic were still hung on front doors, farmers worked with antiquated tools, and electricity appeared to be a privilege here.

"We have to find shelter!" Saint heard Ben shout from behind her. His concerns were barely audible above the rain's pounding cacophony.

Ignoring the plea, she continued on. She had led them away from Bratislava, and was steadily heading west, but was unsure why. Something deep in the back of her mind tugged at the Wraith, as though calling to her. When she closed her eyes she could almost feel an invisible thread pulling her, the end knotted into her ribcage. It compelled her forward despite the pain that gripped her. Saint couldn't stop.

And Ben knew it.

Unsure why or how, there had been a marked change in Saint since killing the angel in Bratislava. He stayed back, keeping a watchful eye on his ward, but his worry had steadily grown. She was a proud, skilled warrior, and he had never seen her like this before, not even after the death of her Master and teacher at the twisted hands of Lord Bane. Saint had always, somehow, been able to keep a level head and retain perspective no matter what the situation, but now...he didn't know what to think. She was like a woman possessed, but of or by what, he didn't know. The wolf did not like this at all.

To make matters worse, the weather was only adding to his sense of dread and paranoia. The constant, overwhelming cacophony was dampening his hearing, while the multitude of odors being dredged up by the storm were confusing his sense of smell. The werewolf knew he was freezing to death, but he felt hot and muggy. Through an act of sheer willpower, he remained focused and fought against the urge to start removing articles of clothing. If Saint kept going, he would too.

But this had to stop.

"Saint," Ben called. "We have to find shelter."

She ignored the werewolf.

Gritting his teeth, he moved quickly past Saint, spun, and backpedaled to stay in her line of sight. "Emily," he barked, "listen to me. We have to get out of the rain. We're going to die out here."

Her eyes seemed glazed and distant. She didn't respond, but instead pushed past her companion.

"Dammit, Emily." Reaching out, Ben grabbed the Wraith by the shoulder.

With a move so quick that Ben had no time to react, Saint spun and lodged her fist in the dead center of the wolf's chest. Knocked off his feet by the ferocity of the blow, Ben sailed back and splashed down in the mud. Wiping the excess from his face, he opened his eyes to find Saint once again walking away.

His temper blossomed and he snapped.

Leaping up, Ben tossed off his waterlogged jacket and charged. Dropping his shoulder, he speared Saint, wrapped his arms around her and knocked her to the ground. As the two splashed into the mud and muck, Ben's head was viciously snapped back by Saint's elbow to his chin. Tumbling backwards, Ben tried to roll with the blow, but she was too fast. If Ben was a tank, Saint was a fighter jet. Drawing up onto her hands, Saint bucked her legs out and tagged Ben again. The wolf skidded back and ended up with a mouth full of mud and rainwater.

Spitting the gritty substance away, Ben watched Saint slowly lift off the ground. Her black hair was a mess over her face, leaving only her unearthly blue eyes visible as they stared at him. Her expression was void of anger or pain. She simply existed.

And that scared him more than any monster ever had.

"Saint," Ben stammered, "what the hell are you doing?"

Her eyes hollow, Saint marched toward the werewolf.

"It's me. It's Ben," he said, almost pleading. He didn't want to hurt her. She was strong, fast, and agile, but in close quarters with a werewolf, she would be shredded. Ben fought against the voice in his brain yelling for him to transform and destroy the woman.

116

She was his friend…and he…

Saint grabbed Ben by the throat and lifted him out of the mud with her supernatural strength. Her fingers were like steel bands around his flesh. Struggling, he couldn't break free of her grasp. He could not…no, would not fight back. Bound by his promise, Ben wouldn't allow Saint to come to harm, especially by his own hand.

The wolf felt gravity slam him back into the mud. Wiping the muddy water quickly from his face, he looked up to see Saint walking away amidst the falling rain. He couldn't help the confusion that set in. He watched her for what felt like an eternity. She made no motions for him to follow, no backward glances over her shoulder. She simply walked away.

Ben sat in the mud, raindrops falling hard around him. As they crashed into the mud and water, it splashed up into his eyes. He felt lost as his eyes tried to track Saint in the gloom. Her dark outline disappeared into the gloom leaving him alone. As the temperature started to drop, he witnessed the rain changing to sleet, and the first massive snowflakes drifting to Earth. Slowly standing, he let his head fall back, closed his eyes, and felt the precipitation hit his face.

Saint was gone.

And Ben let her go.

A black-clad figure watched from a distance. He made no movements as he stood against the elements, waiting. The altercation between the two confused him, but ultimately it made no difference. She would be his. At least now he wouldn't have to kill the wolf. Tossing his leather trench back, his golden eyes flashed as he spun and vanished.

***

They followed the tubular passages as they wound deeper and deeper. There seemed to be no logic to the design as one moment they dropped straight down, curled around, then twisted off in an entirely different direction. Passing through chambers large enough to house aircraft, connecting corridors seemed to egress randomly with no apparent architecture or logic. Specter could only imagine that this was how it felt to be inside an ant colony. But strangely, it seemed deserted. There were no drones scurrying about as they readied for winter, or anxiously tending to the queen. This place, whatever it was, was hard, lifeless, and empty.

Amidst the blue light, Specter followed Metatron closely praying not to get lost. The angel hopped lightly from passage to passage, using his wings for added lift and stability. Specter tried to do the same, but hadn't quite got the mechanics down. He knew with Metatron it had become instinctual, whereas he was still forced to consciously manipulate the feathered appendages. He felt strange, disoriented with the heavy wings hanging off his back. The once agile Wraith had almost tumbled several times as the new wings threw him off.

And despite what they represented, he felt like a mutant. He wasn't a Wraith anymore, and he wasn't an angel. Specter felt like a circus grade freak.

118

The Wraith's body popped, creaked, and ached as he moved. Whatever Metatron had done to him was still happening in his body. His breathing was labored, and his heart raced, but he knew it wasn't from the activity. Despite his actual age, he was in peak physical condition, a benefit of the Wraith virus. Specter felt feverish and nauseated, and what felt like jackhammers pounded in his brain. He was still changing...but into what?

Metatron opened his wings then disappeared, his blue robes billowing. Climbing quickly toward the top of the passage, Specter dropped down on one knee and felt a rush of pain explode in his brain. Slamming his hands to his temples, he pressed hard, hoping to contain the pressure that felt as though it was about to burst free. As it slowly subsided, Specter placed his hands on the edge of a connecting passage and stared into the massive chamber below. It was easily a sixty foot drop to the bottom and he could see Metatron waiting silently for him there.

Standing, Specter spread his wings. Stepping to the edge of the passage, he steadied himself. This was a complex series of events he knew he wasn't ready for. Anxiety gathered in his spine and legs as a deep sense of vertigo gripped him. He was in a place he didn't understand, trusting a being he knew nothing about, and his body was changing in ways he couldn't completely fathom. Images of his body crushed on the chamber floor below flashed in his mind.

He jumped.

Leaning forward, Specter flattened his wings.

As they caught the air, the pull on his muscles was immense. He felt like his entire ribcage was about to be ripped from his flesh as he tried to slow his descent. Gritting his teeth, the Wraith flapped his wings and immediately felt the lift they generated. He strained with all of his strength, but couldn't keep his wings level. Dipping forward, he felt them slice through the air and his fall suddenly accelerated. Roughly fifteen feet from the floor, Specter tumbled feet over head and crashed to the ground.

His arms flailed out wildly as the impact was met with a resounding crack and searing pain up his forearm. Cradling his arm, he grunted but refused to cry out. Specter rolled onto his back.

"I'm sorry," Metatron said apologetically, but made no move to help Specter. "I didn't think to consider if you were ready for this trip. Your body must still be in a state of flux."

"I don't know about flux," Specter grunted as he rolled onto his knees, "but I sure hurt like hell."

"Your bones are brittle," The Voice explained. "A result of them becoming hollow."

"Great." Looking down at his right arm, he cringed. Roughly two inches below the elbow, his arm was cocked at an awkward angle. A sharp bump had formed on the opposite side where the broken bone was threatening to break through. He lifted his eyes to Metatron. "Can you help me?"

"You'll heal," Metatron answered callously. Turning away, The Voice folded his wings back and started across the chamber.

Specter set his jaw. Wrapping his fingers

around the wrist of his broken arm, he exhaled slowly, then yanked firmly. There was a gurgle beneath the skin then a loud, sharp pop as the broken bone snapped back into place. Doubling over, he couldn't help but yelp in pain.

Slowly standing, he breathed as the pain began to dissipate. He knew his Wraith physiology would hasten the injury's repair, but because of the changes he was going through, he wasn't certain that was the case any longer. Folding his arm tightly to his chest, he tried to keep it as still as possible. Moving carefully to avoid any missteps, Specter started after Metatron.

The chamber was cavernous. Passages entered and exited at all angles, while what looked like support struts careened through the empty space creating the appearance of a spider's web. The blue light appeared somehow brighter here, as if it had shifted toward white in the spectrum.

Scanning the chamber's walls, Specter felt his heart drop in horror. "What is this place?"

"This," Metatron spread his arms wide as if presenting his gift to the world, "is the future."

On every surface, in every free space, humans were packed into cocoons. The same skin-like substance that had held Specter now contained these people of every race and color. Arms and legs dangled limp from the cocoons as though the people were dead. A blue crackle of electricity danced over the room causing the immobilized humans to shake as though experiencing a seizure. Far too many to count, Specter surmised the numbers ranged in the thousands.

A single cocoon appeared to be separated from the rest. Located in almost the exact center, it was recessed into the floor. Many of the support columns angled in and terminated around the cocoon. Arcing around it, the floor seemed to be raised like a shrine. Wavy lines radiated away from the shrine in all directions like beams of light in a child's depiction of the sun, and were embedded with oddly styled symbols that looked almost Middle Eastern in design. Held beneath the cocoon's flesh, there was a woman. Specter's eyes settled on her blonde hair and soft, ageless features. He remembered her from earlier when he was cocooned as well. His eyes traced down the barely visible outline of her body, but stopped abruptly when he reached her abdomen.

"She's pregnant," Specter said angrily.

"She is," Metatron confirmed. Walking around the shrine, he stood in the two o'clock position facing her, folded his hands and bowed his head. "She carries our destiny."

Specter couldn't hide his outright dismay. "What are you doing to these people?" He watched another wave of electricity careen over the chamber leaving a seizing mass of humans in its wake. "This is inhumane!"

"We are not human," The Voice pointed out.

Specter thought of his own turn in one of the cocoons and the obvious slapped him hard across the face. "You're creating an army of angels."

"I already have an army." Metatron laughed. "We are not just creating soldiers here," he looked down reverently at the central cocoon, "we are

122

designing the future. Man has proven unworthy of the gifts we have bestowed. His time has passed. He must now step aside for his successor."

"This is genocide!" Specter stared into the darkness of Metatron's hood, but could see nothing. "Who are you to judge mankind? What gives you the right to say when its time's up?"

"It was not my decision," Metatron answered. "I am merely The Voice. As has happened six times on this planet already, God has chosen another species for extinction. This time," the angel returned his gaze to the pregnant woman cocooned at his feet, "the Maker has chosen the talking monkeys."

Specter felt the rage in Metatron's voice, and it was deeply unsettling.

"The Father blessed you with reason and free will, and what do you do with it? Monkey killing monkey over patches of dirt. And ironically, the instrument of man's destruction has not come from the stars, or plague, or an age of ice, it comes from the Wraith who swore to protect them."

Specter felt suddenly sick. He dropped down on his knees before the shrine and stared at the woman. "Who is she?"

"A vampire," Metatron replied, "who was impregnated by a Wraith."

Specter stared at the blonde woman's face. He wanted to reach out and touch her, if only to prove in his mind that she was real. "That isn't possible."

"The Prophecy has come to pass," Metatron answered. "A Saint's blood has created a new race."

Already ill, Specter felt his face flush as the words met his ears. He knew the words all too well.

All Wraith did. It was their prophecy. He didn't know how to respond.

"Her name is Kat," Metatron spoke quietly and evenly. "Much as Mary before, she will be spoken of in song and praise as the Mother. She will give birth to the Savior."

Specter felt suddenly as though he had sided with the enemy. "And what is to be my role in this?"

"You will train the Savior," The Voice said without hesitation. "With your advanced fighting techniques, our Savior will be a warrior."

Specter's broken arm throbbed and he wanted to vomit. "And if I refuse?"

Metatron laughed, turned, spread his wings and lifted off the ground.

Specter watched The Voice vanish into one of the passages, leaving him alone with Kat, and the thousands of comatose humans cocooned there. He stared at Kat's face. She was beautiful. He was having a difficult time fathoming that she was a vampire, his sworn enemy. There was something off about her, but he couldn't quite put his finger on what. This woman, a pregnant vampire, was not exactly what she seemed. He was immediately sorry, and felt an overwhelming sense of loss as he looked upon her face. As another wave of electricity skittered across the nest, Specter dropped his face into his hand. As he replayed Metatron's words in his mind, one thought emerged:

What had he done?

Chapter Eleven

"Well, this is a fine mess you've gotten us in to."

Conrad tried not to laugh, but did in spite of himself. The statement was far too ridiculous to not be enjoyed.

Stark ignored the High Wraith and continued to pace in his borrowed clothes. Not many Wraith were built like the werewolf chieftain, so he had been forced to settle for a brown robe to wrap around his massive frame. The tranquilizers had worn off some time ago, leaving the wolf to rage ever since.

Conrad couldn't blame him, though. The last place he expected to end up was in a prison cell, but this wouldn't last long. Soon he would be forced to face Alexander's Tribunal, Conrad sighed, and shortly after that, he would certainly be dead. Convicted on charges of treason, the sentence was death. It was really pretty cut and dried at this point. He would spend his final days in a cell, waiting to die, and all of his accomplishments and teachings would be forgotten or erased.

History did not reflect well on traitors.

They were locked away deep in the bowels of the Academy, so should they accidentally be "forgotten," no one would ever see them again. No more than ten by fifteen, Stark's massive frame occupied much of the cell, leaving Conrad relegated to one of the back corners. Sitting against the wall, the High Wraith had his knees pulled up with his forearms resting on top of them. He rolled a small bit of concrete recovered from the floor between his thumb and fingers. Probably a result of Bane's attack, the cells in this area still showed the scars of the bomb that ripped open the Academy. Scorch marks streaked down the walls like Death's bony fingers creeping in for the kill. He wondered if Alexander left the damage there to make this place more intimidating, or as symbolic proof that it took more than an entire vampire army to destroy the Wraith.

A faint tapping caught Conrad's attention. It seemed to appear, vanish, then reappear and was very rhythmic in nature. It sounded almost as though something was banging against a pipe just beyond the back of the cell. The Wraith dismissed the sounds. This place was old, and damaged. That would more than account for the noises.

Leaning against the thick iron bars that crossed the cell, Stark lifted a meaty paw and ran his fingers over his shaved head feeling the stubble that grew there. Stark spun on his heels and faced Conrad. "What are we supposed to do now?"

The High Wraith tossed the piece of debris away, watching it skitter across the floor and bounce out of the cell. He drew a breath in through his nose and slowly exhaled. "We wait," he answered finally.

"Wait?" Stark asked, obviously incensed by the answer. "Wait here to die, you mean?"

Conrad didn't reply.

"This is stupid," Stark hissed. "We came for help, and now we're prisoners? I escaped death at the hands of the angels, only to walk willingly back at your side. I knew I never should have trusted you damned Wraith." The wolf paused. "We have to do something."

The High Wraith cocked his head slightly.

"Say something!"

Locking eyes with the beast looming before him, Conrad remained still. He finally let his gaze fall to the floor.

With an angry grunt, Stark spun back to the bars and clamped his hands around them. Shaking them hard, a fine dust of concrete fell free, but the bars refused to budge. The werewolf knew he could break free, but the question remained, to where? He was deep in a Wraith stronghold, and despite the ferocity of a fully transformed werewolf, the enemy's numbers were far too great for him to escape. He would be struck down before he reached the front gates. Turning, he slumped against the wall and slid to the floor into a position mirroring Conrad's.

Conrad stared at the wolf. His body language screamed "defeated," very strange for the chieftain of a werewolf tribe. Werewolf society was much more animalistic and savage than almost any other on the planet. One didn't become chieftain simply by being born into it, a wolf had to prove they were worthy of being the alpha male, and to do that, they had to fight. To hold the title of chieftain, a wolf must be strong, powerful, determined, and fierce. None of those described Stark now.

The faint tapping returned. Conrad cocked his head and listened. "Do you hear that?"

Stark lifted his head. "Hear what?"

"That tapping sound," Conrad answered. "I've heard it on and off for the past ten minutes or so."

The wolf turned away from Conrad. "I don't hear anything."

Straining his hearing, Conrad listened intently but the sound had vanished again. He was starting to think his earlier theory about this place being old and damaged was correct. He gave up and returned his attention to the wolf. "Like I said," Conrad paused, "we have to wait."

Stark glared at Conrad. He pulled in a breath to retort, but let the thought go. It probably wouldn't do any good anyway. Anger compelled him to slam his elbow back against the wall. He felt a burst of pain up his forearm, but chewed it back. It was stupid, but at least the pain distracted him for a moment.

"Master Wraith?"

Conrad lifted his eyes to find a young woman standing outside the cell. Her hands were folded neatly at her waist, her brunette hair immaculately styled. The chocolate leather trench she wore glistened in the fluorescent light, as if it were brand new, and hung down to her ankles which were beautifully encased in a pair of black high-heeled shoes. The black dress she wore left little to the imagination, and displayed her cleavage beautifully. She looked more like she had been called away from a cocktail party than a Wraith.

"My name is Michelle Stewart," she said matter-of-factly.

"Ah," Conrad smiled, recognizing her accent,

128

"the American Wraith." She had trained as a warrior, but elected to serve a more political role within the Order. Stewart had joined the Academy here after Bane's attack. "I had been wanting to meet you."

Stewart smiled. "And you, the head of the Council of Seven."

"Former," Conrad corrected.

"Right," Stewart said almost apologetically. She batted her long, beautiful eyelashes. "I've been assigned by the Tribunal as your counsel."

"So," Conrad exhaled and smiled, "I'm actually getting a chance to defend myself?"

"Certainly," Stewart replied. "But we have to face facts, Master Verge."

Conrad cocked an eyebrow. "Which are?"

"You and your pet werewolf blasted into the Wraith Academy, on your way to do God knows what," Stewart spat.

So much for a fair trial, Conrad thought.

"Pet?" Stark stood off the floor and faced the counselor.

"That isn't going to sit well with the Tribunal, no matter what your reasons are," Stewart finished, ignoring Stark. "We are facing a war on two fronts, and the Chancellor has been forced to take emergency measures."

Conrad felt as though he was listening to Alexander's press secretary instead of his legal counsel. He lifted his hand and pulled it down his face.

"But your reputation could save you," Stewart said finally. "You are one of the most respected

Wraith in the Order, Master Verge. Your service has been exemplary. That will not be forgotten."

"It seems like my fate has already been decided," Conrad said. "Why, then, do I need you?"

"The Chancellor is pushing for a death sentence," she scanned over to the wolf, "for both of you. I personally think you're worth saving, despite the circumstances."

"Thank you," Conrad exhaled.

"I'm going to meet with the Chancellor immediately," Stewart said, "and argue for your immediate release. If that fails, we must begin on your defense right away. The Tribunal is set to convene on the 31st. That doesn't leave us a lot of time."

"Happy Halloween," Stark snorted with amusement.

Stewart didn't seem to enjoy the irony as much as Stark. Her dark eyes hardened. Pulling a breath in through her nose, she brought her attention back to Conrad. "I'll return as soon as I can."

"Take your time." Conrad laughed. "We're not going anywhere."

Stewart stood in awe of the two men in the cell. Her expression was that of disgust and confusion.

"You don't like me," Conrad said.

"That's irrelevant."

"To hell it is," the High Wraith barked.

"No," Stewart spat back, "I don't like you. I've read the files on you. I think you're a cowboy, and you're reckless. Many Wraith have died at your side, including Thomas Cross who was considered one of the most promising students this Academy,

130

or any other for that matter, has ever produced. Add that to the fact you allowed Emily St. Louise to go AWOL, and I see one very sloppy Wraith and a poor leader. I don't think you're fit to carry a scythe, let alone lead the Council of Seven."

"Indeed." Conrad tried to recover from the verbal slap he had just received.

"Now, if you'll excuse me," Stewart quickly composed herself, "I have to meet with the Chancellor."

Turning, she walked quickly away from the cell, the click of her heels echoing as she went. The two listened to a heavy door opening, then slamming closed. They were alone again.

Stark looked to Conrad with a bemused expression on his face. "We're boned, right?"

Conrad nodded. "Pretty thoroughly."

***

Walking slowly through the streets of Vienna, he was literally soaked to the bone. The rain hadn't stopped, and showed no signs of abating. But the weather matched his mood. He had stumbled, almost randomly, into the Donaustadt, north of the Danube River. Looming in the rain haze was Millennium Tower. Designed in the mid-ninties, the tower looked like an alien obelisk in the center of the city. Constructed of concrete, steel, and glass, the tower rose over six hundred and sixty-two feet into the atmosphere, and came to a sharp point that looked very much like a scalpel. Standing below it, his feelings of insignificance only grew.

Ben felt completely lost and alone for the first time in memory. Thoughts of Saint's attack kept flashing in his mind's eye. He had never seen her behave that way, and hoped to never see it again. He was her sworn protector, a vow he had taken in the spirit realm, but how was he supposed to fulfill that promise now? That vow was everything to him. So much, in fact, that he had given up his birthright to become chieftain of his clan. Stark had been named chieftain in his stead, but Ben knew things wouldn't be the same. His father had led them for nearly a century, and for him to turn his back on his legacy was an insult to the clan, to say the least.

Now, he had nothing.

His eyes wandered from the Millennium Tower to the slowly moving waters of the Danube. Vienna's lights reflected on the shimmering surface making it look like there was another city, another world, underwater. Behind him, he heard the sounds of civilization. Engines hummed, industry churned, and people moved about their lives despite the weather. He couldn't escape the images of the charred remains of Bratislava in his mind, and wondered why the angels had not done the same here.

Turning away from the mighty river, the werewolf staggered almost drunkenly through the masses trying to escape the weather. Ahead, he spotted a gathering of people crowded around the large display windows of a department store. Some cowered under umbrellas, or damp newspapers, while others stood defiantly against the rain, but they all refused to move. Ben spotted a telltale blue flicker against the front row of people. It seemed like something out of the past: a crowd gathered around televisions in a store window waiting for updates on the moon landing, or the war effort.

Ben caught a man in his peripheral vision watching him. Wearing a short, worn, leather jacket with orange bands on the sleeves, and a black baseball cap featuring a team Ben didn't recognize, the man suspiciously turned away as quickly as the wolf directed his attention toward him. Ben paused and sniffed the air. The rain, people, and urban landscape were interfering, but something bit at his nostrils, something familiar. The hairs on the back of his neck stood up as danger signals registered in Ben's mind. The man nervously glanced back to Ben, found he was still being watched, pulled his baseball cap low, stuffed his hands in his pockets and walked away.

Ben watched the man go, but couldn't escape the unease he had created.

Shaking some of the rain off his black leather jacket, Ben moved into the crowd and tried to catch a glimpse of the televisions. At first, through the forest of people, he only caught blurred glimpses. As he moved deeper into the crowd, he was disheartened to see the images on the screen.

It was Bratislava. The devastation was exactly as he remembered it. The camera panned slowly over scenes of carnage and death, then to a wide shot of the city that showed billowing black smoke blotting out the heavens. The city was completely destroyed.

Ben turned away. "I can't watch anymore. I was there."

"How were you there?" a woman asked in

shock.

"That's Bratislava," Ben answered.

"No," the woman answered. Reaching out, she turned Ben back toward the televisions. "Look," she said, pointing.

Ben read the legend at the bottom and stood horrified. His mind seemed somehow unable to process the information at hand. "How can this be?"

Against a blue background, bold white lettering clearly read San Francisco, California.

The image on the screen transitioned to the more familiar Golden Gate Bridge that spanned the bay, and then to the smoking ruins of the Transamerica Building. Ben understood instantly that the devastation he witnessed in Bratislava had been repeated all over the world. The angels weren't just localized to Europe…they were everywhere.

No one was safe.

Ben turned and pushed his way out of the crowd. On the sidewalk, he stared worriedly up into the rainy sky scanning for the dark outline of angels. He wiped rain from his eyes, but saw nothing. As the sky flashed blue with lightning, the werewolf remained vigilant. He would fight until he couldn't.

"Why do you protect them?"

Ben spun wildly to find a man in a black trench coat watching him. The man's long, dark hair hung in wet strands around his face, making his skin look extraordinarily pale. His irises were a haunting shade of sea-foam green that appeared somehow unearthly. His face was handsome, cleanly shaven, yet unnerving in a way that Ben couldn't understand. It was almost as if he was too perfect. Every face has slight defects—perhaps one eye is a little higher, the nose might be a bit crooked, or the mouth might slant slightly—but this man had none. He was immaculately symmetrical.

But Ben immediately trusted him. "Because it's the right thing to do," he replied.

"Good answer." The man smiled, showing his perfect teeth. "I only ask because you, a werewolf, are traditionally considered an outlaw, a renegade. Yet you fight on the side of the light. Marvelous."

Ben was slightly taken back by the man's statements. "How do you know I'm a werewolf?" he asked in a hushed voice, still aware of the crowd gathered around the televisions just feet away.

"I know many things. I had expected two of you," he said in a sullen tone, "but it seems his song was too strong. We will have to make do." He presented his open hand to Ben. "Take my hand. I will explain."

Ben hesitated, but only for a moment. Reaching out he took the man's hand and felt an instant wave of electricity flow through his body. The world around him began to spin wildly, yet the man stayed still before him, his expression unchanged. Feeling the contents of his stomach begin to rise, Ben wanted to release the man's hand but found that he could not. The muscles of his hand, wrist, and forearm felt as though they were locked.

Panic gripped him.

As the world stopped spinning, he felt his muscles relax and was finally able to let go. Stumbling back, he clamped his arms around his guts hoping to hold back the vomit. Slowly, as he gained control, he realized he wasn't in Vienna anymore.

He returned his attention immediately to the man. "Where are we?"

"Golden Gate Park," the man said. He lifted his hand and presented the Golden Gate Bridge peeking through the fog as though he were a model on a game show offering the latest model sedan as a prize.

Ben's eyes settled on the bridge, then scanned around to the smoking ruins of the city by the bay. The wolf had been here once before, when he had rescued Saint from the werewolf bounty hunter Talon Creed, and returned his father's axe to his clan. He watched the dark outlines of angels flitting through the darkened sky as they continued their rampage. This wasn't a fitting end for this city.

"I'm sorry," the man apologized. "I should have warned you about the trip. It can be difficult your first time."

Ben stared at the man warily. "How did you do that?"

"I believe introductions are in order." The man smiled. He began unbuttoning his trench coat. Letting it fall away from his shoulders, he lifted his arms, and unfolded his raven-black wings.

Ben stumbled back, threw off his coat, and held ready to attack. "Angel," he spat.

"Archangel," the man corrected.

"Why are you killing people and destroying cities?"

"You have it all wrong," the man said. "My

136

name is Michael, and like you, I am a soldier of the light."

"You're a killer," Ben growled, despite recognizing the name. He gritted his teeth and focused to hold his transformation at bay.

"That is true," Michael admitted, "from a certain point of view. Yes, deaths have been attributed to me, but they were always for the right reasons." He folded his wings back and stepped toward Ben. "I'm here to help."

Ben remained wary, hesitant. "Why should I believe you? I've watched what I believed to be angels kill for no reason."

"There is always a reason," Michael said quietly, knowingly, and pointed upward. "He works in mysterious ways."

Ben set his jaw, and stared at the archangel. "You didn't answer my question."

"I'm sorry, but I cannot," Michael replied. "But trust your feelings. Your heart knows."

"Don't give me that cryptic garbage," Ben said, but inside he knew the truth. Michael wasn't lying. The werewolf was standing before St. Michael the Archangel, who led his Army of Light against Lucifer, and cast him into Hell. This was The Messenger, and the Left Hand of God.

And suddenly Ben's world was split wide open.

"I'll help," the werewolf breathed.

"Good," Michael said, then let out a hearty laugh. Patting Ben on the shoulder approvingly, he stepped close and his jovialness quickly faded. In the gloom of the storm, his face was deadly serious. "You must find the Lance," the archangel paused.

137

"It's our only hope. That's all I can offer."

Michael looked into the cloudy sky. Holding out his hand, he cupped his palm, allowed the rain to pool, and showed it to Ben knowingly. "Time is running out, werewolf."

Chapter Twelve

She stared at her palms as she walked. Though it had since washed away, she could still see the angel's blood there. She felt suddenly like Lady Macbeth, decrying, "Out, damned spot, out..." only to realize too late that it was her guilt that kept the blood on her hands. In her life, she had dispatched dozens of vampires, and demons. She was a killer. When one stripped away all the pomp and circumstance of the Gwyliad Wriaeth, that's all that was left: they were an order of trained killers. Yet this kill, even though it was done in self-defense, seemed different. Saint had killed an angel.

Few memories of her life before the Order existed. This was no place for sentiment and weakness. What wasn't needed was discarded to make room for the Order. But she vividly recalled an image of her mother kneeling in a church, candles surrounding her, as she prayed before a stone sculpture of St. Michael. The memory seemed surreal, as if it didn't belong with the rest, or as though it had been ripped from a dream and implanted as real. The candles around her mother shimmered beautifully off her porcelain face, allowing the statue's shadow to seem almost as though it was alive as it danced on the floor. Saint watched her mother's hands work down the rosary beads she wore at her neck, chanting quietly as she went. There was a deep sense of sadness on her mother's face, though Saint didn't know why.

She had almost no memories of her father, and

had been an only child. Born and raised outside of Cardiff, Wales, Saint had been protected since birth, as if her mother knew something of the darkness Saint now hunted. Master Ben Quinn had discovered her at the age of eleven, and had taken her to the Academy. Her early memories were hazy, and distant. Though she hadn't yet reached the age of twenty-five, her childhood seemed hundreds of years in her past, cloaked by the fog of time, as though by dark design.

An outcast for as long as she could recall, Saint had always felt separated from the other students. Her only true friends, Miller Barnes, Thomas Cross, and Master Ben Quinn, were all dead, taken from her by Vampire Lord Bane. Born with a rare condition that neither she nor the Order understood, her body had accepted the Wraith virus, and somehow mutated it. She was something new, and the source of a prophecy dating back thousands of years. Only two known Wraith had ever been able to change the virus, the originator of the Gwyliad Wriaeth, Gwynn, and now her. This was staggering to even consider, and only isolated her further. She was now the ultimate synthesis of vampire and Wraith: the perfect killer.

Yet no one, let alone Saint, knew why.

Stumbling along the bank of an overflowing irrigation canal, she listened to the wet squish of her booted feet in the mud and muck. Long since numb from the wet and cold, she stood defiantly in the rain listening to the beautiful and horrible rhythm. She didn't know what she was doing, or where she was going. Her sole priority now was to find Kat, but with no idea where to look, that was going to be difficult.

And still something tugged at her. Like an invisible thread wound directly to her soul, Saint felt it pulling and directing her toward God-knows-where. Since the angel's death, she had felt it. Persistent, like a voice in a dream, it hovered in the back of her mind, unwilling to be ignored or forgotten. A splinter in her mind, it was starting to become infected, the tendrils of disease slithering deeper and deeper into the flesh. It was growing in strength, and she knew soon, it would become undeniable.

There was another pressing concern: why could she hear the angel's song? Neither Kat nor Ben had heard it. Perhaps it was because she was a Wraith? There was no simple answer, yet she needed one. To be effective against this new adversary, she had to understand why and how to overcome it. She had been able to push past it in Bratislava, but that had been against one, lone angel. What would happen if she came upon a...

She paused. What the hell do you call a group of angels? Crows were called a "murder," geese were a "gaggle," and wolves were a "pack." What were angels? It didn't really matter, anyway.

Stopping, Saint turned. Below she could see the distant lights of Vienna. She had been steadily climbing into the northern edge of the Alps. At this altitude, the rain was starting to freeze and stick to the ground. Thick snowflakes were beginning to mix with the rain, somehow flitting to the ground amidst the huge drops. Vienna looked peaceful and quiet, nothing like the carnage and destruction she had witnessed in Bratislava. The angels didn't appear to have struck there…

Her mind snapped to her werewolf guardian. She hadn't thought of him, even once, since separating from him. Suddenly Saint remembered attacking him…and crumbled to the ground.

What had she done?

Why had she assaulted Ben so savagely? It didn't make any sense. She recalled the memories of the fight, but they felt foreign to her, as though she were seeing them from outside her body. Her stomach twisted and suddenly she felt sick. What was happening to her? She needed Ben…

The hair on the back of her neck stood up. Her eyes widened.

Rolling onto her back, she heard a weapon slice through the air where her head had just been. Continuing the roll, she pushed off the ground, vaulted onto her feet, and drew her scythe. Activating it, her wary eyes scanned the rugged terrain through the rain. There was no sign of any attackers, but plenty of places to hide and snipe from. She glanced at the tree behind where she was seated, and found a silver and black dagger embedded deep in the trunk.

"Not good," Saint whispered.

Before she saw it, she heard the high-pitched whine of a blade slicing through the air.

Bringing her scythe up instinctively, she blocked the attack with a clang that reverberated up her arms. Her hands stinging from the power of the blow, Saint snapped her eyes to her scythe. There,

142

she saw another curved blade, almost identical to hers, locked by her parry. She followed the blade with her eyes, up to the cylindrical shaft, and then to a pair of midnight black gloves grasping the hilt. It seemed to take an eternity to register in her brain, but in reality not even a full second had eclipsed.

Her attacker smiled showing his fangs. Pulling his scythe slowly away, he stepped back and lowered his defenses. Lifting his hand, he called his dagger back to him then sheathed it on his belt. His blue eyes appeared almost gray in the low light, yet luminescent. He wore a black trench coat that hung just past his knees, and a dark sweatshirt beneath, the hood partially hiding his face. In the shadows, Saint saw a slender, jagged, twisting, black tribal tattoo stretching down the right side of his face and terminating just above his jaw.

It was Bane's mark, and Saint knew it well.

Saint gasped.

He laughed.

Saint wanted to take a step toward him, but forcefully stopped herself. She had known this man since she was twelve years old. She had watched him grow from a scared boy who had lost his family to vampires, to one of the most skilled and powerful Wraith in the order under the tutelage of Master Conrad Verge. He had been her friend, competitor, and confidant at the Academy, yet their lives were set on two very different paths. Paths, it seemed, that continually crossed, diverged, and intertwined again. All thought Conrad had destroyed this Wraith last year after he went rogue. It seemed fate had a different plan for him.

"Thomas," Saint said slowly. "You're dead."

He nodded. "Thomas Cross died under Conrad Verge's blade." He lifted his double-bladed scythe—that had been a gift from Conrad—and spun it playfully. "Bane gave me a new life, and a chance for vengeance. You may call me Scourge now."

Her friend was indeed dead.

She felt nauseous. Thomas—now Scourge— was the only Wraith in existence she had given her mutated virus to. It had transformed and gifted all of her strengths and evolutionary changes to him. Now, he had her virus, which perfected the Wraith strain, and Necolamia Morbus, the vampiric equivalent. With no idea how the two related, yet wildly dissimilar viruses combined, she may have had a hand in creating the most perfect vampire ever to exist.

"The Wraith killed Kat," Scourge growled. "For that," he brought his black and silver scythe to bear, "I will kill every last one of you."

In a blur of motion, Scourge charged, and attacked.

He was fast—Saint blocked the waist-high strike and parried it—but she was equally so.

Saint directed all of her mental energy in one burst at Scourge. With an audible pop, the force blew the vampire back. Not wasting a moment, Saint charged bringing her scythe around her body and screaming down over her head.

Landing on his back, Scourge threw his scythe straight up deflecting Saint's attack and rolled out of the way. Jumping to his feet, he predicted the

144

Wraith's next attack and leaned back barely avoiding her blade. He felt one of the strings on the collar of his hoodie slice cleanly off by the singing blade. Dropping back onto his hands, he flipped his legs over in a perfect round off and landed in a solid defense position. His gray eyes snapped to his discarded scythe on the ground behind Saint. He smiled.

Raising his arm, Scourge called his weapon to his hand.

The shaft hit Saint hard behind the knees and upended her. She cursed under her breath as she landed on her shoulder, somersaulted, and brought her scythe up to block. Scourge's blade hit hard enough to cause bright, gold sparks to erupt between the two mystical weapons.

Mere inches from her face, Saint watched a lock of her hair fall away, cut by Scourge's blade.

Rolling backwards, she pulled Scourge off balance, kicked her legs up into his chest, and flipped him easily over her. Her momentum carried her up to her feet. Leaping vertically, she narrowly avoided Scourge's scythe slicing horizontally through the air where her legs had just been.

Hitting the ground, Saint spun on her toes, and locked her eyes on Scourge. "We don't have to do this, Thomas. I can save you."

Scourge's gray eyes flashed gold for a moment. "Save me? From what?"

"We have the Troika Serum," Saint offered. "We can make you human again."

"Are you kidding?" Thomas lifted his arm and flexed it like a body builder, "I feel fantastic! Why would I ever go back to being human? I have more power than I've ever dreamt of."

Saint frowned. "Kat's alive."

If his heart still beat, it would have skipped in that moment. The smile of enjoyment finally faded from his lips, leaving only pain on his face. "Lies," he hissed.

"She's alive," Saint said again.

His face contorted in anger. "Liar."

Saint held her breath for a beat. "You can be with her. She needs you, Thomas."

"Stop calling me that!" Scourge charged.

He attacked out of anger and became sloppy. Slamming his scythe straight down at Saint, she easily blocked and repelled the attack. Scourge had lost focus in his rage. He wasn't letting his weapon work as an extension of himself, rather, he was using it like a club trying to beat her down with sheer force. Blow after blow Saint was easily able to fend them off with little effort. Stepping lightly like a boxer, she moved left to avoid another awkward strike. Kicking Scourge's scythe blade to the side, the force of his attack sent him sailing into the ground face first. Hitting hard, he bounced left and tumbled into the irrigation canal with a splash.

Spitting and gagging, Scourge rose out of the icy water and clawed his way back onto the bank. His eyes focused on her with a raw hatred that sent a shiver down her spine.

Deep sadness overtook her as she stepped back. His arm shot out trying to grab her, but didn't come close, even once. Stabbing the end of her scythe into the ground, the Wraith flipped her wet hair out of her eyes and watched Scourge skitter to his feet. "Thomas," she breathed, "Kat needs you. She's..." Saint paused, unsure if she should tell him. His possible salvation was worth the risk. "Kat's pregnant."

Scourge stopped dead in his tracks.

"It's the truth, Thomas," Saint said evenly. "She's nine months pregnant."

Scourge said something inaudible, even to Saint's ears, stumbled back, turned and fled.

Saint charged after him, but quickly lost him in the trees. He was fast, possibly faster than she was. Slowing to a trot, Saint scanned the tree line amidst the softly falling snow. There were no tracks and no sounds. Scourge was gone. She stood, once again staring at the lights of Vienna below. All was quiet.

For now...

She needed to find Ben, and tell Conrad Thomas was alive. She headed down into the city.

**

"Please wake up," Specter said quietly as he caressed Kat's cheek.

She showed no signs of movement. Perfectly still, not even her eyes twitched. Kat wasn't even dreaming...and what would a pregnant vampire dream about, anyway? Bred of Wraith and vampire, this child's future had already been predestined. It would walk the line between shadow and light, uniting all, or destroying everything. This could be the single most important epoch in the long history of humanity, or the end of all things.

He had no idea how long he had been with her. Time seemed to lose its meaning and importance here. As though it had somehow been ripped from the timeline of the rest of the universe, this place seemed to simply exist. Yet the fate of the world was being decided here.

And that scared the hell out of Specter.

Lifting his face, the Wraith looked over the hive of humans, and was swallowed by a deep sense of regret. Electricity skittered over the cocoons, causing many to shake violently. These people were victims of circumstance. In the wrong place at the wrong time, they were now facing the same uncertain future he was.

He realized the truth.

The wings on Specter's back hadn't given him an identity, they had instead stripped it away. He was nothing now. Not Wraith. Not human. Not angel. He had wanted answers, needed to somehow understand the grand scheme of it all, but had instead thrown away the last thread that made him who he was. Specter was still lost, now even more so than before.

He had to escape.

But he wasn't leaving without her. Not again. Not ever again.

Chapter Thirteen

Ben was again in the shadow of the Millennium Tower in Vienna. Turning, he found the same crowd of people gathered watching televised reports of worldwide carnage. Spinning, he searched the street for Michael, but already knew what he would find. The archangel was gone, leaving only cryptic references to a lance, and that somehow time was running out.

Ben was facing an entirely new world now. No longer did he believe this was the beginning and end of life, but just another plane of existence on some grand journey. For the first time in as long as he could remember, the werewolf experienced hope. He had heard the old legends of Gods, magic, and war, but had never truly believed them. But now, there was no other choice. St. Michael, the archangel, had just drafted Ben into his Army of Light.

He felt alive.

But confusion ran rampant over his brain. The wolf had just met the archangel St. Michael but wasn't ready to deal with all the ramifications. Believing in all those things that went bump in the night was easy, he was one after all, but God... That was something altogether different. How could any rational, somewhat logical human being believe in an omnipotent life form who existed before all things, and had allegedly created everything? The idea was simply too archaic and offered far too many loopholes. The concept of God, to him, was an ouroboros, forever eating its own tail.

It simply wasn't possible.

And yet moments ago, Ben was having a chat with an archangel in Golden Gate Park. An angel so high in the order, Ben reminded himself, that he was God's personal messenger and had expelled Lucifer from Heaven. And there wasn't a shred of doubt in the wolf's mind that Michael was telling the truth. Ben didn't know if he should start on the quest Michael had set before him, or head straight to church and repent, for if there truly was a God, Heaven, and Hell, he was completely screwed.

At least the absurdity of the moment made him smile.

Preoccupied with memories and worries, he didn't see the man in the baseball cap reaching inside his black leather jacket ominously.

There was a sharp sting in the back of his neck.

His head felt thick as a dense fog settled over his brain. A mixture of confusion and something he couldn't identify, the werewolf pressed the meaty part of his hand to his head hoping for release. He leaned forward slightly and wobbled on his heels as his heart raced. Trying to recover, Ben overcompensated and crumbled to the wet street as though drunk. Hitting his elbow, he felt a surge of pain up his arm and suddenly wanted to retch. Hauling himself up on his hands and knees, the wolf gritted his teeth and fought back the nausea. What the hell was wrong with him? Leaning back, he placed his hands on his hips and fought to control his breathing. In and out with each breath, he felt his pulse slow.

150

Watching his breath freeze as he exhaled, he felt each massive raindrop smack his flesh. Rainwater poured down his face and chest. Beyond cold, he was almost starting to feel warm. Not a good sign. Even with his werewolf physiology he was as susceptible to hypothermia as any other living creature. Lifting his hand, he pulled it through his drenched hair then down to his neck, and felt something small and metallic lodged there. Grabbing it, he gritted his teeth and tore it free of his flesh. Holding it up, he tried to focus on it, but could only make out that it was small and silver, with some sort of brightly colored material on one end. Letting his head fall back, Ben felt the cold rain on his face.

Blinking to try and clear the cobwebs in his mind, the werewolf thought he saw the sky growing darker, as though insects were swarming and chewing away the light. Falling back, he splashed into a puddle and felt his head crack against the asphalt. His left arm ached, and he felt as if a dagger had pierced his chest and was slowly being twisted. He heard a scream, but it sounded distant, removed. Pain exploded up into his brain and he lost consciousness almost instantly.

"Ben?"

The wolf opened his eyes and saw the vague outline of a person, but details were blurred.

"Ben, you have to get up."

He felt himself being lifted off the ground. "What's happening?" Trying to wipe the rain from his face, he fought for balance. Ben reached wildly, trying to latch onto anything, or anyone, to stay upright. He felt sick and tired, his body weak. "I feel terrible…"

"Stay with me, Ben," the voice said firmly.

He recognized it. "Saint?"

"Come on," she said, slipping her arm around his waist. Then putting his arm over her shoulders. "We have to move. Now!"

Lurching forward, his legs skittered clumsily to keep up. His chest ached and burned, as though it had been set on fire and was threatening to consume him. His vision was a mottled palette of gray, black, and white. Dark shapes moved in and out of his field of view, but his reactions were far too slow to actually follow and discern what they might be. Cries of agony and anguish met his ears, but sounded so distant they might as well be half a world away. Ben felt Saint pull him to the left and nearly spilled to the ground. He just wanted to lie down and rest. He wanted that so badly. Yes, rest…

Broadsided by something that felt as solid as a Peterbilt truck, Ben was knocked easily to the ground like a discarded rag doll. Skidding on the wet asphalt, he felt Saint's body crash down onto his legs. The familiar metallic sound of her scythe activating came next, then she was up. Leaning his head back, Ben listened to the song of Saint's blade as it whipped through the air in precise, controlled attacks. He tried to roll out of the way, but he was fading again.

A hand like iron grabbed his chest and lifted Ben from the ground. He tried to fight, but his arms fell limp to his sides.

Saint's blade screamed past Ben's head and he

suddenly felt the grip release. He felt weightless for a moment, but gravity seized him with all of its strength and dragged him back to Earth. Hitting hard, his head snapped back and cracked against the pavement. Stars sparkled before his eyes but were quickly replaced by blackness.

"Ben..."

He heard Saint's voice, weak and hurt.

"I need you."

Rolling onto his side, Ben opened his eyes again. With his vision still blurred, he could almost make out Saint's form. Huddled on the ground next to him, Saint's fists were pressed hard against her temples, and she was rocking back and forth like a caged animal that wanted release. Her discarded scythe was on the concrete between them.

The angel's song...it was killing her.

He had no choice.

Ben started to transform.

The pain in his chest instantly intensified as his body began to reconfigure. Ben roared in agony as bones snapped then reshaped themselves. The werewolf's heightened metabolism sped up and fought whatever was happening in his body. He felt his skin tear away revealing his dark fur as fingers ripped at him. The angels were on him. Lifting his face, Ben howled as his muzzle formed. Throwing his massive arms back, he knocked away the attackers and spun on his clawed feet.

His vision was clear and sharp, and he felt powerful. The werewolf let out a long, slow, sorrowful growl as he took in the scene.

Vienna was suddenly a war zone. Angels

swooped about killing and destroying all that they could. Flames licked the sky, despite the pounding rain. The sky was dark with the shadows of the creatures. The chug of machine guns overrode the chaos, while glowing red tracer bullets screamed wildly into the air from all directions.

Snapping his focus down, Ben saw three angels on the ground where he had just knocked them. Picking the closest, the werewolf lunged and crashed down on the being with talons fully extended. Digging into the angel's flesh, he heard it scream as he clamped his jaws around its throat. Biting into the soft flesh, Ben felt a warm font of blood on his tongue. Locking his jaw, he pulled back and ripped the angel's throat out. Lifting into a crouch, Ben felt the angel's blood spill down his throat as he spit the mouthful of flesh, muscle, and windpipe away.

He watched one of the two remaining angels back away, but the other one wasn't as smart.

The angel spread its wings, hardened its gaze, and charged. Leaping off its toes, it pushed itself into the air and flapped its massive wings. Ben pulled his lips back into a horrible sneer of fangs and blood. The angel was fast, but Ben was faster. Throwing himself into the air, the werewolf met the angel head on. The two met with a resounding thud, but before the other being had a chance to react, Ben was already clawing, biting and ripping. Slamming to the ground, Ben spun onto the angel's back and dug his claws into the being's powerful shoulder muscles.

Breaking free, Ben dug his leg in for leverage

and tore the wings from the angel's back. The being loosed a high-pitched scream that cut through every other noise in Vienna. As the last breath escaped its lungs, the angel's head fell forward onto the concrete, dead.

Tossing the wings down with satisfaction, Ben rose up and howled triumphantly.

Lowering his gaze, he saw a multitude of angry eyes locked on him. He knew he could take a few, but not all of them. They would easily overwhelm him. He gritted his teeth. This was a battle he wasn't going to win.

They charged the wolf.

Spinning, Ben scooped Saint into his arms and slung her over his shoulder. Dropping low to the ground, Ben ran as hard and as fast as he could. Leaping over objects, he vaulted off the roofs of vehicles as he avoided angels. One swooped down before him, barely missing him and crashing into a street lamp. Jumping into the air, Ben threw his legs out and slammed his claws into another striking the angel's head. Momentum brought them down to the ground. Feeling the satisfying crunch of bone beneath his feet, Ben released and charged ahead. Another attack caught him blindsided, and knocked him wildly to the concrete. Pulling Saint down into his arms, Ben rolled and came back up running.

He had to get out of the open.

Weaving from street to alley and back again, the werewolf moved quickly and easily through the urban jungle. Bursting from the mouth of an alley, Ben erupted into a squad of soldiers. He looked quickly over the fresh-faced men and women, as they did him. He heard one yell in terror and the first black assault rifle swing in his direction. He was already up and moving before the first bullet was fully chambered and fired. Breaking through the soldiers like a battering ram, Ben tried to knock them down, but didn't want to hurt them.

Skittering into an adjoining alley, he swung up onto a fire escape as a volley of bullets screamed past him. He heard one of the shells hit the metal just to his right and ricochet wildly. Growling angrily, Ben vaulted over the railing and climbed quickly to the roof and out of the line of fire.

Before he could even breathe, the angels were on him again. Swatting one away, he watched it hit the roof's ledge, bounce, and disappear into the alley below. The sound of artillery sealed its fate. Ben dashed over the roof, his strides long. Leaping from roof to roof with ease, he skidded left to avoid another attack, snatched an angel out of the sky by its wing, and smashed it to the ground. Digging his foot into the creature's back, he twisted his arm and broke the angel's wing with a crack.

He felt claws rake his back.

Grunting, Ben swung wildly, but missed the attacker.

Ahead, he saw safety.

With his arm clamped over Saint, Ben charged as several angels dove toward him. Leaping off the roof, the werewolf sailed through the air, the wind screaming in his ears. Hitting the ground, he felt the concrete crater below his feet. He hit a dead sprint. He would not look back. It was roughly fifty yards across the courtyard to the front gates and they

156

would be inside Hofburg Palace, the winter capitol of Austria. It was tightly guarded, and there was a good chance the soldiers would fire on the charging werewolf, but at least Saint would be safe. There were no other options left. Ben had to get Saint away from the angels.

Cutting left, then breaking right, the wolf weaved across the courtyard like a running back charging for the end zone. Ben could feel angels bearing down on him, but the wolf pushed himself harder. His heart thumped loudly in his ears, and his blood burned like battery acid in his veins. Every part of him hurt, and the rain felt like icy stones slamming into his face and chest. Ben charged forward with every last ounce of strength.

He was almost there.

***

The two prisoners sat silently in the cell. Stark had been trying to rest, but couldn't seem to relax enough to drift off. He was wound tightly, as almost anyone would be facing imminent death. Conrad, by comparison, was resting against the wall, his legs crossed, and his battered leather trench draped over him like a blanket. The Wraith had fallen asleep some time ago.

Stark didn't like this place, and he certainly didn't like the people. Wraith were the pompous, arrogant, self-appointed police of the preternatural world. Through their interference, vampires had not been eradicated, but rather transformed into a powerful dark plague that was threatening to consume the entire world. It was sheer idiocy and ego that kept this pitiful band of cops, with their stolen power, operating. Before the Wraith, supernatural beings had taken care of themselves, and vampires had been nothing more than a nuisance, like an infestation of insects, and just as easily disposed of.

Stark had witnessed entire clans of werewolves destroyed by the Wraith on claims that they were too dangerous, or that they had gone rogue. What gave the Wraith the right to decide the fate of other species? Who asked them to step in anyway? There was a long-standing peace between wolves and wraith, but it was tenuous at best. His kin believed their goals matched the Wraiths', but Stark never believed that to be true. The Order had caused more harm than it had ever remedied.

Stark hated the Wraith.

But he had saved Conrad. Why?

Because even though he was a Wraith, the wolves respected Conrad. And he was a good man. Stark believed that. The High Wraith had helped return his clan's ceremonial axe that had been stolen, and had aided in the defeat of Talon Creed, one of the most notorious, outlaw, werewolf bounty hunters in the world. And Stark knew, deep in his gut, that Conrad would have saved him if the situation were reversed.

Still, for every one good Wraith, there were a multitude who abused their power and position. They claimed they were protecting humanity, but to what end? Where was the line drawn between salvation, and genocide? Stark had hoped to watch the Academies burn in glorious, cleansing fire, but that didn't seem likely now. His fate had already been decided.

Conrad stirred, but didn't awaken.

Stark's eyes settled on him. How easy it would be to climb across the cell and break the Wraith's neck...of course, what purpose would that serve? They were both already condemned to death, and Stark would have no more innocent blood on his conscience. He had already witnessed the death of his entire clan. Perhaps it was better this way in the end. The flame of the werewolf would die out, leaving the younger races to finally fend for themselves. It seemed appropriate. The old ones were nearly gone, and these new, younger species—humans, Wraiths, and vampires—would no doubt destroy each other. Life could start anew on this planet, as it had done so many times, and it would be free of the hypocritical, pompous Wraith.

Quiet settled in the cell. Above, the buzz of electricity radiated out from the fluorescent lights, while the intermittent rush of water came muffled from pipes behind the walls. The muted muttering of another prisoner bounced from cell to cell, and had become all but incomprehensible by the time it met Stark's ears. Somewhere in the background, the sound of water rhythmically dripping echoed off the cool concrete. This was Hell.

The lights flickered as the concrete rumbled.

Conrad shot forward, his eyes wide and instantly alert. He waited.

Another rumble washed through the walls and into the floor. Dust wafted to the floor as the lights sputtered and died.

Engulfed by darkness, Stark could hear the

Wraith's steady breathing. Pressing his hands to the wall, the wolf waited for his eyes to adjust as he slowly stood. "What's happening?"

Everything shook again, this time much more violently.

Conrad turned to the wolf. "The Academy is under attack."

Chapter Fourteen

Another wave of electricity danced across the cocoons in the hive. He hadn't left her side since discovering her. With no concept of time in this place, Specter didn't know how long that was. Staring at her face in the blue light, he took a long, slow breath. Kat hadn't moved, blinked, or stirred at all. Only the rhythmic rise and fall of her chest signified she was even alive. She was so beautiful, even in this state.

Specter smiled.

Leaning forward, he placed his hands on the skin-like mesh of the cocoon. Running his fingers up the glistening, rubbery surface, he came to an edge and wrapped them tightly around it. Peering beneath, he tried to see if she was connected to the pod in anyway. He knew very well that if he took her out it could kill her instantly...but he had to get her out of here. This was the mouth of madness, and Metatron was the forked tongue.

Throwing his leg over the cocoon, he stood on both sides of the altar. Reaching down, he grabbed the edge again. Digging his heels in, Specter pulled with all of his strength. The flesh stretched, creaked, and groaned, but refused to break. He took a step back and curled his arms up to his chest, his biceps shaking beneath the strain. He heard the flesh pop, then again. Specter spread his wings and took one more step back. His arms shook violently against the cocoon. Throwing his head back, the Wraith roared at the top of his lungs as he pulled. He almost had it.

The flesh snapped.

Specter lost his footing and sailed backwards. Skidding as he hit the floor, he felt a massive chunk of the flesh land on him with a heavy smack. With a yelp, he tossed it away and skittered to his feet.

Rushing back to Kat's side, his heart dropped when he stared into the open cocoon. A mass of tubes surrounded her body and she was partially immersed in some sort of dark fluid. He watched as one of the tubes slithered over Kat's naked body and disappeared into the fluid as though alive. The sight sent shivers up his spine. Peering in, he tried to determine if any of the tubes were connected or penetrating the pregnant vampire in any way, but couldn't tell. Kneeling next to the pod, he lifted his hands but hesitated, unsure what would happen when he reached in.

He had to. He'd already come this far. Pulling in a breath, the Wraith guided his hands into the fluid, and beneath Kat. It was warm, and sticky, and disgusting. Lifting her carefully, he saw several of the tubes slide away. He felt a wave of relief. There were no marks on her flesh where the tubes had been. They seemed to be acting as restraints. Getting her body above the fluid, Specter saw her eyes flutter for the first time.

Then several tubes snapped around his arms.

The tendrils yanked hard pulling Specter and Kat back down into the pod. It seemed the cocoon was not as willing to give up its prize as Specter thought. A surge of pain chewed up the side of Specter's head as it slammed against the side of the altar. He felt the warm, sticky goo on his arms and face and tried not to panic. His mouth and nose were submerged in the fluid. Struggling against the tendrils, he writhed and pulled, trying to draw breath. His lungs ached, and he could hear his pulse pounding in his ears as he fought. He was suffocating.

His head emerged from the fluid. Exhaling audibly, he opened his mouth and pulled in a breath along with a gulp of the fluid before the tendrils yanked him back down. The fluid's bitter, metallic taste burned his tongue and gums. Desperate to breathe, anger blossomed in his brain and surged like adrenaline through his veins.

Specter had just about enough of this place.

He had already lost so many. The image of his wife and daughter filled his thoughts. Drained of blood, their flesh was pale, cold, and lifeless. Locked in an embrace, arranged that way by the vampire who killed them, they had journeyed into death violently and unnecessarily. The worst part came after though, at his own hands. To ensure they didn't join the ranks of the undead, Specter had been forced to decapitate the bodies, and remove their hearts before burying them in the garden. He remembered holding his wife's heart in his hand and wondering if this was truly where love came from… The thought both saddened and sickened him.

Specter wouldn't lose another innocent life. He would not abandon Kat to this fate. He would not.

He swung his legs up, braced them against the sides of the cocoon and pushed with all of his strength. The muscles in his lower back quivered under the strain as the tendrils fought against him, determined to keep him there. The tubes creaked as the flesh had under the strain. The Wraith focused every bit of his strength. His body shook against the pressure, as he pulled free of the fluid. Catching his breath, he heard the first tendril snap like a rubber band.

He pulled again.

Another tube snapped, and he heard what he thought was the cocoon whimpering. Specter was unable to hide his surprise.

Is it alive…?

Flipping onto his back, he squatted down like a weightlifter and tried to maneuver the tendrils onto his shoulders. Tossing his head back he roared at the top of his voice and pushed with his legs. The tubes moaned as they stretched, but finally broke free.

Scooping Kat out of the fluid, he leapt into the air before the tubes could grab them again. Turning back, he watched the cocoon search blindly for its occupant, and finally withdraw the mess of tendrils.

Looking down at Kat's stomach, he admired the beautiful bulge. At least eight or nine months along, she was beautiful. Her eyes fluttered and opened slightly, but she was too groggy to say or do anything. Kat hung limp in the Wraith's arms. Leaning her forward, he searched her back for the telltale bumps of wings growing, but saw nothing. Perhaps the transformation hadn't been complete?

That's when Specter realized he was hovering in the center of the chamber.

His mighty wings flapped, keeping him aloft. He had done it involuntarily, and realized that scared the hell out of him. They were starting to become a part of him, and his brain was able to use them unconsciously. He cursed under his breath, but knew not to look a gift horse in the mouth.

Lifting his head, Specter held Kat tightly in his arms and flew toward the passage at the top of the hive.

A figure emerged from a dark corner of the room below. His eyes, hidden by the heavy hood of his robes, watched approvingly as Specter and Kat vanished from the cocoon chamber. The Wraith was everything he wanted, and would be the perfect teacher for the King of Kings. He had indeed chosen well.

Metatron was pleased.

***

Ben collapsed.

Saint hit hard and slid along the polished marble floor. Choking down a breath, she slammed her fists to her head again. The angel's song was screaming in her mind, and it felt as though any moment her head was going to burst. Rolling onto her side she saw several people and guards rushing toward her amidst cries of "monster." The people, dressed in white with a red cross on their shoulders, immediately started to tend to Saint while the guards in red surrounded Ben and held him at gunpoint.

"No," Saint cried when she heard the weapons' bolt click and release.

Pushing away the nearest medic who had just

snapped on a pair of latex gloves and was trying to hold a stethoscope to Saint's chest, the Wraith fought through the angel's song in her head and crawled toward the werewolf. Ben was writhing on the floor, whimpering softly. He tried to get to his feet, but collapsed again.

"Don't hurt him!" Saint yelled as she fought against the medics trying to hold her in place. "Ben!"

Ben's wolf eyes snapped to Saint and he howled painfully. He reached for her, but his strength was completely gone.

Frustrated and terrified, Saint rolled onto her back and kicked one of the medics hard across the face. As the man's head snapped back, the Wraith grabbed the other by the throat and tossed him away. Skittering onto her feet, Saint launched herself into the circle of guards and onto Ben.

"Don't hurt him!" she screamed, doing her best to shield the werewolf. The angel's song was becoming unbearable. Blood spilled from her nose. "Please."

A chunk of hair fell away from the werewolf, and he lost consciousness.

The massive palace gates closed with a thud. Men barked orders calling for the doors to be barricaded.

Saint watched the guards.

Their gaze was fixed on the wolf.

There was another shout for assistance amidst the chaos.

Finally one of the guards snapped his rifle up and slung it over his shoulder. Spinning away, he commanded the others to follow and help barricade the doors.

Saint wanted to roll into the fetal position and cry, but wouldn't let herself. She had to take care of Ben now. He had saved her life, again. Sliding off him, she focused her thoughts and pushed the angel's song as far to the back of her mind as she could. Taking off her leather trench, she draped it over Ben's naked flesh. He had reverted to human form and looked like hell. Several large, black bruises were forming on his arms and chest, and his back was bloody from numerous deep scratches.

Lifting her eyes, she spotted the two medics she had been forced to attack. One was still rubbing his jaw. "Please," she breathed, "he needs medical attention."

As the two medics looked to each other, their fear was palpable. Neither was more than twenty-five years old, and looked as though they were doing everything possible not to simply run and hide. She couldn't blame them. Turning back to Saint, they grabbed their equipment off the floor and walked quickly over. Yes, they were scared, but their oath to save and heal was more important. Dropping down, they snapped on their latex gloves and went to work on Ben. Standing, Saint stepped back to get out of their way.

Listening to the wolf's chest, the medic's eyes widened. "Arrhythmia," he said to the other.

"B.P. is through the roof," the second added, pulling the black blood pressure cuff off Ben's arm.

"What does that mean?" Saint asked nervously.

The second medic pulled back his sleeves and

167

knelt behind Ben intending to work on his back, but something else caught his attention. "Look at this."

The other medic leaned over and examined the back of Ben's neck. "Puncture wound?"

The first medic agreed, then turned to Saint. "We need to get this man to the palace Infirmary."

"What's happening?" Saint almost shouted.

"Looks like a heart attack," the medic answered as they started to lift Ben off the floor. Pulling the werewolf's arm over his shoulder, he waited for the other medic to do the same. "But there's a puncture wound at the base of the skull," he added. "Could have been poisoned."

The two medics started carrying Ben off without another word.

Two loud thuds echoed through the palace entrance. Spinning, Saint watched all the remaining guards and palace personnel holding the massive gates closed against the angels. Anything that wasn't attached to the floor was being fetched and stacked against the doors. Their barricade was flimsy at best, and wasn't going to hold long against the onslaught of angels.

A vision appeared in Saint's thoughts. She clearly saw herself walking to the door, slaughtering the guards with her scythe, and knocking down the barricade.

Saint was appalled by the thought. Why would…

She stopped and something clicked in her mind. The angels were trying to control her with their song. It was the reason she saw the vision, and why she attacked Ben outside of Bratislava. She suddenly felt sick and angry, and understood the song's purpose was twofold: if the angels could not control her, they would kill her with it.

She felt weak and powerless.

But it only lasted for a moment, as she became more determined than ever before. The angels had taken Kat from her, and tried to take Ben. The Wraith gritted her teeth. These creatures would not control her. Whatever they were, she would see every last one of them dead for what they had done. Starting now.

A door opened may be walked through in either direction.

Saint dropped down on the marble floor and sat Indian style. Saint was the most unique Wraith ever created, with abilities well beyond the scope of her brethren. And she was going to prove that to the angels. Placing her hands on her knees, she closed her eyes and regulated her breathing. In through her nose, hold, and slowly out through her mouth. She repeated it. Moving the angel's song from the back of her mind, she listened to the haunting melody, and began to visualize it in her mind's eye. As the music spread out, she saw tiny, barely visible threads extending out from her head like spider's silk. Following one of the threads, she was pleased when she found it terminated in a nearby angel's brain.

Moving among the creature's thoughts, she was amazed and frightened by how alien it was. Thoughts and memories were not organized rationally, but broken down into base components and stored in separate places. If one were to try and read an angel's thoughts, they would most likely only uncover random strings that appeared to be nothing more than gibberish. From the angel's mind, Saint saw the same invisible thread webbing out in all directions. Pulses of electricity danced along the threads, going to and from other angels. They were all connected by a group conscience. Each had their own thoughts, but the angels seemed to be governed externally.

Fascinating, Saint thought, and useful.

In her own mind, the Wraith started to build up what could basically be compared to as a static shock. Collecting energy from every corner of her brain and nervous system, it started to snowball in the base of her skull. The Wraith was careful not to allow it to touch her connection to the angels just yet. She didn't want the door to be prematurely closed. As the ball of energy grew, she listened to the terrible and beautiful Angel's song, wondering if this was what every mind in the hive heard.

Outside, in what felt like the distance, she heard men's voices calling for more to barricade the doors. They were losing control. The angels were about to break through.

It wasn't as big as Saint wanted it, but the ball of energy would have to do. She balled her fists and steeled herself. She had no idea what this would do, but she had to try. Moving the ball into the center of her brain, she felt her fingertips tingling as tiny bits of energy escaped and surged down her limbs. One more breath. Lifting the ball, she pushed it into the exact center of the angel's song and watched it split and radiate up the threads in all directions.

She waited.

The Wraith's mind was suddenly filled with hundreds of voices screaming in unison. Saint fell back on the floor, writhing in agony. If the song's volume knob was turned to five, the screams were at eleven. She felt as though the sides of her head were about to split wide open. As she rolled onto her stomach, Saint realized one of the screams was her own.

Just as quickly as it started, the screams stopped.

Flipping onto her back, Saint felt the pain in her head start to abate. Looking inward, she saw that all the angel's threads had been removed. She had been disconnected from the hive...at least for the moment. Slowly sitting up, she wiped her hand under her nose and saw a wide crimson streak on the side of her hand. Her nose was bleeding profusely.

She turned her attention to the palace doors.

Silence.

The guards were still there, holding them in place, but there were no sounds beyond. The constant thrum of weapons firing had also fallen silent. There was only the patter of rain on the windowpanes.

Holding her hand to her nose to try and quell the bleeding, Saint stood slowly. She felt woozy and weak for a moment, but found her balance. Walking carefully across the beautiful marble floors, her ears were perked, and her senses were stretched out trying to discern what had happened. Stepping easily around the confused guards, the Wraith peered through the gap between the gates.

Nothing.

She stepped back, uncertain what to do. Looking down, she watched the rainwater pooling beneath the doors slowly turning black. It was blood.

Grabbing the doors, Saint instructed the guards to get behind her. The old doors groaned as they were pulled open. The cold rain pelted Saint as she moved around the doors and stepped outside. Her mouth fell agape. Bodies of dead angels were littered everywhere she looked. Most were in awkward, broken positions as though they had fallen like rocks from the sky. Blood pooled around the bodies despite the rain, staining the white feathers black.

It was horrific, and Saint had caused it.

Saint lifted her eyes to the sky, scanning. The angels were gone. At least they were safe, for now.

Turning back, she pulled her hand away from her nose to find it drenched with blood. But that didn't matter right now. She had to get to Ben. Taking a step past the guards, Saint felt her head spin and she crumbled to the floor. She felt a pair of hands on her shoulder.

"We need to get you to the infirmary," one of the guards said.

"Yes," Saint muttered. "I think that would be best."

Signaling another to help, the guard slipped his arm around Saint's back and the two escorted her out of the palace lobby. "I don't know what you did," the guard said quietly, "but thank you."

172

Saint nodded and flashed a brief smile. "It's what I do."

Chapter Fifteen

Another tremor shook the cell, and they could hear the muted clamor of battle above. Stark paced the floor like a caged animal with the smell of fresh blood on the air, while Conrad stood near the bars quietly observing. Crossing his arms, the High Wraith listened to the squeak of his leather trench then turned his attention to the werewolf. With each passing moment Stark was becoming increasingly agitated. Conrad wasn't sure if it was anticipation, or outright fear.

"Will you stop?"

Stark shot Conrad the stink eye and continued to pace. Lifting his beefy paws, he cracked his knuckles one by one.

"This isn't helping," Conrad argued. "You're only succeeding in getting on my nerves."

Stopping, Stark turned, stepped up to Conrad, and stood staring down at him. The wolf wasn't that much taller, but he seemed to tower over Conrad. Still, Conrad had taken down bigger opponents than Stark. Battle was about control, focus, and discipline, and rarely decided by brute force.

Conrad waited. "Well?"

Stark huffed in disgust and turned away. "How can you stand this? Your people could very well be dying up there, and we're stuck in the dungeon. Isn't it driving you mad?"

"Point of reference," Conrad breathed, "those aren't my people anymore. They've made that abundantly clear. And there really isn't much we

174

can do, now is there?"

"You can't tell me that you've given up on the Order that easily," Stark shot back. "You're a company man, if there is such a thing."

Conrad felt his temper flare. "What would you have me do? Gallop in on my white horse and save those who have imprisoned us?"

Stark threw his head back and laughed derisively. "How the hell should I know? I just don't want to be in this little box when the angel of death comes calling."

Dropping his head, Conrad turned away from the wolf. Stark was, amazingly, right. Just because the head of the Order had become drunk with power didn't mean all had to be sacrificed. Conrad still believed in the Order. He knew what they fought, and died for, was right. Maybe they had lost their way somewhere, and maybe the path wasn't so clear anymore… But were they really worth saving?

He had to believe that. It was all he had left.

The Wraith lifted his hands and wrapped them around the cool, iron bars. He leaned close and rested his forehead, enjoying the momentary sensation of coolness. Another shout echoed through the concrete, this time louder.

The angels were inside the Academy.

"Conrad." Stark stepped near and waited.

Turning his head, he brought his eyes up to the wolf's.

"We have to do something," Stark said. "I need you to stand back." He started to pull away the Wraith robe.

Conrad understood, and shrank into the back of

the cell.

Dropping down to his knees, Stark initiated the change. Almost immediately the flesh of his powerful back ripped open revealing the wolf. He yelled, but his human voice was quickly changed to a wolf's howl. Lifting his head, he pinned his ears back and sprang off the floor. Hitting the bars with almost unimaginable force, they bent outward, but refused to break. Stark shook his head, and backed up for a second attempt. Huffing like a bull, Stark lowered himself and coiled for the strike. With a roar the likes of which Conrad had never heard, Stark launched into the bars, tearing the anchors completely from the concrete. The bars, and Stark, flew outward and crashed into the empty cell opposite theirs.

Before Conrad was out of the cell, Stark was already back on his feet and had hit a dead sprint for the end of the cellblock. He watched the werewolf haul up, rip the metal door from its hinges, and disappear beyond.

For a moment he wondered if the wolf was rushing to battle, or escape.

Reaching instinctively for his scythe, Conrad remembered it had been confiscated. Not entirely eager to join the battle without a weapon, he had to follow Stark. Charging through the debris that used to be the doorway, Conrad threw himself to the floor to avoid a body sailing in his direction. Looking over his shoulder, he saw a bloody mass that was formerly an angel. He recognized the wings, and that was about it. He returned his gaze forward and found himself in complete awe.

Stark's massive, black form stood in the center of the room annihilating wave after wave of angels. It was a blood bath. Each attack was a killing blow, and every move was perfectly executed. Body parts were torn free, torsos eviscerated, and bones broken as Stark raged. This wasn't to save the Wraith. This wasn't even to stop the angels. This was revenge, pure and simple, for the death of his clan. This was every bit of anger and pain unleashed in a blinding blood rage that could not be satisfied.

Conrad knew better than to get in the middle of it.

The Wraith scanned the room. Octagonal in shape, he knew a control desk had once sat in the center, but had been almost completely obliterated by either the angels, or Stark. Each wall contained another heavy iron door, leading to another tier of cells. To the far right was the main entrance, once sealed by two bulletproof glass doors. Both lay shattered on the floor, destroyed.

Conrad had to get to the entrance, but one pissed off werewolf and a lot of angels were in his way.

Rolling up on his knees, Conrad watched the attack. Angels emptied out of the entrance, completely focused on Stark. Skittering along the wall, he peered carefully around the corner, and found the passage to the next area was clear. Looking back at Stark, Conrad paused. He couldn't just leave the wolf, could he?

Stark's eyes snapped to Conrad as he tossed another angel aside. The wolf didn't say anything, but his message was clear.

177

He was buying Conrad time.

Without hesitation, the Wraith jumped to his feet and raced down the exit as fast as his legs could carry him. He wouldn't waste this opportunity. He had to get to his people and see what the angels had done.

Coming to a blind corner, Conrad felt a nervous tingle in his chest. He reacted instantly, throwing his feet forward and sliding like a baseball player stealing second. As he rounded the corner, he watched an angel leap off the wall and drop into the corridor.

Swiping wildly, the angel's hand grazed Conrad's forehead.

Using his momentum, Conrad dug his heels in and threw himself forward. He ricocheted off the wall, and hit the floor running, not bothering to look back. He already knew the angel was in pursuit. An almost animalistic, high-pitched scream erupted from behind him. It sounded somehow otherworldly, and sent a shiver down his spine.

Ahead, he saw the lobby and the recently rebuilt bank of lifts. Before Bane's attack and the destruction of the original Academy, most Wraith didn't know this sublevel existed. But with a gaping hole looking down into it created by Bane's bomb, it was hard to keep secret. Chancellor Alexander had redesigned it for use by all personnel, despite having large sections designated off-limits. Covered in cream tile and paint, it was supposed to be inviting and friendly, but right now it was a death trap.

Broken corpses littered the floor, and three

angels stood guard in front of the elevators. Like sentries, they stood motionless in their black robes with their wings folded to their shoulders. The darkness that shrouded their faces only made the beings more ominous. Blood dripped from their fingers and was splattered angrily on their white feathers.

Fear compelled Conrad to stop, but he didn't. His loss at the hands of the angels earlier in Trafalgar Square was still fresh in his mind.

But he couldn't stop. He wouldn't.

Charging in, he saw the angels snap around and lock onto him. Unfurling their wings, he heard the same alien cries.

They moved. Conrad reacted.

Diving forward into the corpses, Conrad grabbed a discarded scythe and activated it as he rolled to his feet. Bringing the scythe across his body, he felt the curved blade connect with the closest angel's arm and easily slice through. The angel threw itself back, cradling the damaged limb.

But the other two were already on Conrad.

The weapon vibrated oddly in Conrad's hands, as it was designed for another Wraith, but it was still powerful. Spinning it around his body, he brought it over and lodged the long, curved blade into the nearest angel's head. Spinning the handle, he hit the other angel square in the ribcage, knocking it down. Ripping the scythe free, Conrad knocked the dead angel away and pressed his attack.

The scythe screamed through the air as Conrad swung it over, then up into the chest of the angel he had already wounded. The blade slid into the

179

angel's torso with little to no resistance and sliced cleanly up to the creature's throat. Within its hood, Conrad could hear the angel choking and gagging. Kicking straight ahead, Conrad held his scythe in place as his opponent was pushed away, cleanly eviscerating it. Bringing the weapon around his body in a flourish, he stabbed the shaft into the angel on the floor, killing it almost instantly.

Conrad dropped to one knee next to the angel. "Let's see what you look like." Expecting to be completely shocked, he ripped back the angel's hood.

And found a human face.

It looked like any other person, but its face appeared gentle and loving, yet with no discernable expression Conrad could read. Its hair fell in golden waves down past its shoulders while the lips and eyes seemed eerily androgynous, but were nevertheless beautiful. Its eyes, open in death, were an unearthly blue the same soft shade as a newborn's. A black substance trickled down from its mouth.

Standing, Conrad stared at the angel for a long time. He wasn't sure what to expect beneath the hood, but a beautiful, androgynous human wasn't it. He was confused, and saddened at the same time, as though this being was too beautiful to be dead.

The High Wraith wrapped his fingers around the scythe's hilt and pulled it free. Staring at the blade, he saw the same black substance that was coming from the angel's mouth. Reasoning it must be their blood, he wasn't sure he wanted to touch it. Deactivating the scythe with his thumb, he held it in his hand for a moment longer. The weapon's vibrations were starting to match his own. It didn't take long for a scythe to realign to a new owner, but it would take years before it was fully tuned. He missed his scythe. Sliding it onto his belt, he tugged on his battered leather trench to hide it.

Stepping over the corpses, he started toward the elevator, but stopped short. It was quiet. He didn't hear the sounds of battle from the detention area, and his heart sank. Spinning, Conrad rocketed back down the hallway, his ears perked for any signs of life. Only the click of his booted feet filled his ears. He mentally scolded himself for leaving Stark. But he had no other choice, and it was what Stark wanted…right?

Coming back to the blind corner that led into the detention area, Conrad skidded to a stop as a hulking black form emerged. "Stark? Are you all right?"

The werewolf's eyes settled on Conrad, but they looked distant and glazed. He nodded.

Peering into the detention area, he saw corpses of angels littering the floor. Drawing his attention back to Stark, he spotted glimmering patches of hair wet with blood. He couldn't tell if it was Stark's, or the angel's.

Sliding off the wall, the wolf stumbled forward. His massive paw was clamped over his stomach, and soaked with blood. Crumbling to his knees, Stark whimpered softly.

"No," Conrad said, dropping down next to Stark. He reached for the wolf's hand, but Stark bared his teeth and growled. Conrad cocked his head and his face became stern as though addressing a disobedient pet. "Let me look."

Stark growled again, this time more fiercely.

"Stark," Conrad snapped, "I need to look at it if I'm going to help you." He reached in and grabbed the werewolf's hand. To his amazement, and relief, Stark let him.

Holding Stark's paw, Conrad gently pulled it away to find three deep gashes. Blood welled from the wounds and spilled into the wolf's fur. Small globules of fat oozed beneath the torn flesh, and there were at least two places Conrad could see into Stark's torso. The wounds weren't fatal, but damned close. Combined with Stark's other wounds, they probably would be.

"Damn," Conrad breathed. This wasn't a simple matter of stitches and gauze; werewolf physiology demanded its own remedies. But there was another problem: only werewolves could tend to each other, and Stark's clan was dead. That didn't leave them a lot of options. Conrad looked into the wolf's eyes, and realized that Stark had already worked through the problem. He knew he was going to die. "We need to find Ben."

Stark whimpered again.

"I know," Conrad said, answering the imagined question, "but we'll find him. He has to be alive."

Pulling his paw free of Conrad's hand, the werewolf sank back and lay on the floor. Both he and Conrad knew the only thing keeping him alive was his werewolf state, and he couldn't hold that forever. Curling up like a dog, he closed his eyes and sighed.

Conrad scooted closer and placed his hand on the wolf's forehead. Scratching the wolf gently behind the ear, he started to pet Stark's neck. "Thank you."

Stark opened his eyes, but only for a moment.

Conrad drew a breath. "I'll find Ben. I promise."

***

He was lost...in more ways than one.

Certain he had passed this same junction three times before, Specter stopped and cursed. He felt like he was trapped in a funhouse, but without any of the fun. Angry, frustrated, and tired, he looked down at Kat's face. Still unconscious, her eyes fluttered from time to time behind her eyelids. He had to get her out of here. He would not let her child be perverted by some madman. Specter returned his eyes to the junction of passages. Each led off in a different direction, while one dropped straight down. The blue light of the hive was getting to his eyes, and all he could see was darkness.

"Where are you going, Marcus?"

Metatron's voice boomed. It sounded as though it was coming from every direction at once. Specter couldn't get a bead on it.

Turning right, Specter started down another passage quickly and quietly.

"You must realize that I will not allow you to leave with the Savior," Metatron said.

Specter remained silent as he navigated the passage. Twisting to the left, it dropped off sharply. Stepping off the edge without a second thought, he used his wings to slow his descent and guide him to the ground. Touching down softly, Specter adjusted his grip on Kat and moved deeper into the hive.

"You will not get out," Metatron assured him.

Unnerved by Metatron's taunts, Specter slipped and almost fell. Hitting the side of the passage with his shoulder, he somehow remained upright. He looked nervously at Kat, watching for any signs that the trip had jarred her and the baby, but she remained comatose. Lifting his hand, he gently brushed an errant lock of hair from the vampire's face.

"I have given you a new life, and this is how you repay my kindness?"

Specter gritted his teeth. "You haven't given," he shouted, "only taken!" Pulling in a breath, he headed deeper into the passage.

"What a harsh assessment," Metatron boomed. "Yes, drastic measures were needed, but I assure you, for all that has been lost, it will return to this world tenfold."

Cutting left, Specter dove into a connecting passage and quickened his pace. He had no idea if he was actually making headway, or just running around in circles.

"We are witnessing the seventh extinction," The Voice continued, "and the fulfillment of our birthright. Father made us first," Metatron said proudly, "but then He created you talking monkeys. You fought, killed, polluted, and ruined Eden. This was a gift! It was paradise."

Specter maintained his pace, despite Metatron's words. He knew it was true. Mankind was capable of such beauty and ingenuity, yet spent all their time

184

devising ways to kill each other.

"They always say it was a serpent who tempted Eve," Metatron continued, "but that is a perversion of the truth. Yes, it was a serpent, but it was firmly attached between Adam's legs. Humans were exiled from the Garden of Eden by being filthy, talking monkeys."

Specter could hear the anger in Metatron's voice, and understood why the angel hated mankind. In many ways, Wraith and angels were kindred. They were both created to protect, but kept their presence hidden. They were silent guardians of humanity, from a darkness those they protected weren't even cognizant of.

The Wraith's pace slowed. Maybe he was running for the wrong reason. He looked down at Kat again. Specter felt ashamed, but he wasn't sure humanity was worth saving.

"Every gift received has been twisted into something evil. Humans were given free will, and they chose to kill themselves and each other." Metatron's voice echoed through the passages, and reverberated off the walls. "My people went to war for the talking monkeys. We overthrew those who believed we were superior and deserved to be the sole bearers of God's love." The Voice paused. "I can see now that we were wrong. Humans do not deserve to live."

Shocked by Metatron's admission, Specter stopped. "Lucifer thought the same way you do once, and look what happened to him, Metatron." He knew in that moment the archangel wasn't acting as The Voice of God, but his own design.

"You can't do this. It isn't your choice. It isn't your right."

"Right?" Metatron roared. "We were created first! This is not about rights anymore. We deserve this."

"Go to Hell," Specter spat as he charged down another passage. "You deserve that too."

Specter was knocked to the ground in a searing flash of pain. Landing on his back, he did his best to save Kat from the fall. Rolling onto his side, he pressed his hand to his throbbing face. Looking up, he saw Metatron standing silently before him.

"Perhaps I was wrong about you," The Voice said softly. "Perhaps I have chosen poorly."

Pulling his hand away from his cheek, he found his fingers covered in his blood. The cut on his face radiated pain in every direction, but he pushed past it. He was a Wraith, and he would do his duty. Specter stood defiantly. "I won't let you do this."

Metatron disappeared before his eyes and again the Wraith found himself on the ground. Pain erupted from his chest. Looking down, he saw another sizeable cut spilling blood.

"You cannot stop me," Metatron promised.

Holding his chest, Specter lifted himself off the floor and turned to face the archangel. "Maybe not," the Wraith admitted, "but I'll sure as hell try."

The Voice disappeared again, but this time Specter was ready for it.

Throwing a punch straight out, he guessed that the archangel wasn't merely vanishing and reappearing, but moving quickly. He felt his knuckles connect solidly, and suddenly Metatron's

186

form slammed to the floor at Specter's feet. Specter kicked, but The Voice recovered too quickly.

Specter felt Metatron's arm clamp around his throat, while the other dug into the soft flesh of his side. Grunting, Specter maneuvered an elbow up and connected with the angel's head. Grabbing Metatron's arm, Specter adjusted his stance, twisted, and pulled with every bit of his strength tossing the angel to the ground. Dropping down, Specter jammed his knee into the angel's chest and heard bones crack.

Throwing the Wraith off, Metatron was almost immediately on his feet. "You can't kill me," he promised, "but you shall pay for this little insurrection of yours." He stepped back and waved his hand horizontally.

Tendrils, similar to those restraining Kat in her cocoon, lifted out of the passage and snapped around Specter's arms and legs. The Wraith twisted and bucked, but couldn't get any leverage. As he fought, more and more tendrils slithered out of the floor to restrain him. Several wrapped around his throat and slowly began to constrict his airway.

"I should kill you," Metatron said ominously, "but I still have need of you." He turned his attention to Kat. "Just pray that the Savior is unhurt."

"Why does an angel need a talking monkey to be the Savior?" Specter gasped.

Metatron snapped his fingers and the tendrils clenched down on Specter's throat. "Yours is not to understand; yours is to follow."

Kneeling, Metatron slipped his arms gently

under Kat and lifted her off the floor. Cradling her like a newborn baby, he brushed her hair from her face tenderly. Turning away, he disappeared into the darkness.

Leaving Specter alone.

188

Chapter Sixteen

The palace infirmary wasn't designed with full-scale war in mind. Basically used for small emergencies, all others had to be handed over to the nearby hospital, so it was ill-equipped for nearly everything it was dealing with now. A handful of nurses and one general practitioner were on hand and doing the best they could, but it just wasn't enough. Too many were coming in too fast.

People, bloodied and battered, stood shoulder-to-shoulder waiting for their turn to be seen. The noise was becoming overwhelming again, despite the staff's repeated attempts to keep them quiet. Some complained, others told of their harrowing adventures, while still more simply cried. It had been a massacre out there, and even though it was hard to believe, these were the lucky ones. The others, mothers, fathers, sons, and daughters, lay dead in the streets, victims of a war they didn't even know they were involved in.

Saint sat in the far corner, a wad of gauze held under her nose, watching the organized chaos. Scanning the crowd, she stopped on a man in a black leather jacket with orange stripes on the biceps, and baseball cap, that seemed to be eyeing Ben warily. His eyes lifted, finally aware he was being watched. Locking eyes with Saint for a moment, he pulled his cap low and sank back into the crowd of people. Perhaps he had seen Ben in werewolf form, or was just curious why Ben was getting immediate attention and he was forced to stand in line. She couldn't be sure. Still, Saint had an ominous feeling about him.

Her eyes settled on Ben's unconscious body stretched out on one of the few available beds. Two nurses were attending to him. While one was trying to insert a needle to start an intravenous drip, the other was tending to his lacerations. She worked quickly with needle and thread, closing wounds and repairing flesh. The doctor had instructed that Ben be given an injection, but Saint hadn't been able to hear what cocktail had been ordered.

Standing, Saint pulled the gauze away from her nose to check it. She was still bleeding, but it had lightened considerably. Refolding the square of gauze, she tried to find a clean side and held it to her nose again. Moving across the floor, she stopped at Ben's feet. "How is he?"

The nurse applying the sutures glanced up at Saint, recognized her, then returned her attention to her work. The blue scrubs she wore complimented her blond hair and light eyes. Probably in her early thirties, her face was free of wrinkles and blemishes. She was lovely in a very natural way. "It's too early to say. We may have caught it in time."

"Caught what?" Saint asked.

"I'm sorry, I just don't have time for questions," the nurse replied. "You can see we're extremely busy, but I promise we're doing everything for your friend we can."

Saint nodded. She looked at her werewolf guardian lying helplessly on the table, and realized that once again he had placed her life above his own. Two other times he had nearly died protecting her, once at the hands of Vampire Lord Bane, the other while rescuing her from the bounty hunter, Talon Creed, and yet he never asked for anything in return. She reached down and placed her fingers gently on his exposed foot and was dismayed by the coolness of his flesh. She felt the urge to cry, but fought it with everything she had left. She would not mourn the living. Grabbing the edge of the blanket, she pulled it over and tucked it beneath his feet. It was the least, and only thing, she could do.

Turning away, she waded through the crowd toward the exit. She had to get out of here…to anywhere.

Wandering into the lobby, she daubed the gauze to her nose again and checked for blood. At least her nose had stopped bleeding. It was something, anyway. Dropping the gauze into her coat pocket, she walked slowly listening to her steps echo deep into The Hofburg. The once Imperial Palace had been home to some of the most influential and powerful families in Europe, and it showed in its architecture and decoration. Lavish didn't even begin to describe it. It was well beyond that.

Stopping short of the main entrance, she stared at the open doors. Furniture was still piled on either side, probably in case the angels decided to mount another attack. Gray clouds loomed beyond, releasing sheets of rain on the city and rumbling as lightning crackled through. Crews worked against the weather, doing their best to clean up some of the carnage. Bodies were piled and then moved by heavy machinery. The sight was sickening to Saint. It was so undignified, yet she understood that this was the only viable option at present.

A deep sense of sadness gripped her as the angels and humans were piled together. They had been humanity's protectors, now they were its killers. What had caused the angels to fall from grace?

And what could keep the Wraith from doing the same?

Saint brushed her dark hair away from her face. She needed to get back to Ben. No one would know to come find her if...she stopped herself. She wouldn't even consider it. He would pull through.

He had to.

Turning back, Saint walked the route back to the infirmary with barely an upward glance. Walking around the line of waiting people, she ignored their angry protests as she scooted inside. She wasn't here for medical attention after all. Plus, she had saved most of their lives, so they could shut the hell up as far as she was concerned. The Wraith bit her lip, and realized the gravity of the situation was starting to get to her. Exhausted from running, she was becoming punchy. She needed sleep, or better yet, a vacation.

Scanning across the infirmary, she spotted Ben, unsurprisingly, exactly where she had left him. The nurses were gone, but he had been attached to several machines in the interim. A monitor beeped rhythmically, and showed the beats of the werewolf's heart in jagged valleys and peaks, while a tube beneath his nose fed him a direct supply of oxygen. He was holding on.

Her eyes were drawn to the man in the leather jacket and baseball cap standing at the foot of Ben's bed. She saw a glimmer as he pulled something from his coat.

Gun? Knife?

She didn't have time to ascertain what it was. Saint reacted. Charging across the room, she reached for her scythe, but found it missing. She remembered losing it in the battle.

Throwing herself forward, she tackled the man hard and sent both of them skidding into the wall. The man recovered quickly and delivered two quick jabs to Saint's midsection, and then a brutal uppercut that connected with her jaw and snapped her head back. She felt another impact to her sternum that knocked the wind out of her, and threw her back.

He was strong...and definitely not human.

Gasping for air, Saint rolled onto her knees and snapped her eyes back to the man. He was charging again, this time the knife was clearly visible in his hand. He meant to kill Ben, and now her. But who was he?

Bringing her arms up across her face, she blocked the attacker's downward thrust and the knife only inches from her face. He was good. He wasn't wasting any time, instead going right for the killing blow. She stared into his golden eyes and smiled.

Vampire...

Knocking his arm up, Saint dropped down and swept the vampire's legs from beneath him. Spilling

193

to the ground, the vampire hissed and tried to roll off his back before Saint could finish him. He cursed as he got to his feet. Saint stood quietly, waiting, because he was backed into a corner.

"You kill me, Wraith, and the werewolf dies," the vampire hissed.

"I think you're a little confused," Saint said playfully. She was back in her element, with an enemy she understood. He was good, but she was better.

The vampire patted the breast of his jacket with a toothy grin. "I poisoned the wolf. But I also have the antidote right here."

"Good to know. Now I'll just kill you and take it." Saint started toward him.

"Whoa," the vampire barked, "hold up, big boots. I'll break the vial. Then the wolf will surely die."

Saint stopped. The vampire's bargaining posture was a little better than she thought. Still, she knew he was about to die. Glancing nervously to Ben, she wondered how much time he had. With the poison coursing through his body, it could take effect any moment. Still, she had to know. "Who sent you?"

The vampire only smiled. "Seems I'm holding all the cards." He dug into his jacket and produced a vial filled with an amber fluid. Holding it up, he watched the light reflecting through it. "I'm leaving. Once I'm out the door, I'll place the vial on the floor. You try to stop me, and I break the vial. I see you following me," he pulled his coat back and showed the chrome, 9mm pistol on his belt, "I destroy the vial. And trust me, I'm a very good shot."

"Seems like you've got it all worked out," Saint admitted. "Okay." She stepped out of his way.

The vampire cocked his eyebrow surprised it had been that easy. It shouldn't have been. "Really?"

"Yup." Saint nodded. He was a good fighter, but the vampire was, thankfully, dumb. "Oh, just one other thing."

The vampire waited expectantly.

Saint lifted her arm and called the vial to her hand telepathically. She smiled. "I forgot to mention," she lifted her other arm and presented her hand as though she were holding an invisible object, "I don't make deals with vampires."

Gasping and clutching his chest, the vampire instantly dropped to his knees. His mental camouflage faltered, as he lost control. The decayed corpse that was his true form was revealed amidst of chorus of gasps and screams from the people in the infirmary. His golden eyes locked on Saint. "What are you?"

"Death," Saint replied, the smile fading from her face. She clenched her fist, crushing the vampire's heart mentally.

Its eyes rolled back as the vampire dropped dead to the floor. Wisps of blue flame erupted from its flesh, and quickly consumed the creature.

Moving through the glowing embers kicked up by the palace's ventilation system, Saint handed the antidote to the nearest nurse. "Inject him," she said, pointing to Ben, "now."

"How much?" the nurse stammered, still staring at the lingering flames that had claimed the vampire.

Saint shrugged and turned to look at Ben. "All of it."

Walking around the table, she stood before the pile of ashes on the floor. There wasn't much left, just a few chunks of bone, and charred bits of flesh and muscle. Tossing her trench back, she knelt down and lifted the chrome-plated handgun from the ash. Wiping it clean, she considered it for a moment. It was a beautiful weapon, and the vampire wasn't going to need it anymore. Ensuring the safety was clicked, she slid it into the back of her pants, the way she had seen it worn in so many cop movies. There were no clues left to the vampire's identity, or whom he worked for. And unfortunately, dead vampires tell no tales.

Standing, Saint watched the nurse pushing a syringe filled with the antidote into Ben's IV. Pushing slowly on the plunger, she watched the amber liquid move down the clear tube and into Ben.

"You know, this could be more of the poison," the nurse considered.

Her stomach gurgled nervously. She hadn't considered that. Why had she been so eager to take the vampire at his word? Because she wanted to believe…but she may have killed Ben. She scowled at the pile of ash on the floor, but knew it was her own fault. Saint slipped her fingers around the werewolf's hand as the last of the amber substance drained into his arm. Watching the nurse expectantly, she waited.

Ben's body convulsed, arching his back painfully.

As the heart monitor went insane, nurses across the infirmary scrambled to Ben's side. Charging into the room, the attending physician started barking orders in rapid succession.

Working furiously, one of the nurses pushed Saint out of the way without a word as Ben's body continued to shake. The rhythmic beeping of the heart monitor had almost become one, solid sound as it tried to register the wolf's wildly erratic heartbeats. Trying their best, the nurses were trying to restrain the werewolf but failing miserably. He was about to hurt someone, or himself.

Saint stepped in and put her hand on his chest. Pushing down with what looked like little effort, the Wraith held the convulsing werewolf. "Do what you have to do," she said quietly.

Exchanging strange glances, the nurses and physician went to work on Ben.

Watching, almost numb, Saint felt distant and disconnected from the scene, as though she were seeing it on television with only a passing interest. Her eyes fell on Ben's rugged, battered, but handsome face. The wolf had mysteriously appeared in her life during Bane's attack on the Academy, and saved her when she had been forced to face the Vampire Lord in single combat. He had protected her nearly every day since, and asked for nothing. And now her carelessness was about to claim his life. In that moment she realized the truth. He was more than her protector. He was meant for her. Saint lov—

"He's stabilizing."

Saint snapped her head toward the physician and watched him, his hands hovering cautiously above Ben's chest. His eyes jumped back and forth from the displays to Ben's face.

"What did you do?" Saint asked.

The doctor looked up at Saint, confusion obvious on his face. "Nothing. Yet."

Saint's expression echoed the doctor's. "What?"

"We hadn't got anything into him yet," one of the nurses confirmed.

The Wraith took a breath, and lifted her hand away from the werewolf's chest. He was still, except for the rise and fall of his chest as he breathed.

Everyone watched, expectantly, as though they had entered the eye of the storm and the other side was approaching.

Ben's eyelids fluttered, then opened. His eyes were dark, and looked glazed.

Saint slipped her fingers around his hand again. "Ben?"

Silence.

Squeezing his hand gently, Saint leaned closer and ran her hand over his forehead. "Can you hear me, puppy?"

His eyes searched, as if confused.

Saint's mind was gripped with anxiety. Had the poison done something to his body, even more insidious than death? Had it destroyed his brain? She stared at her protector, tears welling in her eyes.

198

"I need a vacation," the wolf whispered, almost painfully.

Saint laughed and felt the tears streak down her cheeks, as her anxiety, pain, and fear released in one burst. After kissing Ben on the forehead, she pulled back slightly and stared into his strong eyes, tears still falling from hers. "No vacations," she whispered, "we still have work to do." Running her fingers through his hair, she smiled softly. "Get some rest. You deserve it."

Ben nodded, and his eyelids fell shut.

Squeezing his hand once, the Wraith slowly let go and straightened up. She looked each of the nurses and the physicians in the eye with a nod that said thank you. She started to turn away, but felt Ben reach out and touch her side. Looking down, she found his eyes open again and a worried expression on his face. "What is it?"

"The Lance," Ben breathed. "Michael said we need the Lance to stop this. Time is running out."

"What does that mean? What Lance?" Saint paused. "And who is Michael?"

"The archangel," Ben answered. He blinked hard, as though fighting against the weight of his eyelids.

Lifting the werewolf's hand, she held it in her own and kissed the back softly. "Get some rest," she said again, but he had already drifted away.

"We'll keep an eye on him," the nurse promised.

"Thank you," Saint said with a half-hearted smile. She turned and started toward the door.

"Miss?"

Saint paused and turned to see the physician walking after her. Pulling off his glasses, he rubbed the lenses with his white lab coat. "The Lance," he breathed.

"Yes?" Saint waited.

"I never used to believe in all of this garbage," he said with a nervous laugh. "You know, angels and devils, and the like. I thought it was all just kid's stuff," he explained, his unease becoming more and more apparent. "But it's all real, isn't it? All of it?"

Saint nodded. "What about the Lance?"

"It's here," the doctor said. "Well, I can't think of many other famous lances, so your friend must be talking about the Holy Lance, right? That would make sense, considering I've always thought it was a bunch of garbage too."

He was rambling. Saint put her hands on his shoulders to try and focus him. "Tell me about the Lance."

"It's here, in the Hofburg, over in the Royal Treasury."

Saint recalled seeing a sign that had directions to the treasury in the lobby. "What is it?"

"Jesus didn't die on the cross," the doctor answered and slipped his glasses back on. "Well, at least according to one account. A Roman soldier killed Jesus with his lance. They have the spear in the Schatzkammer. It's on display."

He stood for a moment, sizing up the Wraith. He wanted to say more, to ask questions, but couldn't bring himself to.

Saint smiled. "Thank you."

The doctor nodded, turned, and walked back to Ben's bedside.

Saint saw the threads of the past few weeks starting to come together, and why she had been drawn to Vienna. With angels filling the skies, it made sense that an artifact supposedly tied to Jesus' death had importance. Of course, that meant she had to believe Jesus actually lived, and was the Son of God. Well, that made as much sense as anything else in Saint's life. Why not? If this was truly the Lance Ben was talking about, maybe they had finally caught a break.

Of course, really, what were the odds?

***

Kat woke and found a dark hooded figure standing over her. Her eyes keyed on its wings, and she felt an immediate rush of fear. Her body wanted to flee, but found it was restrained. Looking down, she saw a rubbery, skin-like sheet restrained her, and she could feel something wrapped tightly around her arms and legs beneath it. Struggling with all her strength, Kat discovered that she could not break free. Her panic increased exponentially as memories of her decades of imprisonment by the Troika vampire clan flooded her thoughts. She had been a guinea pig once, and would not live through that again. She felt her baby move in her womb, and knew she would not subject her child to any of this.

"Let me go!" Kat screamed at the silent, hooded figure. Straining, kicking, and writhing with all of her strength, the pregnant vampire tried again to break free. "If you don't release me," she growled and her eyes shifted horribly to gold, "I promise I'll break free and rip out your goddamned heart. Do you hear me, you son of a bitch? Let me go!"

"I cannot," The Voice answered. "You are far too important, and we are too near transformation."

The word hit Kat like a rock between the eyes. She was doomed to the same fate…again. Her anger was replaced with raw terror. "I'm pregnant," she pleaded. "Please, don't hurt my baby."

"I would not dream of it," Metatron promised. He lifted his hands and gestured to the rest of the hive. "She is the hope of us all."

Kat's eyes wandered frantically over the others cocooned there, hanging motionless on the ceiling and walls. Her hatred for the cloaked figure increased. "Why are you doing this?"

"You are," Metatron paused, considering his words, "unique. There is no being like you in the entire world. We have awaited your arrival for thousands of years, watching in the background, ensuring events we set in motion came to fruition."

"What?"

"This child," Metatron folded his hands, "is the end product of all our hopes and dreams. She is the perfect synthesis of all my machinations. She is the Savior; she is Nephilim."

The word sat like sour milk in Kat's gut. It registered deep in her mind, in a place time had buried, somewhere primal. Not fully cognizant of what the word meant, she had an instant hatred of it. Anger and confusion swirled in her mind. "The Troika serum did this to me…not you. You're a liar."

202

"Am I?" Metatron laughed. "The Troika? Do you think three incompetent, Russian vampires could be responsible for such advanced genetic manipulation? They were idiots, merely tools I used to see my will realized. Everything was done to my design."

"No," Kat said, shaking her head.

So many events... The war between the vampires and the Wraith, Kat's death and rebirth, Saint's evolution, experimentation by the Troika, Thomas' transformation, and becoming impregnated were all too random to be planned. She could not, or would not, believe it.

It was simply impossible.

"I won't let you take my baby," Kat said, her voice trembling with fear. "It's all I have left of Thomas. It's mine."

"Your concerns matter little," Metatron assured Kat. "You are inconsequential. Your part in my grand production has been played, and after you give birth, you will be unnecessary."

Kat glanced down at her bulbous belly, and had the sudden fear that the Antichrist was growing in her womb. Her unborn baby was the result of some master plan...that thought alone scared the Hell out of her. And for the first time since becoming pregnant, she questioned her decision to carry it to term.

She didn't want to die.

Then the first labor pains gripped her abdomen and her water broke.

Chapter Seventeen

His borrowed scythe gripped tightly, Conrad moved quickly and quietly through the halls of the Wraith Academy. The battle was over. As quickly as the angels struck, they had retreated, leaving only death in their wake. Bodies, of both Wraith and angels, were scattered everywhere, and it appeared that both sides suffered heavy casualties. It was obvious the angels weren't expecting this level of resistance. Many had lost their lives, but the Wraith had struck a blow to this enemy that would not be soon forgotten.

Conrad scanned for survivors, but there weren't any to be found. Lifeless eyes stared relentlessly, asking to understand why they had fought and died this way. But the High Wraith didn't have any answers. Each man and woman knew what it meant to serve the Order, but the choice to give up his or her life for it was never an easy one. There were many old ones, but more young. They were all dead.

The Order's flame had been extinguished.

And Conrad knew it. It had remained strong for thousands of years, but now, in the dawning of the new century, it stood against too many foes, and too many had been lost. There would be no grand redesign like Chancellor Alexander promised, nor would there be a return to the old ways as Conrad wished for. Their demise had begun with Bane and ended with the angels. It seemed as though the hand of God had reached down from Heaven and smote the Gwyliad Wriaeth. Their time had come and gone.

A barely audible moan pulled Conrad from his morose state. Scanning the hallway beyond the Council Chambers, the Wraith moved methodically over every body, hoping for the best, but prepared for the worst. As he searched for signs of life, he saw something move, just barely, beneath an angel's corpse. He held his breath and position. Bringing his scythe up, he watched patiently for any other sign.

Nothing.

Silence...nothing more.

As Conrad circled around, his eyes locked, and he waited. There was another groan and the angel's body moved. Conrad tightened the grip on his scythe. He didn't have time for this. Stark was dying. Conrad had to move.

Moving carefully to the angel, the Wraith lifted his weapon to strike. All it would take was one blow to silence the fallen angel... As the angel's eyes stared vacantly into the great beyond, it lifted, and fell limp to the floor.

"Dear Lord," Conrad breathed as he deactivated the weapon and slung it onto his belt. Pulling the angel's corpse aside, he knelt down. "Xavier..."

"Conrad," the Wraith gurgled as blood spilled from his mouth. He tried to lift his hand, but found his strength had left him.

Conrad's eyes wandered down Xavier's body and found a dark, ever-growing bloodstain over his friend's stomach. He returned his gaze to Xavier's and tried to smile, but knew he was about to lose a

205

dear friend. "What did you do now?"

"Something foolish," Xavier sputtered and gagged painfully.

Conrad laughed and lifted Xavier's good hand into his own.

"They struck without warning," Xavier said to Conrad, though it looked as though he was focusing on something in the distance, his eyes glazed and dilated. "I tried to get to you, but," he coughed again, "we were pinned..."

Conrad held Xavier's hand tightly. "Is there anything I can do?"

"No." Xavier coughed. "It's a little late for that."

The two High Wraith stared at each other. There was a mutual admiration and respect between the two. They had fought side by side more times than each could recall, and most often walked out of the battle completely unscathed. Xavier had faced down Bane and one of his most powerful minions in the defense of the Council, and only lost a hand, but this time he wasn't so fortunate.

Xavier tried to draw breath, but was failing. "Where does one go," his eyes started to roll back, "when killed by an angel...?"

Conrad wanted to answer, but nothing seemed appropriate. Xavier was facing the last, great unknown, and he had to do it alone. Theology was pedantic at this point. Placing his free hand on Xavier's chest, Conrad smiled. "You did good."

Xavier wheezed, smiled, and nodded. "I did..."

"Thank you," Conrad added, knowing it was probably the last thing he would ever say to his friend.

Xavier's grip weakened and he started to slip.

Placing his hand behind Xavier's head, Conrad lowered the High Wraith gently to the floor. He listened to the last breath escape Xavier's lungs, and knew the High Wraith was gone.

Conrad let his head fall as Xavier died.

He wasn't a religious man, but in that moment Conrad whispered a prayer, asking that Xavier be delivered to Heaven for his lifetimes of service. As the words tumbled off his lips, they felt foreign and foolish. Desperate words from a desperate man. He wanted to believe...but Xavier's question about angels and death still unsettled him, and cast doubt on any absolution Xavier, or any other Wraith, would find in the great beyond. Ending the prayer, he gently closed Xavier's eyes.

The High Wraith stood and tried to hold back the anger that raged through his veins. Turning, he drew his scythe and charged. He knew exactly where he was going, and who he was looking for. Conrad wanted answers, and there was only one man who might have them.

Coming around a corner, he spied his destination. The double doors were closed, and most likely locked, but that wasn't going to stop him. Kicking hard, Conrad destroyed the locking mechanism and knocked the doors wide open.

The massive office was empty and dark. The emergency metal shutters that had been installed during the redesign were locked down, letting only a sliver of light spill inside. Nothing seemed out of place, or damaged. The angels didn't seem to get this far…but the shutters could only be closed from inside this room, and the door was locked from the inside.

He was here.

Conrad thumbed the stud on the hilt of his scythe and activated it. The weapon shuddered and doubled in length. Hitting the activation stud one more time, its long, thin, curved blade snapped into place. Holding the weapon lightly in his hands, the High Wraith felt it vibrating, more in tune with his body now. Each scythe was designed by a master weaponsmith for an individual Wraith, so it was tuned perfectly, and became an extension of the Wraith's body. Using another Wraith's scythe was difficult, but not impossible, and it could even prove to be dangerous.

His anger wanted him to rush, to charge blindly in and destroy the office, but his training overrode the urge. Stepping softly, heel to toe, he was silent as he moved into the office. He scanned the room, carefully noting shadows, and furniture that could obstruct his view, or hide someone. Passing a decorative statue that stood in the center, Conrad circled around chairs toward the large, opulent desk sitting before the massive windows. Papers were sprawled across the surface, as well as a small, ancient-looking scroll, held closed with a bit of twine.

His curiosity overwhelmed him.

Picking up the scroll, Conrad slipped off the twine and carefully unrolled the fragile paper. Jagged black lettering, of a type that seemed vaguely familiar but unreadable, occupied much of the surface. Elegant, hand-drawn designs framed the text, and the drop caps were done in a beautiful, medieval style with large, colored boxes behind them. As the Wraith's eyes wandered down the scroll, they stopped on the words "Gwyliad Wriaeth," and he felt the hair on his neck stand up.

Was this what he thought it was? It had to be. Then he saw the Gaelic word that roughly translated as "Saint," and his questions were answered.

"Oh my…"

"That's what I thought the first time I held it too."

Conrad spun at the sound of the voice, angered that he had lost his focus so completely. His eyes settled on a large couch that sat against the far wall of the office, and the figure that occupied it. He wanted to reach for his scythe, but couldn't seem to let go of the scroll.

"It's magnificent," Alexander commented. "Isn't it?" His legs crossed, one elbow was propped on the edge of the couch and he was leaning his head on his knuckles.

"Yes," Conrad agreed. "Is this," he hesitated, "the original?"

Alexander nodded. "It is the past, and the future of the Wraith. It is our everything."

Conrad looked at the fragile piece of parchment in his hands. He had the overwhelming urge to crush it and toss it to the floor, as it, and what it represented cost Saint everything…yet how could a prophecy this important be disregarded? If she was truly the progenitor of a new race, how could that be ignored? Did the needs of the many outweigh the

209

needs of the one?

"What language is this?" Conrad asked, his eyes falling back to the text.

"It's a mixture of nearly fifty different languages," Alexander answered. "One of which is Angelic."

The statement stunned Conrad. He scanned over the scroll again, searching for something, anything, that looked angelic. He shook his head and looked up at Alexander, "How can a Wraith prophecy contain angelic script?"

"That's a question we've never been able to answer," Alexander stated, "but there it is. Perhaps the writer chose to encode the document, much like Nostradamus did with his predictions. I can't speak to the motives of the prophecy writer."

"Incredible," Conrad breathed reverently. "It's amazing that a Wraith created this document."

"It wasn't a Wraith," Alexander answered.

The admission stunned Conrad. "What?"

"No one truly knows where the prophecy came from," Alexander admitted. He rubbed his fingers through his hair. "Or how it came to be so revered by our forefathers." The Chancellor smiled at Conrad. He knew the High Wraith had come to either kill him or remove him from power, but he was slowly working his way around it. He didn't get where he was by being daft. "It's a bit of a mystery."

Conrad wasn't comfortable with where this conversation was heading. "You've ruined Saint's life, forced her to run from her own people, all because of a prophecy that may or may not actually have been written by a Wraith, or even be true?"

"We know it's true," Alexander countered. "So many things have already come to pass. The prophecy is upon us, and a Saint's blood will create a new race. Simply put, we need Saint, and the Wraith will be reborn, stronger, faster, and more powerful than ever before."

"I hate to quote movies," Conrad said, "but with great power comes great responsibility. I believe Saint is responsible enough to wield this gift, but you," the High Wraith leveled his stare at Alexander, "are not."

"You dare judge me? What gives you that right?" Alexander started to stand.

But Conrad pulled his scythe and stepped back.

"I only want what's right," Alexander held his position. "I will recreate the Wraith with the prophecy as my guide. We will quell the vampire uprising once and for all, and protect humanity—"

"Through force," Conrad finished.

Alexander paused then smiled. "If that is necessary." He opened his arms. "We can bring an end to the war, my friend. To all wars."

Conrad nodded and took a long, slow breath. "Peace on Earth?" The High Wraith almost laughed at the words. "At what cost?"

"No cost," Alexander replied. "We will simply step in and combat the forces of evil, in whatever form they may take, human or inhuman."

"Do you actually think before you speak?" Conrad scoffed. "Do you really understand what you're proposing? Not only would the sheer manpower involved in something like this be staggering, but you would basically be installing yourself as dictator."

"What must be done for the good of the many," Alexander answered. His eyes twinkled as one of the slices of light fell across him. "I can save lives, if you help me." He paused. "Give me Saint."

"No," Conrad gritted his teeth. "Not ever. Wraith died just outside your door! And what did you do? Sat in your little fortress and waited. I would never put the fate of the world in the hands of a coward!"

Alexander's brow furrowed, and his face turned almost demonic. His eyes shifted to icy blue—like Saint's.

Conrad pulled up his scythe defensively, but Alexander had already drawn his weapon, activated it, and was on the High Wraith with incredible speed. The Chancellor attacked with a viciousness and total abandon that Conrad had never witnessed before. His attacks were quick and precise, expending as little energy as possible to wield his scythe. If Conrad could not bring down the Chancellor, Alexander would certainly outlast him.

Moving backward, knocking blow after blow away, Conrad tried not to get cornered. Alexander's skill and fighting acumen was certainly beyond anything he expected from the politician.

Blocking another strike, Conrad brought his scythe down and over, tying up the Chancellor. The two Wraith stood shoulder to shoulder. "How did you do it?"

"There were tests done on Saint before the destruction of the Academy. The head of the

Council saw to those personally," Alexander answered, allowing Conrad to believe he had the upper hand for a moment. "The blood samples survived."

Conrad was horrified. "You injected yourself with Saint's blood?"

"I had to," Alexander lowered his voice ominously, "to ensure peace."

Lurching forward, Alexander threw his head into the bridge of Conrad's nose. Conrad's head snapped back and he lost control of the block. Alexander pressed forward and swung his blade laterally, barely missing Conrad's midsection. Dodging the next swing, Conrad dropped and swept Alexander's legs out from under him, knocking the Chancellor to the ground.

Throwing his scythe over his head, the Chancellor rolled backwards and flipped onto his feet in one fluid motion. Bringing his scythe down slowly, he dropped into a defensive stance that Conrad had never seen before.

"This is already over, Master Verge," Alexander gloated. "You're merely delaying the inevitable. Lay down your weapon, and I won't kill you."

Conrad's resolve was unwavering. He stood ready.

"So be it," Alexander spat.

The Chancellor charged and attacked. Swinging high, his weapon met Conrad's with a clang that reverberated painfully back into each of the warrior's hands. His hands stinging, Conrad fought through the pain and repelled another of

Alexander's strikes. Spinning, Alexander brought his scythe back around and attacked again. Conrad fell back beneath the power of the hit and was barely able to maintain his footing. Alexander struck again, and again. Conrad yelled in agony as his hands throbbed in pain.

Conrad's defense fell.

Alexander lifted his weapon for what would surely be the killing blow.

But stopped.

Taking a step back, Alexander's scowl softened, and a curious expression washed over his face. His eyebrows lifted and his mouth twisted into an awkward smile. "Can you hear it?"

Conrad brought up his scythe, barely able to hold it with his aching hands. Backing slowly away from the Chancellor, he tried to give himself time to recover. "Hear what?"

"It's almost like," Alexander paused and cocked his head as if straining his ears, "music."

The High Wraith drew a breath, and listened. The silence of the Academy was almost overwhelming. Where once had been life, now was a dead tomb.

Alexander's face twisted in pain. "It's beautiful, and horrible." His scythe clattered to the floor as he clapped his hands over his ears. "Make it stop!"

Conrad couldn't hide his confusion. "I don't hear anything."

Dropping to his knees, Alexander balled his fists and pressed them hard into his temples. "I can't hear anything else." A tear rolled down his cheek.

"It hurts."

Conrad's eyes were drawn to the doors he had kicked wide open. Silently, an angel stood watching, wings folded at its side. Blood dripped from its fingers, and Conrad was certain, beneath the darkness that hid the angel's face, it was smiling.

Alexander collapsed into the fetal position, and drew his knees hard to his chest. The man who had nearly bested one of the most competent warriors the Order had ever produced was now openly sobbing.

Conrad put two and two together, understanding that the angel was the source of Alexander's pain, but why? And why could only Alexander hear it? Was the Chancellor being singled out for some reason? Conrad couldn't wait for an explanation.

Lifting his scythe, Conrad charged the angel.

Slashing across, the High Wraith missed the angel as it dodged backward. His momentum carrying him forward, Conrad spun, brought his scythe over, and down across the angel's chest. The creature shrieked as its robe and flesh were splayed open by the Wraith's blade. Black blood spurted from the wound angrily.

But Conrad's body was heavy with exhaustion. Unable to dodge the retaliatory strike, he winced and fell back as the angel's claws ripped across his throat. Pain surged up his neck as the cuts felt like a cat's scratch, warm and itching. Leaning back, he avoided the angel's next strike at his face. The High Wraith tumbled backwards and spilled to the ground. Landing flat on his back, he skittered like a crab trying to get out of the angel's reach. He was tired and weak. This was a battle he wasn't going to win.

The angel launched itself into the Chancellor's office, its wings spread wide.

He made a split-second decision. If this didn't work, he would be dead. Pushing back hard, Conrad skidded on the tile floor, righted himself, and rolled onto his knees. Holding his scythe like a spear, he deactivated the curved reaping blade, and launched it with every bit of strength he had remaining.

Not designed for throwing, the weapon wobbled and whistled oddly in the air as it spun.

It hit.

Conrad's scythe pierced the angel's chest, very near where Conrad hoped its heart was, and erupted from its back with a spray of black blood. Screaming, the angel fell like a rock and collapsed on the floor. Clawing, scratching, with its wings flapping pointlessly, it seemed as though the creature refused to die. Its body shook violently as it tried to rip the scythe from its chest, feathers flitting around it like snowflakes.

The High Wraith lifted himself slowly to his feet. His body was in agony. If this didn't work, and the angel didn't die, Conrad knew he was done for.

The Wraith watched, nervously.

Shrieking again, the angel flopped and rolled onto its side. A pool of black tar-like blood pooled on the floor beneath it as it finally fell silent.

Conrad breathed a sigh of relief...

...then felt pain rip through his back and his

216

chest. Stunned, Conrad looked down to see the silver, bloody tip of a scythe jutting from his chest. He tried to take a breath, but it was too painful. Looking over his shoulder, he saw Alexander holding the other end of the weapon, blood spilling down his face from his nose and eyes. The Chancellor's mouth was pulled up into a horrible sneer, his teeth bloodied, and his eyes like horrible blue flames.

Conrad dropped to his knees and wrapped his hands around the scythe.

***

His personality, his very soul, were being torn away. Encased in darkness, Specter struggled to hold onto what was his. Unseen claws tore at him, dug deeply into his flesh, scratched at his bones, and chewed on that which made him human. Terror washed through him like he had never experienced before. Even at the hands of the vampiress Caitlin, when he was repeatedly tortured, killed, and brought back to life, the Wraith never felt this desperate and lost.

He was being torn down, bit by bit.

It was almost as though Metatron was physically forcing his will on Specter. He heard the archangel's voice echoing through his thoughts, telling him what was right, and pushing him to serve, proselytizing on an intimate and undeniable scale. He tried to hold on with every ounce of his being. He had to get out of here. Specter had to get free, for Kat's sake.

Specter started to fight.

Chapter Eighteen

Walking briskly through the Hofburg Palace, Saint listened to her footfalls echo loudly. Normally filled with people, tours, and staff, the palace was eerily empty. Glancing up, she spotted several signs in various languages that pointed toward the Schatzkammer. A German word that translates as "treasury," the Schatzkammer is the Austrian Imperial Museum, and home to some of the most precious artifacts on Earth. From what she had gathered, the collection spanned a thousand years of history, and every item was literally priceless.

But she was only interested in a single piece.

It seemed odd that the object which was going to save the world was sitting in an Austrian museum. Shouldn't things like this have to be quested for, or something idiotic like that? This all seemed too easy. Still, she had no idea if this was the Lance Ben wanted, what it meant in the grand scheme, or how it was going to save the world. The whole thing struck her as stupid...or maybe Saint was just irritated.

Coming around the palace's west wing, she spotted the entrance to the Schatzkammer. Quickening her pace, she moved quickly toward the massive arched entrance. The doors, unsurprisingly, were open and unguarded. During the angel's attack, all able guards and palace staff, no matter what their duties, had been called to help refugees and defend the palace. At least they had chosen correctly. In this instance, humanity had tried to save each other, instead of protecting what they possessed.

Stepping inside, she scanned the massive museum. Glass cases, filled with glittering artifacts, filled the floor. Saint took a step and realized she had no idea what she was looking for. She had learned a long time ago that just because an object was named "Lance," did not mean it was actually a lance. Moving quickly down the rows, she scanned through the glass to the German labels that surrounded each object. Her eyes wandered over jewels, crowns, and other sacred artifacts.

"Took you long enough."

Almost jumping out of her skin, Saint snapped her attention toward the voice. A shadowed figure rested against the wall on the far side of the room, his arms crossed and a smoldering cigarette in his hand. His eyes were fierce, and seemed to have an orange glimmer in the museum's low light.

"I have been calling for days," the man added then took a drag from his cigarette. "I should know better." He laughed and exhaled the blue-gray smoke. "Talking monkeys aren't especially bright. Next time, if there is one, I'll send an engraved invitation." He smiled. "Map included."

Saint watched the man warily. Still without her scythe, she felt naked and defenseless. He created a sense of dread in her that she had never experienced before. Deep down, on some primal level, she already knew who he was...and that scared her more than any vampire or monster she had ever faced.

The man took another drag of his cigarette then

flicked it away. Pushing off the wall, he adjusted the blood-red tie knotted at his throat, then ran his hand down it, flattening it beneath his immaculately tailored black suit. Checking his cuff links, he moved briskly deeper into the museum. Pausing, he turned and looked back over his shoulder. "Well? You coming, Emily?"

The sound of her name coming from his mouth made her shudder. She took a breath. Alarms blared in her brain, screaming for her to turn and flee, but she didn't. Ben was right. And finding him here only confirmed it. She wasn't going to run. She forced herself to take a step, and then another. Saint followed him, but kept a healthy distance.

He chuckled softly and shook his head. She was brave, but stupid... Saint was merely a talking monkey. There wasn't much more he should expect. Slicking back his shoulder-length black hair, the man turned and moved deeper into the Schatzkammer.

Saint followed. She watched the man walk. Every movement was precise and fluid, expending the precise amount of energy, and no more. Not a thread was out of place either. Everything about him was perfect, from the double-breasted Armani suit, to the beautifully polished gleam on his shoes, the glittering gold ring he wore on his pinky, and the immaculately sculpted goatee that clung to his chin. He was beautiful, and yet horrific. It was as though he was a grotesque parody of humanity as he tried to be one of them, but couldn't hide his true monstrous nature. He was perfectly evil, pure and simple.

Moving through another row, he stopped. Folding his hands behind his back, he waited for Saint. She approached, but kept a healthy distance, as if it really mattered. If he wanted her, he could have taken her long ago. But that wasn't the way he rolled. He would much rather objects of his desire give themselves willingly to his power. That was always so much better...and much more satisfying to leave them broken afterward, a victim of their own desire.

He motioned toward a case. "Here."

Saint took another step and stopped. Leaning ever so slightly, she caught sight of it and her breath was taken away. Clearly Roman in design, the Lance had a gold sleeve around the center that shined like the sun. The metal of the spearhead had almost been completely blackened by time. Long, narrow, and curved in the middle, metal filaments like twine wrapped around the base, then criss-crossed like shoelaces. It appeared fragile, but had proven strong enough to stand the test of time.

"See the words on the gold?" he asked.

Saint spotted letters engraved in the gold sleeve, and nodded.

"Lancea et clavus Domini," he read, then looked up at Saint, "Lance and nail of the Lord."

Saint felt humbled standing before the implement that had killed Jesus Christ. She drew a breath. "Is it true?" She paused. "I mean, you were there, right?"

"Contrary to popular belief, and the Rolling Stones song, I had nothing to do with that." He smiled. "I don't make men do evil things. I simply

provide a home for them when they have finished."
Laughing, he reached over the case, balled his fist, and smashed through the glass.

Saint jumped back, unsure what to think. Why aren't there any alarms?

Reaching in, he snatched the Lance from its cradle and lifted it to his face. "The craftsmanship is remarkable." He sniffed the Lance, then licked it. His face cringed as though tasting something unpleasant. Turning, he spit and repeatedly smacked his lips. "Too bad this is a fake," he said, tossing it to Saint.

Grabbing it out of the air, Saint cradled it gently in her hands as though protecting a child. She felt the weight, and ran her thumb over the gold sleeve. It was heavier than it looked. "How can this be a fake? This is the Holy Lance."

"Nope." He laughed. "Replica. I bet if you look hard enough you'll find 'made in China' stamped somewhere on it. Everything's made in China now," he muttered angrily. "Anyway," he digressed and snatched the Lance from Saint, "over time, there have been numerous weapons believed to be the Holy Lance. This one," he said, holding it up, "was even stolen by Hitler during World War II."

"But why?" Saint asked, "if it's a fake?"

"Oh," he smiled devilishly, "it wasn't then. It was the real deal."

Saint shook her head, obviously lost.

"When Hitler fell, the Lance was recovered by American General Patton and returned here to Vienna," he explained, "or so the legend goes." He considered the Lance for a moment then tossed it over his shoulder like a piece of trash. "Turns out my boy Patton—with whom I have had many, many wonderful conversations—knew what he had in the Lance. So before sending it back to Vienna, he had a replica made."

"So Patton kept the true Lance," Saint worked through it, "and had the replica returned here. He had his cake and ate it too. He had the Lance, and was celebrated as a hero for returning a national treasure."

"You're sharp," he smiled. "Not as sharp as Miller was, but he served his purpose."

Saint felt as if a weight dropped directly on her heart at the mention of her best friend and lover's name. She had killed him during Bane's attack on the Academy after it was revealed he was working with the Vampire Lord. Saint had been crushed, to say the least. He was her everything.

"Sorry," he said, leaning forward slightly. "Did I reopen an old wound? I'm bad about that," he said apologetically. "You know, forked tongue and all."

She wasn't amused.

He sighed and shrugged. "Oh well. My bad." He looked around the museum. "You want to get out of here? Satan needs a Cherry Coke." He extended his hand to the Wraith. "Take my hand."

Saint looked from his face to the hand, and back to his face.

"Come on," he laughed, "no strings attached." He held up two fingers on his opposite hand. "Scout's honor."

"You were never a scout." Saint frowned. Reaching out, she took his hand.

"No, you're right. Never a scout. But I have had quite a few scout leaders." He laughed. "Let me buy you a drink."

Saint stumbled back and almost fell. Flipping and flopping in her torso, her guts seemed angry, as though they wanted out. Her eyes tried to adjust to being outside after standing in the darkened museum only moments before. Sneezing, she forced a mouthful of dust out.

She had no idea where she was, but this certainly wasn't Vienna. Adobe and stucco buildings were on all sides, and in the distance, she could see a huge, glittering body of water. It had to be a sea, or possibly an ocean. Palm trees dotted the shoreline as far as she could see. This would be paradise if there weren't old, junked cars and rusting trucks behind her. The sky was overcast and it was raining ever so softly.

Saint's eyes turned back to him. "Where are we?"

He had wandered to a small building and was waiting just beyond the arched entrance. "America's heartland, Mexico. Now can we get a drink?" He paused. "Please?"

She was about to have a drink with the Lucifer, so why was it so hard to believe that she had traveled thousands of miles from Europe to Mexico in the blink of an eye? "So the Devil does have manners," Saint said, regaining a bit of her composure.

"When I have to." He chuckled. Turning, he walked into the archway.

Saint waited for a moment, then followed him

224

inside. Inside, it took a moment for her eyes to adjust, but once they had, she wished they hadn't. The bar was a dive, in every sense of the word. Dirt covered the floors, which was good, because it hid the vomit and urine stains. A long bar, which looked like wood, but was more likely cockroaches holding hands, stretched along the center. A smattering of Mexicans looked up from their drinks to Saint, but quickly lost interest. The bartender, a portly man with a thick mustache, stood quietly watching as he cleaned a mug, a chewed toothpick hanging from his thick lips.

Lucifer had already taken a seat at the bar and was signaling the barkeep. Walking cautiously, Saint chose a seat next to him, and slid onto it. She folded her hands nervously on the bar and waited.

"What'll you have?" he asked.

Saint shrugged. "Beer."

He looked from the Wraith up to the bartender. "Beer," he said slowly pointing to Saint in that slow, loud, obnoxious American way when someone thinks the person they're speaking to is an imbecile. He then pointed to himself and said, "Cherry Coke."

The bartender sighed in disgust but moved to fill the order.

"In a clean glass, Pedro," the Devil added.

Saint waited until the bartender was hopefully out of earshot and looked to the Devil. "You don't speak Spanish?"

"Flawless, actually," he answered. "I just like to annoy people." He smiled wryly. "It's a little hobby of mine."

Saint made the same disgusted sigh the bartender had a few moments ago. "Look, what is it that you want with me?"

"Straight to business," he commented, "I like that. Okay, here's the scoop, sweetheart: I'm here to help you."

"But you're the devil," Saint pointed out.

"Exactly," he said, "and the only one."

The bartender returned and set the drinks on the bar. He muttered something, probably derogatory to the Devil, then waited for a response. Smiling softly, the Devil leaned forward and motioned for the bartender to do the same. As the Mexican did, the Devil whispered in his ear. The bartender jumped back as though he had been shocked, knocking glasses and bottles from the bar behind him. His face became white, almost as white as Saint's, and the toothpick fell out of his mouth. He started repeating something beneath his breath, which was probably a prayer of some sort, turned and charged away.

"What the hell was that?" Saint asked in awe.

"A little personal business." The Devil smiled. "I did a favor for Pedro back in '78. He still owes me." The Devil winked. "And I always collect. Anyway," he waved his hand dismissively, "on to other things." He snatched his soda from the bar and took a heady drink. "Smooth."

Saint shook her head and put her fingers around her glass, but didn't take a drink.

"Metatron is creating Hell on Earth," the Devil said, almost as if discussing the weather in passing. "I can't have that."

226

Saint nodded. "And Metatron would be who?"

"The archangel?" the Devil asked and waited. "The Voice of God?"

Saint shrugged.

"Don't you talking monkeys read the Bible anymore? Christ." He sighed. "Metatron is seraphim, one of the highest orders of angels, and in fact the daft bastard is one of the most important archangels. He speaks for God, since it's impossible for God to speak to His creations without killing them. Personally, I think Mr. Omnipotent just likes to feel important. He's like Michael Jackson, but without the peppy tunes."

"While this little conversation is lovely," Saint smiled snidely, "I fail to see the point."

"Settle down there, Killer." He laughed. "I'm getting there."

Saint writhed on her barstool under the nickname. She never thought of herself as a killer, even though she was. The thought made her more than a little uncomfortable. "Look, all I know is that Michael appeared to Ben and told him to get the Lance. That's it."

"Ah, Michael," Lucifer breathed. "The good little soldier." He paused and considered the archangel, and his expulsion from Heaven. "Michael should be cleaning up this mess instead of me. But no." He frowned and took another drink of his beverage. "I think he's retired now. Spends most of his time in Palm Beach. I heard he actually played a round of golf with Tiger Woods recently while I'm working my ass off. Bastard."

"Still no point," Saint pointed out.

"Fine," he said flatly. "Apparently the art of conversation is dead."

Saint shrugged, took a sip of her beer then promptly spit it back into her glass. She pushed the mug away.

"Metatron serves only as the messenger," he said. "That is, until recently apparently. A couple of thousand years ago he went MIA."

Saint laughed. "That's recently?"

"Stay with me," he said quickly. "Metatron's been up to something, but none of us knew what it was. The dirtbag's been sneaking around right under my nose. He's trying to recreate the Nephilim." Lucifer waited, hoping the word would resonate with the Wraith. Seeing her blank expression, he rolled his eyes and continued.

"At the beginning, God, in His infinite wisdom, sent a legion of angels down to earth to help guide and teach man. Instead, Azaziel and his idiot cohorts taught men how to make war, and started drilling the men's women while they were away making said war." He laughed. "It's really kind of funny if you think about it."

"Yeah," Saint breathed, "a real knee-slapper."

"Bah." He waved his hand at Saint. "You have no idea what good comedy is. Anyway, something happened that no one, not even God, expected. The women were impregnated by the angels."

"Talk about an interesting paternity suit," Saint commented.

"Hey." The Devil smiled and laughed. "That was good! You are funny!"

Saint didn't laugh.

228

"Okay, maybe not," the Devil reconsidered. "So the babies born of angels and humans were called Nephilim. They were incredible... Titans among men, and practically Gods. It became clear, very quickly, that they were too powerful. They made war against humans and angels, and when that got boring, they started killing each other, and drinking each other's blood. So the All-Mighty stepped in and took care of business, in His usual flamboyant way."

"What happened?" Saint asked, amazingly engrossed in the tale.

"You know Noah and that whole ark thing?"

Saint nodded.

"God flooded the Earth to kill off the Nephilim, Azaziel, and all of their followers. Nice, huh?" Lucifer laughed. "He could have just shoved a lightning bolt up their ass, but instead he basically wipes out everything on Earth and starts over. You have to admit, He does have style."

"So what now?" Saint asked. "Why is Metatron trying to recreate the Nephilim?"

"Jealousy," Lucifer said.

"Ah." Saint laughed. "He's marching to your drum now?"

"Metatron fought at Michael's side in the war," Lucifer said. "And now he wants to kill you talking monkeys. Does the word 'hypocrite' mean anything to him?"

"Apparently not." Saint shrugged.

"He's tired of serving you monkeys," Lucifer summarized. "He's decided to wipe you out instead, and in doing so, he's pissed in my Cheerios. I won't have it. And neither will the big guy upstairs."

"What?"

The Devil pointed his thumb over his shoulder at the door. "It's raining."

Saint shrugged. "So?"

"It's raining," he said again, adding, "all over the world. Do the words 'Great Flood' mean anything to you?"

Saint's eyes widened, "Again?"

"Seems so," Lucifer said.

Saint grabbed her beer and chugged it. "How do we stop it?"

"That's where the Lance comes in," Lucifer answered. "Metatron knew he had to be a bit sneakier than Azaziel this time around, so he didn't come here and randomly start screwing women. He knew His Majesty wouldn't stand for that again. He basically went mad scientist on us, and genetically manipulated two races over thousands of years, for the eventual purpose of creating a Nephilim without direct angelic intervention." The Devil turned on his stool and looked directly at Saint. "How does it feel to be a tool?"

In that moment, Saint understood everything, and saw the Prophecy in its complete and terrible nature. Everything she held important was, in fact, pointless. She felt violated.

"I know. It sucks." He took another sip of his Cherry Coke.

"So Kat and Thomas…"

He nodded.

"…and her baby is…"

"Yup," he breathed.

230

Saint grasped the ultimate solution the Devil was presenting. "And I have to kill it, or the world will be destroyed?"

The Devil smiled and nodded. "Neat, huh?"

"Why me?"

"Because you, my perfectly named Saint, are responsible. Not in a direct way obviously," the Devil said, "but you were basically the end result of Metatron's experiment." He paused. "You are the perfect hybrid of human and angel."

Saint shook her head. "I'm a Nephilim?"

"No." The Devil laughed. "You have all the best qualities of angel and human, with none of either's drawbacks. This was always the path of the Wraith. Metatron created you, and the Prophecy."

"And the other race?"

"Vampires." The Devil smiled. "Which accounts for the blood drinking. Nephilim were the most bloodthirsty bastards I've ever seen." He finished his beverage, and signaled Pedro the bartender for another. "Kat has become the perfect hybrid of human, and Nephilim. So once this synthesis of the three species was complete, Metatron had only to step aside, and let human nature finish his job. Didn't take long either," he added, then laughed.

Saint's head swam as she tried to process the new information. She could see the interlocking webs between Metatron, the prophecy, her, Thomas, Kat, Conrad, the Troika, Bane, and even the progenitor, Gwyn ap Nudd. Somehow it seemed to make sense in a twisted way. Every piece had to fall into place of its own accord, but had done so by

Metatron's design. It was a tangled, fragile web that could have collapsed at any moment...but hadn't.

Which also explained why she could hear the angel's song in her mind. She was one of them...part of the hive.

She wasn't the Chosen One, but merely the end result of a grand experiment. Saint felt angry and devastated about being lied to her entire life, but somehow relieved. She wasn't the Chosen One.

"Why do you care?" Saint asked. "Seems like Metatron is fighting your war now. Shouldn't you be helping him?"

"No," he barked and leapt off his stool. Lucifer slammed his hands on the bar and pushed into Saint's face. She could feel his breath on her skin, and the sulfurous odor of his flesh. "This is my war, and the talking monkeys are mine to destroy. He thinks you're so much better than me..." His eyes wandered away and flashed orange. "This place, and all of its people, are mine."

"Settle down, Sparky," Saint soothed. "It was just a question." She saw Pedro deliver Satan's Cherry Coke then skitter away like a frightened child. "Look, sit down and enjoy your soda, okay?"

He took a breath, composed himself, and retook his seat. Smoothing his hair back, he lifted the glass and took a deep drink from the small red straw. "They have the best Cherry Coke here," the Devil commented, smacking his lips with satisfaction. "That's why I keep coming back."

Saint understood that during his expulsion, he had become completely mad. "Why are you here with me?"

232

"I can't interfere directly," he answered. "None of us can anymore. We can influence, but not control. We have to let you stupid talking monkeys make your own choices, good or bad."

"That's why Metatron did what he did," Saint understood.

"Bingo." He snapped his fingers. "And that's why we're having a drink together in Mexico. Make sense?"

"In a roundabout sort of way," Saint answered.

"Well, that's the way these things work now." He shrugged and finished his second beverage. Sliding off his stool, he adjusted his suit jacket. "Ready to head back?"

"Wait." Saint stood. "What about the Lance?"

"Oh," the Devil smiled, "right. Almost forgot. Come on." He turned and walked out of the bar without another word.

Shaking her head, Saint turned and followed him feeling as though she was dealing with a child. Which, in truth, was probably a pretty good description of Lucifer. He was a spoiled brat, trying to win back his daddy's love in the only way he knew how.

Stepping outside the bar, she felt the rain on her face. Looking up, she saw lightning skitter along the clouds. Drawing in a long, slow breath, she let her gaze fall back to Earth and found the Devil standing in the center of what could probably be considered this town's 'Main Street.'

He waited. As Saint approached, he pointed down to the ground. "Dig here."

Nodding, Saint dropped to her knees and

233

clawed at the dirt.

"Patton lost the Lance," he explained. "It went through dozens of hands before it was hidden here. They thought no one would think to look for it in Mexico." The Devil laughed. "And who can blame them?" He knelt down next to Saint. "But I'm always watching."

She tried to ignore the ominous warning, and the realization that Heaven and Hell were real. It sent a shudder straight to her soul. As the hole deepened beneath her, her nails scratched against wood.

The Devil ran his fingers through Saint's hair and leaned close. "Thank you for helping me. I won't forget this." His black, forked tongue slithered out of his mouth and he licked up Saint's face.

Saint shivered, but refused to pull away.

His eyes flashed again. "I'll be seeing you." He waited. "Very soon."

And he was gone.

The urge to fall back on the ground and cry gripped her and she felt tears spill from her eyes. Her stomach churned and her head ached. Everything Saint was, was gone. An hour ago, she had been a Wraith, and the Chosen One, a being spoken of in prophecy who would create a new race and hopefully end the war between vampires and the Wraith. Now, she knew she was nothing more than a jealous angel's tool for retribution. She felt weak, an empty shell cracked and broken.

She wanted to give up.

Let the rain come, she decided.

234

The Earth would once again be cleansed of evil and nonbelievers. No more vampires. No more Nephilim. No more Wraith. And that seemed somehow appropriate and just. She looked down at the hole she had been digging, and made up her mind. Pushing the loose dirt back into the hole, she covered it up the best she could. Standing Saint turned and headed back toward the bar.

If this was truly the end of all things, she needed a drink.

***

Kat howled as her body shook with contractions. Gritting her teeth, her body wanted to push, but she fought against it. Running her hands through the inside of the cocoon, she grabbed onto several of the tubes and squeezed with every bit of her strength. The living cocoon squealed like a pig and slid several tendrils around the vampire's throat in protest. Kat started to see stars before her eyes as the tubes constricted around her neck.

She clamped her fists closed, choosing death over delivering the baby, and hopefully taking it down with her. But she already knew that wouldn't happen. She was so close they would simply cut her open and take the baby if it came to that. Kat didn't have any choice.

Her child was about to be born.

Chapter Nineteen

Conrad felt his heart struggle. Falling, he held onto Alexander's scythe and tried to keep it still in his flesh. Every movement radiated pain out in all directions. It hurt to breathe. The High Wraith crumbled to his knees, and crawled toward the door. He had to get away from this place, but he was so tired... Conrad simply wanted to lie down. To shut his eyes, to rest, only for a moment...

The Chancellor's cackle echoed off the walls.

He had to fight. Conrad couldn't let this be the end of all things. Clawing with every bit of his strength, he inched forward. He slipped as his fingers lost their grip in the pool of blood growing larger beneath him. Slipping down, his face smacked the floor and splattered his blood. Conrad gritted his teeth, reached behind him awkwardly, and wrapped his hand around the scythe. Yanking hard, he cried in agony as the weapon moved, but refused to come free. Blood sputtered around his lips as he breathed hard and tried to focus. He tried again, this time with every ounce of his remaining strength. With a sickening slurp of muscle and blood, he wrenched the weapon free.

The scythe clattered to the floor leaving Conrad with a pain-filled cavern in his torso.

Wheezing, he drew a slow breath while doing his best to ignore the whistling emanating from the hole in his chest. There was a very good chance Alexander had punctured one of his lungs. Forcing himself off the floor, Conrad rolled back slowly onto his knees. Every heartbeat felt like a hammer strike to his head, and he knew that each could be his last. The High Wraith focused on the exit.

"Where are you going?" Alexander's voice sounded distant, and haunting. "You won't make it to the door. I promise you that."

Conrad ignored the threat. Placing his fingers on the floor, he rolled onto the balls of his feet and stood. The world around him wobbled as though he were on an amusement park ride. He fought for balance and clarity. Squinting, he thought he saw a dark form pass outside the doors.

The sound of a scythe blade scraping against the floor sent a shiver straight down his spine.

"Master Verge," Alexander cooed.

Wavering for a moment, Conrad took a step and almost slipped on his blood. He tried to stop the bleeding by pressing his hand to the wound, but only succeeded in slowing it. His red life spilled onto his fist and down the front of his shirt. He took another step, but saw the Chancellor move to block the door.

Alexander sneered, blood running down his face. "We have arrived at the end." He licked his lips, tasting his own blood. "You are the old Order." He spun his scythe. "I am the new."

Conrad coughed, the spasm sent pain rippling through his body. He wanted to fall, but somehow remained standing. "You can't even banter," the Wraith croaked as blood spilled down his lips. "You're an idiot."

"Now we've reverted to name calling?" Alexander laughed. "Are we going to meet at the tetherball court at lunch to fight? Better be careful or you might hurt my feelings."

Behind Alexander, Conrad saw the dark form again. He locked eyes with the Chancellor, and smiled. "If you strike me down, I shall become more pow—"

Alexander punched Conrad solidly in the nose, dropping him. "Were you seriously just quoting Star Wars?"

Conrad grabbed his nose, and moaned. But his pain slowly started to turn. From somewhere deep inside, it started to roll out of him. Despite the pain, he laughed.

Alexander furrowed his brow. "What are you doing?"

Conrad laughed.

"Stop it," Alexander growled. "Stop it!"

But Conrad couldn't. He laughed.

"I said stop!" The Chancellor spun his scythe, lifted it over his head, and prepared the killing strike.

The dark form grew massive behind the Chancellor. Its red eyes flashed angrily in the low light and it bared its huge teeth.

Conrad lifted his arm and pointed over the Chancellor's shoulder. "Goodbye, Chancellor."

Alexander's icy blue eyes shot wide. He was fast, but it was already too late. The Chancellor swung his scythe around and started his attack.

The werewolf struck savagely. Clamping his powerful jaws onto the back of Alexander's neck, the wolf bit down with deadly force. Alexander screamed and fought, but the wolf shook him like a dog toy. Vertebrae were crushed beneath the wolf's power. With one final shake, the wolf snapped his head back severing Alexander's spine.

It was over.

The werewolf released Alexander, letting him crumble to the floor like a discarded toy. Blood coated his muzzle and dripped away horrifically. Its red eyes settled on Conrad. They were filled with anger, pain, and amazingly, sorrow. Taking a step, the wolf whimpered and fell.

"Stark," Conrad breathed, "thank you." Scooting painfully across the floor, the Wraith placed his hand on the back of the werewolf's neck. "You did what you had to."

The wolf whined softly. It wasn't his intention to come here and kill Wraith, and certainly not the Chancellor of the Order. Still, Stark knew Conrad was right...but it might already be too late. His eyes settled on the bloody wound in Conrad's chest. His sensitive ears could hear the Wraith's heart slowing, and a distinct flutter in one of its chambers. Conrad didn't have long.

That's when they saw him.

"Hello, boys," he greeted coolly.

Stark drew his muzzle back into a sneer and growled fiercely. He tried to draw to his feet, but slipped back to the floor. He was absolutely spent.

"Bad, doggy," the man scolded and adjusted his blood-red tie. He turned to Conrad and his eyes flashed orange. "Aren't there leash laws in this country, Master Wraith?"

Conrad couldn't find the words to reply.

The man stepped around the wolf and Wraith,

239

and stopped at Alexander's body. Kneeling down, but making certain his suit pants didn't touch the pool of blood, he pressed two fingers to the Chancellor's throat. "Mauled by a werewolf," he muttered. "Not a good way to go."

Pushing his ears back, Stark growled louder, almost protectively, over his kill.

Lifting his head, the man stared at Stark then turned to Conrad. His expression has lost much of its jovialness. "Will you shut him up?"

"He does his own thing," Conrad explained, "and under the circumstances, I wouldn't mess with him." He stroked Stark's neck like a beloved pet. "Nothing more dangerous than a wounded wolf."

"Yeah, yeah," he dismissed. Grabbing Alexander's leg, he started to pull the body toward the door.

Conrad's vision was growing dark, and he was feeling sleepier by the moment. "What exactly are you doing?"

"There aren't many souls I would come to personally collect," he answered, straightening his double-breasted suit jacket.

As if the proverbial lightbulb flashed above Conrad's head, his eyes widened then his back straightened uncomfortably. In that moment, he knew who he was talking to and felt fear wash through his brain. He scooted slightly closer to Stark.

"Listen," Lucifer breathed as he neared the exit, "I'm not usually one to take sides, except for my own, but this is important and Saint needs you alive." He unbuttoned his jacket and shook it. A

240

metal cylinder fell from the pocket and hit the floor with a hollow clang. "Oops," he said as he rebuttoned his jacket. "How clumsy of me to have dropped that priceless, ancient artifact. I really should be more careful." He turned and started out the door with Alexander in tow. "See you around, boys."

"Wait," Conrad gasped.

The Devil turned and glared at the High Wraith.

Conrad drew a pain-filled breath into his chest. "Alexander made a deal with you?"

"Obviously." The Devil rolled his eyes. "Now, if you don't mind, I really am very busy. Oh, and, Stark?"

The wolf's eyes flashed red and he growled.

The Devil smiled. "This doesn't change anything. I'll be waiting."

Conrad turned and looked at his werewolf companion in shock.

Stark lowered his head and whimpered.

The Devil turned and walked away leaving a bloody trail as he dragged Alexander's body.

The Wraith couldn't seem to tear his eyes from Stark. He felt angry and ashamed at the same time. He had no idea what the wolf dealt with the Devil for, but it didn't make any difference. All of his respect for the werewolf, all that had built up over the past few days, was gone.

Conrad shifted his gaze to the artifact the Devil had "accidentally" dropped. It was cylindrical, roughly six inches long, and no more than two in diameter. It was gold, and embossed with an intricate pattern of woven designs, but was aged and worn. A seam stretched the entire length of the artifact, but there were no visible hinges, locking mechanisms, or discernable means of opening it. There was an air about it, though, that felt powerful, and dangerous.

"He said Saint needs help," Conrad said, still considering the artifact, "and he gave us this. What do you think?"

Stark was quiet, his eyes closed.

Pressing his hand to the wolf's chest, Conrad searched for breathing and a heartbeat. They were there, but very weak. He didn't know what to do, as he couldn't very well give a werewolf mouth-to-mouth resuscitation.

The artifact had to mean something.

Then again, the Devil had given it to them.

Conrad had to take the chance. Stark was almost gone, and he was fading quickly. Neither had much time left.

Leaning forward, Conrad's body screamed in pain. Every move and every breath felt like another stab wound. He was tired. Conrad had been fighting for so long, he had actually forgotten what life was like before the Order, and what it meant to be human. His life was war, and had been for longer than he would ever admit to any living soul. He'd watched those he loved die too many times, and even struck down the closest thing he'd ever had to a brother. Still, there was no sympathy for this devil. He just wanted to rest…but what awaited him, salvation or damnation?

Conrad didn't want to know…but he didn't want to die either.

He clawed toward the artifact. Pulling with every ounce of his strength, Conrad dragged his body over the tile and through the blood. The darkness encroaching at the edges of his vision was steadily growing…and he wasn't certain, but he believed the light above him was growing brighter. Pausing, he turned his head up. His jaw dropped open as his eyes fell on the beautiful light that stretched out as far as he could see and warmth radiated over his tired, aching body. It was welcoming him home. Rolling onto his side, he lifted his hand and started to reach for the light. He wanted to go home.

But his mind turned to Saint and Kat.

Conrad's hand fell away.

He still had work to do.

Twisting onto his stomach, he reached out and felt his fingers brush the artifact. A wave of electricity charged down his arm, exploded in his chest, and suddenly the heavenly light above vanished. Conrad lifted onto his knees curiously. He still hurt, but the pain was clearly diminished. Glancing down at the wound in his chest, he was amazed to find it in an advanced stage of healing. With a smile, he glanced over his shoulder at Stark. "We're going to be okay."

Turning back, he reached for the artifact only to see it kicked away by a heavy, black boot.

Conrad stared at the figure before him, and realized it was like something out of a dream, or a nightmare. Jumping to his feet, he took an uneasy step back, and then another. This couldn't be happening…

The dark figure drew his weapon and his eyes flashed gold.

The Wraith didn't want to believe his eyes. He knew, for certain, that he had left this man for dead almost a year ago. Conrad took in the features that he had known for a lifetime, but they looked alien now, twisted by hatred. This was not the man he knew. "Thomas?"

***

Saint sat alone at the bar, nursing a beer that could have been warm piss. In this place, it probably wouldn't have tasted much different. She could feel Pedro watching her from his place behind the bar, but she couldn't seem to care. He had already signed his life away. She knew where he was headed. This was life at the end of all things, and she couldn't care less.

Glancing over her shoulder, she watched the rain fall in sheets outside. It had been steadily growing in strength since Lucifer brought her here, and now it was a solid drizzle. The Earth in front of the door had already been washed away, leaving an ever growing pool that was threatening to backwash into the bar at any moment. She shrugged. It might actually be an improvement. Angry and disgusted with herself, she chugged the remainder of her beer and ordered another. She wanted to hide, but there wasn't a hole deep enough. It would be over soon enough.

"What wrong with you?"

Saint spun angrily on her barstool, ready to unleash hell on whoever had the gall to actually speak to her. Twisting, mouth open, and finger

244

pointed, Saint found herself without words, staring at someone she never expected to see again.

"You aren't the Saint I know," Ben Quinn stated sincerely. "What happened to you?"

Saint cocked her eyebrow, and tried to remember to breathe. Reaching out slowly, she pressed her finger against Quinn's shoulder and found it very solid. Somehow, some way, this wasn't a dream. He was here. "But you're dead," was all that Saint could think to say.

"Quite," Quinn acknowledged as he seated himself at the bar next to her. Brushing the long, slender braid of hair that hung from his sideburn behind his ear, he adjusted his worn black leather coat and ordered a drink.

He looked every bit as she remembered, from his messy brown hair, to the small mole below his right eye. Quinn was the closest thing she had ever had to a father as her Master and teacher, but Bane had taken him away. She missed him every day, so much that it hurt. She often wished for one more day to learn from him, to simply talk to him, but now she was faced with that very thing, and had nothing to say.

"So," Quinn breathed, "you're just going to sit here while the world ends?"

"But you're dead," Saint repeated.

"Again, yes." Quinn laughed. "But let's move past that. I've been given a day pass, so to speak. I'm told it's a once-in-a-lifetime experience."

Saint couldn't handle it anymore. Lurching forward, she wrapped her arms around Quinn and buried her face in his chest. Her tears immediately started to flow and she sobbed uncontrollably. "I miss you so much."

Quinn smiled and returned the embrace, gently stroking her hair. "It's going to be okay," he comforted her as he had so many times before.

He had known this girl since she was eleven, watched her grow, and become everything she was destined to. Handpicked, Quinn had taken her from her mother, watched over her, and trained her in the ways of the Wraith. He loved her like a daughter, and was extremely proud of her. Saint had been the best student, and friend, he could have hoped for. He only wished he was here for different reasons.

Lifting Saint back into her seat, he gently wiped the tears from her cheeks. "I miss you ,too," Quinn smiled. "I'm very proud of you."

Sighing, Saint sniffed trying to control her emotions. "Thank you."

"I understand you had a visit from the Lord of the Underworld?" Quinn asked.

Saint nodded. "That was an interesting discussion. I went from prophesized Chosen One, to zero in ten minutes flat. I don't even know what to think."

"You're missing the point," Quinn admonished her sweetly. "Despite what you have been chosen to do, you are still the Chosen One. The prophecy has come to pass. Just because you know the whole story, doesn't change anything."

"I'm a lab rat," Saint argued.

"No," Quinn breathed, "you're a Wraith, and a damned good one. That's something no one can take away from you. Not ever."

246

Saint started to retort, but stopped.

Quinn took a long breath and considered his student. "You worked hard to get where you are, did you not?"

She nodded.

"Don't ever let anyone take that away from you." He looked Saint directly in the eyes. "And don't you ever forget that. You are amazing, Emily." He paused. "So what are you doing sitting in this bar when there's work to be done?"

A tear slipped from Saint's eye, but she quickly wiped it away with the back of her hand.

"This isn't the Saint that I know," Quinn added.

Saint shook her head, desperately trying to fight back the tears. "I can't do it!"

Quinn knew how to push her effectively, but also when to let up. "Can't do what?"

"I'm supposed to kill Kat's child!" she shouted, two tears falling free. "How am I supposed to do that?"

Quinn leaned on the bar and rubbed his chin. "You have to do what you think is right."

"That's it?" Saint shouted. "I have to do what I think is right? That's the best you have to offer?"

"What is it you want me to say?" Quinn asked quietly. "You already know what's at stake. Lucifer, amazingly, wasn't lying to you. The choice seems pretty clear to me: do what you have to, or watch the world end."

"I can't take that away from Kat," Saint argued. "That's all she has left of Thomas." She thought of her encounter outside of Vienna with the Wraith turned vampire. "All she has left of what Thomas

247

was."

"I know the whole sordid tale," Quinn admitted. "But that baby doesn't belong to Thomas and Kat. It's Metatron's. That's all."

Leaning back on her barstool, Saint took a long look at her Master. She wanted him to tell her that everything was going to be all right, that she was doing the right thing. Instead, he was scolding her. This wasn't what she wanted to hear.

"Emily," Quinn said slowly. He placed his hand on hers. "I love you. You know that, right?"

Saint nodded and bit her lip.

"You are a champion," Quinn said proudly. "I know you'll do the right thing. It won't be easy, but I know you will."

Wiping away another tear, Saint tried to force a smile. "Do you have to go?"

Quinn shook his head. "Soon. But, I think I have time for another drink."

"Good." Saint laughed through her tears. She signaled Pedro. "Two margaritas."

The bartender nodded and set about making the drinks.

"How's Ben?" Quinn asked.

The question struck Saint curiously. She wasn't aware that the two Bens knew each other. "He's going to be okay. How do you know my Ben?"

"He didn't tell you?" Quinn asked.

She shook her head. "Tell me what?"

"We fought together years ago," Quinn explained then laughed. "Longer ago than I care to admit. But he battled by my side valiantly, and without hesitation. Ben is one of the purest souls I

248

have ever encountered."

"I had no idea," Saint replied.

"He's an amazing man, and like you, he's a champion." Quinn nodded. "After I passed, I asked him to look after you."

Saint was shocked by the admission. She always knew there was something binding the werewolf to her, but she had no idea it was her Master's doing. A flutter of anger erupted in her heart, but she quickly quelled it. It was not because of a lack of confidence in her skills, but because Quinn loved her. Her heart melted, making the darkness that clung there slip away. Even in death, Quinn had found a way to take care of her.

And for a moment, only a moment, Saint knew everything was going to be all right. As their drinks were delivered, the two talked about old times, and friends long gone. Saint and Quinn laughed and enjoyed every minute they had left. She had been given a second chance to say goodbye, and she was not going to waste it.

The end of all things could wait, if only for a moment longer.

Chapter Twenty

As the baby moved down the birth canal, the emptiness forming in her abdomen was startling. It felt as though a piece of her was being ripped away. Kat coughed and sputtered as the cocoon's tendrils gripped her throat. It was just enough to keep her subdued, but not enough to kill. Digging her fingers into the cocoon's flesh, it rumbled and squealed in anger, but refused to tighten its grip any further.

As another wave of contractions gripped the vampire, her eyes wandered up to the robed figure watching her. It hadn't moved, or spoken, but she knew what he was there for. The dark, raven wings were held high on its back, making it all the more ominous.

His hands folded, Metatron waited for the Savior's arrival.

It all seemed so simple once. But life is never, ever that easy. It seemed like a lifetime ago, that she had been on the cusp of her dreams and had it all taken away by a random act of violence. But it hadn't ended there. Her life had been taken, but a new one had taken hold even as the last was drained away. And then that one was taken by the Troika. Just as Kat found freedom, she found a man who loved her unconditionally, and surrendered completely. Fate twisted on her again, though, and took him away.

And Kat had finally had enough. She was tired of being the fates' chew toy. In that moment Kat decided that this was her life, such as it was, and she had enough of being kicked and beaten down.

She was going to fight.

Clenching her jaw, she clamped down on the tendrils and pulled as hard as she could. She felt two pops as they gave way and broke. The tendrils around her throat constricted angrily, choking her. Kat raked her claws along the inside of the cocoon, causing it to scream painfully.

Metatron knelt down, seeming to enjoy the high-pitched squeals of the cocoon. "You can struggle all you want. It will not make a difference. The Savior is coming."

Kat felt the baby beginning to crest, and cried in agony.

***

Conrad watched the dark figure in disbelief. This man was once his friend, his student, his companion, and his brother. Now he had been twisted by anger into an enemy, and all because of a mistake. Thomas believed that Conrad had killed Kat, the woman of his dreams, but nothing could have been further from the truth. Pride and arrogance hastened his turn from the light, and in his anger, Thomas had sought to destroy Conrad. While he was the superior warrior, Thomas lacked patience and experience, which allowed Conrad to best him. He thought he had left his student for dead, but apparently someone intervened.

"You don't have to do this," Conrad said. "Let me help you, Thomas."

Thomas' blue eyes flashed vampiric gold. "My name is Scourge now."

The High Wraith placed a hand on his chest

251

over the wound Alexander had given him. It was healed, but not entirely. A dull ache throbbed behind it, sending ripples of pain across his body. He wasn't in any condition for battle, and certainly not with one of the best warriors the Academy had ever produced. He let his hand fall away and stood tall, trying not to display weakness. His eyes fell to Stark. The wolf's eyes were closed, and he was bleeding heavily. Scanning the room, he spotted the Devil's artifact in the corner.

"You lied to me," Scourge hissed.

"What is it this time, Thomas?" Conrad asked, refusing to speak the vampiric name. "I'm getting a bit tired of this bloody game."

"Kat's alive," Scourge said and started slipping off his coat.

Thomas had every intention of killing Conrad, right here, and right now.

"I told you that," Conrad said. "If you recall, that was the basis for our original argument."

"Where is she?" Scourge stared at his former Master, unyielding.

Conrad paused. "I'm afraid I don't—"

"Where is she?" Scourge asked again. "I will tear this place apart until I find her. I promise you that."

"Fine," Conrad spat. "Tear it down then. It won't do you any good. She's not here." He spied Alexander's scythe on the floor, a little beyond arm's length. He had to get to it, and he had to keep Thomas talking. "I'm so tired of this garbage, Thomas."

"Don't call me that," Scourge barked.

252

"If you weren't so pigheaded, we would still be fighting the good fight, Thomas." Conrad started to circle toward the scythe, but knew Thomas was aware of the maneuver. "Instead, you've become everything you used to hate. You're a vampire, a leech. All because you flew off the handle and went insane instead of giving me the chance to explain."

"You were my brother," Thomas said quietly, his pain palpable. "How could you do this to me?"

"To you?" Conrad asked. "You tried to kill me!"

Scourge nodded. "A mistake I'm willing to correct."

Scourge lunged, quicker than Conrad expected.

Throwing himself out of the way, Conrad hit the floor and rolled. Grabbing Alexander's scythe, with his blood still on it, Conrad got to his feet and activated the weapon in enough time to block Scourge's next attack. Deflecting Scourge's scythe, Conrad's body cried in pain. He wasn't going to last long. He had to get to the artifact.

Whipping his blade laterally, he barely missed Scourge's midsection, but his tired attack left him wide open.

Leaping back, Scourge kicked straight up and connected with Conrad's chin. The High Wraith's head snapped back with a crack and he instantly crumbled. Hitting the floor, Conrad knew enough to roll or Thomas would deliver the killing blow. He heard Scourge's scythe slam into the tile with teeth-rattling force. Spinning on his back, Conrad kicked out and knocked Scourge's scythe away, leaving the vampire off balance. Sliding the blade behind

Scourge's knees, Conrad yanked hard sending the vampire to the floor.

Ignoring the searing pain in his chest, Conrad vaulted onto his feet and charged toward the Devil's artifact, only to have Scourge snatch his ankle and tackle him. Clawing ahead, Conrad felt the vampire grab his legs and start to climb up his back.

Conrad flipped over to see Scourge's golden eyes and fangs bearing down on him. Punching awkwardly across his body, he caught the vampire in the mouth and knocked him back. Ripping his leg free, the High Wraith kicked Scourge as hard as he could. The impact shattered Scourge's right fang, and split his lip.

Scourge howled and fell back, clutching his face.

Rolling onto his hands and knees, Conrad took the opportunity. He skittered across the floor toward the artifact, moving as fast as he could. He was almost there. Throwing himself forward, he felt searing pain in his thigh and his momentum was abruptly stopped. He looked back to see Scourge's scythe blade dug deep into his leg, and then into the floor below.

Scourge stood above him, blood splattered across his face and dripping from his chin. "This ends," he breathed, "now."

"Thomas," Conrad said through gritted teeth, "don't do this. I can help you."

"Bane has given me everything I need," Scourge replied coolly.

"But not Kat," Conrad argued. "I can help you find her, and with the Troika's serum, you can both

254

be human again."

Scourge laughed. "Why would I want to be human again? I have all the power I've ever wanted." He lifted his arm and called the Devil's artifact to his hand with his telekinesis. Holding the gold cylinder, he studied it carefully then returned his attention to Conrad. "You want this?"

Conrad was silent, waiting to see if it had any effect on the vampire.

Nothing happened.

Then Conrad remembered. He lifted his hand carefully to his jacket. He could feel the small cylinder behind the leather, and it appeared to be intact. This was it: the final solution…but he needed a distraction.

As if on cue, Stark opened his eyes, roared, and lifted to his feet. The wolf was sluggish, his pain apparent in each movement. Still, it was enough to get Scourge's attention, if only for a moment.

Digging into his leather jacket, Conrad produced his vial of the Troika Serum. Seeing the amber liquid still contained in the vial, he thumbed the activator and armed the injector. Twisting, he felt Scourge's blade dig painfully into his flesh. He drew his arm back.

Stark whimpered and fell.

Scourge snapped his attention back to Conrad.

Whipping the vial forward, Conrad released it. It tumbled, end over end, like a throwing knife heading for its target. Dropping the artifact, Scourge batted wildly trying to knock it away, but he was a millisecond too slow. The vial sailed past his hand and stuck in his throat. The injector hissed, releasing the serum into Scourge's body almost instantly.

The vampire knocked the vial from his flesh, but it was already too late. He stumbled back, eyes wide with shock and rage. "What have you done?"

Conrad grabbed Scourge's scythe, and pulled it from his leg. Deactivating Thomas' scythe, he slid it onto his belt. Rolling onto his back, he wrapped his hands around the wound, trying to stop the bleeding.

Scourge fell to the ground in agony, his body seizing.

Watching, Conrad prayed he had made the right decision. If it worked, the serum would cause Thomas to revert back to human, and render his body incapable of accepting either the vampire or the Wraith virus ever again. But there was nothing to be done now. Once started, the reaction could not be stopped.

The Wraith's eyes fell to the Devil's artifact on the floor. Reaching out, he took it into his hand and was gripped by another jolt of electricity. Pulling his torn pant leg aside, he watched the wound in his leg quickly closing, and felt his chest stop throbbing. Whatever this thing was, it was miraculous. Conrad stood and quickly crossed the floor to Stark. The artifact had no effect on a vampire. He hoped it would work on a werewolf.

Dropping down to his knees, Conrad lifted one of Stark's massive paws and placed the artifact beneath it. Wrapping Stark's clawed fingers around it, Conrad scooted back and waited.

The wolf's body suddenly convulsed violently,

arched then froze in a contorted position.

And Conrad had a terrible feeling he had just killed the wolf.

Flipping onto his back, Stark howled and shook, much in the same way Scourge still was. Twisting and grinding on the floor, the werewolf pulled himself into a tight ball and wrapped his arms around his knees. Chunks of bloody, dark hair fell away revealing human flesh beneath. His lips peeled back on his muzzle as he tossed his head and howled.

Watching the two writhe in pain, Conrad took an uncomfortable step back. He could very well be watching both of them die, and there was nothing he could do. Each second was an eternity as he waited.

Thomas fell silent.

Then Stark did.

Conrad waited.

Sitting straight up, Thomas stared at his hands then turned his angry gaze to Conrad. His icy blue eyes gone, he looked through his original brown ones. "What have you done...?"

Thomas was completely human again.

Conrad didn't have the words. He could feel Thomas' pain, and anger, and knew he had completely and utterly failed him as a teacher, and a friend. "I'm sorry." Conrad hung his head. "So sorry."

The disgust on Thomas' face told Conrad everything he needed to know.

Thomas collapsed to the floor, and drew his knees to his chin. There was nothing to be done now. Thomas knew for certain he couldn't take on a

Wraith and werewolf in combat, and there was no point in running. He glared at his former Master. "I hate you."

The words cut deeper into Conrad than any blade ever had. He wanted to say something, anything, that would make this better...but he knew those words didn't exist. He had to deal with the repercussions as they came, no matter what they were.

"I feel fantastic!"

Conrad shifted his gaze to Stark, thankful for the distraction, and that the wolf wasn't dead.

Stark stood, stretched his arms wide and flexed his muscled, naked frame. Every wound was healed, and there were no scars visible. He was in perfect health. "I don't know what you did," Stark said, running his fingers over his chest with astonishment, "but thank you. I was almost a goner there."

Conrad nodded. "Don't thank me. Thank your old friend Lucifer."

The name hit Stark like a slap. His face paled and his mouth dropped into a deep frown.

"I don't want to know," Conrad said, letting Stark off the hook. "It's none of my business, and I know you'll have to atone for your sins someday. That's good enough for me."

Stark took a breath and nodded. "Thank you. We all have things in our pasts that we're not proud of." He turned and looked at Thomas. "I only hope I can make up for them before the end."

"A very noble gesture," Conrad offered half-heartedly.

258

"You don't believe me?" Stark asked.

"What I believe makes little difference," Conrad answered. "You have a higher power to answer to." The Wraith let his eyes fall to Thomas. "We all do."

Stark shook his head, trying to ignore the maudlin Wraith. He looked at the gold artifact still in his hand. "What is this anyway?" Lifting it, he flipped it to Conrad.

As it landed in Conrad's hands, the artifact sprang open along the seams he spotted earlier. Shocked, he held his breath for a moment waiting to see if anything would happen...but nothing did.

"You broke it." Stark laughed.

Conrad shot the wolf the stink eye, then returned his attention to the artifact. Sitting in the hollow interior was a rolled piece of paper. Plucking the paper out carefully, Conrad snapped the artifact closed and set it on the floor. The paper looked relatively new, almost like a plain sheet of A4. Conrad unrolled it to find heavy black lettering, and wondered if the Devil had a laser printer in Hell.

"What does it say?" Stark asked curiously.

Conrad cocked his eyebrow and cleared his throat. He held the paper in two hands as though reading from a proclamation. "This is a free pass," he paused, "to the End of All Things."

The paper burst into flame and vanished from Conrad's hand.

"Bloody hell." Conrad sighed. "It's a spell."

The room was suddenly awash in a horrible red hue, and a deafening wail that dropped all three to the floor. Their world began to spin, faster and faster, until they all lost consciousness.

Chapter Twenty-One

Clawing, biting, and fighting, Specter fought against the darkness. He fought for his wife, he fought for his daughter and he fought for Kat, but most importantly, he fought for himself. Guilt had consumed him for so long, he didn't think he had anything left of himself, but he found a spark. Marcus Specter found that little piece of himself that wanted to do the right thing, which wanted to be a hero. And it didn't need anyone, or anything, to feed it.

He wanted to be free...finally free.

Surging upwards, he broke through like a drowning man gasping for air. He ripped, kicked, and struggled against the hive that sought to keep him down. But it was more than that. He was a dead man trying to reclaim his life. He knew how it tasted, felt, and smelled, but he couldn't actually remember living it. A shell of his former self, Specter sought to fill the emptiness again. And it all started here and now.

Digging his fingers into the soft surface of Metatron's hive, the erstwhile Wraith felt his muscles and joints creaking as he strained against them. Lurching forward into the horrible blue light, Specter howled as he finally broke free. Dragging his body away from the cocoon that sought to reclaim him. Rolling onto his back, he took a long, deep breath, and felt tears stream down his cheeks.

Licking his lips, he rolled onto his knees and peered angrily over his shoulder. His wings hung there, a permanent reminder that he belonged to Metatron now. Specter gritted his teeth.

He belonged to no one.

Grabbing one of his wings, he wrapped his hands around them and pulled. Flesh and bone creaked and popped angrily. Dropping his head, he felt the first joint gave way. Pain surged up his back as skin and muscles ripped free of their anchors. He felt his own blood splatter warm on his hands. Leaning back and straining his body, Specter knew he was running on pure adrenaline and endorphins. With one final surge, he screamed in agony and ripped the wing from his body.

Numb and angry, Specter placed the wing before him and stared at it. The white feathers were splattered with blood, signifying to him, exactly what an angel was.

He felt queasy, and was gripped by the overwhelming urge to vomit, but knew he had done the right thing. This was not who he was, nor would it ever be. He guarded the weak, defended the innocent, and fought for those who could not. He was Marcus Specter, Wraith and protector.

He had to find Kat.

Reaching over his shoulder, he grabbed his remaining wing.

***

The two old friends laughed, and smiled, but time was running out, and both were acutely aware of it. Trying their best to enjoy each moment, they nervously awaited the next, knowing it could be their last together.

"It's time," Quinn said and swallowed the last

gulp of his margarita.

"Already?" Saint asked sadly.

Quinn nodded. "I knew this was only a quickie, but it was worth every moment."

The two sat in silence for a moment, doing their best to memorize every feature on the other's face, though they had seen them a thousand times before. Quinn reached over and wrapped his fingers gently around Saint's hand, hopefully reassuring her.

Smiling as best he could, he let go and stood from the bar. Slipping his hand into his jacket, he produced an embossed, gold cylinder. "Here." Quinn offered it to Saint. "You'll need this."

Accepting the cylinder, Saint studied it for a moment. She felt a static charge on it that made her fingertips tingle. The markings on the shell were beautiful, but she didn't recognize them. A seam ran the length of the cylinder, but there were no visible means of opening it. "What is it?"

"Not sure." Quinn shrugged. "I was told to give that to you before they let me out. That's all I know." He paused. "So, what are you doing to do?"

Saint shrugged sliding the cylinder into her jacket. "I'm not sure." She looked over the sullen, quiet faces in the bar. Was this what she was fighting for? "I'm not entirely certain this world is worth saving."

Quinn sighed. "That's bull, and you know it. You're just so busy feeling sorry for yourself that you won't get off your ass and fight."

It was a verbal slap. Saint had the urge to press her fingers to her cheek, cradling the flesh as though she had been physically struck.

"This isn't you," Quinn continued. "You're a damned fighter. You always have been. The Saint I knew didn't sit around and mope when things got tough. She stepped up and faced it head on."

Saint slipped off her stool, straightened her coat, and stepped toward her Master. She stood, staring him down, anger burning in her eyes. "If this is a pep talk," Saint growled, "you're only pissing me off."

"Good," Quinn shot back. "Then get to work."

Saint threw her arms around Quinn. She hugged him with every ounce of her strength and buried her face in his chest.

"Too tight," Quinn croaked.

"Oh." Saint laughed and wiped a tear from her face. "Sorry. I guess retirement has made you soft." She tried to keep a straight face, but laughter erupted from somewhere deep inside.

"Uncool." Quinn laughed. He touched her face gently, lovingly.

"Can I do this?" Saint asked, looking deep into Quinn's eyes. "I mean, I don't know if I'm good enough."

"It's a heavy burden to bear," Quinn acknowledged, "but you won't be alone. You'll have help."

Saint nodded. "You didn't answer my question."

Quinn took a breath. "You are the most amazing woman I have ever known. You are strong, confident, brilliant, and powerful. I can't see the future, but there's no one I would rather have on the front line than you. The world's in good hands."

Wiping another tear from her face, Saint hugged her Master again. "Thank you."

"Any time, Kiddo," Quinn returned the hug. "You better get going. It's starting to rain harder."

Slipping out of the embrace, Saint stepped around Quinn and stared out into the rain. Her eyes focused on the hole she had already started to dig. Completely filled with water now, she knew there was a distinct possibility of the Lance washing away. Quinn, as always, was right. She had to get to work.

She spun around to say goodbye, and almost crumbled to the floor.

Quinn was gone.

Saint stood for a moment, trying to remember to breathe. Closing her eyes, she did her best to compose herself. He never did like long goodbyes, so why was she so surprised? She had been given a gift few others would ever receive: one more day.

And it was enough. Saint smiled.

Turning back to the door, Saint hiked her collar high on her neck and walked out into the rain. The massive drops pelted her skin almost painfully, and despite the almost tropical location, chilled her to the core. Walking slowly to keep her footing, she locked on the water-filled hole she created.

And she heard their song.

Saint froze.

Her gaze lifted to the dark gray sky and she tried to focus through the rain. Blinking rapidly and shielding her eyes, she could hear her heart thumping in her chest as she scanned the clouds. Lightning crackled and raged toward Earth, lighting

265

the storm. In that instant, she saw the dark outlines of thousands moving through the tempest. Her heart sank.

Charging forward, she skittered frantically through the mud. Tossing herself down, she slid toward the hole, rocks and debris chewing up her knees. The Wraith cupped her hands and tried to scoop the water away, but it was no good. The hole filled up faster than she could divert the water. It wasn't working.

Balling her fist, she plunged it into the puddle with all of her strength, and felt the wood beneath break.

Whirling like a vortex, the water drained into the crate hidden below the surface. Pushing her arm into the box, she reached all the way in to her shoulder before she felt the bottom. With her face in the mud, rainwater rushing up her nose, she quickly searched the bottom with her fingers. As the angel's song grew in strength, she felt something. Grabbing it, she ripped it free and dropped it on the ground next to her.

She stared at the red, black, and white fabric, recognizing it instantly. It sickened her to have even touched this artifact of evil, but she knew in that moment that Lucifer hadn't lied to her.

Unfurling the Nazi flag carefully, she found the Lance in the center, situated on top of the black swastika. It was exactly like the one she had seen in the Schatzkammer, down to the gold sleeve and inscription. Sliding her fingers beneath it, Saint lifted the holy artifact and held it reverently in her hands. She could feel something radiating from the

Lance into her flesh, but wasn't certain what. It was almost like when she held her scythe, but somehow different. It wasn't reverberating with her, but rather she felt as though it was transforming her. This was truly the Holy Lance, the Spear of Destiny.

Slipping it into her coat pocket, Saint let her eyes fall to the flag again. Snatching it up, she balled it and stuffed it back into the hole. A pit covered in mud...a fitting resting place for the insignia of evil.

She felt a twinge of electricity in her chest. Rolling back onto her knees, she could feel the cylinder Quinn had given her buzzing in her pocket, almost like a mobile phone set on silent mode. Saint reached into her coat. As it hit her hand, she felt electricity radiate up her arm. Fighting her instinct to drop it, she held on as the artifact snapped open revealing a slip of paper inside. It looked old, fragile, and tattered. Grabbing it out, she tried to protect it from the rain, but it was almost pointless. The ink started to run on the lettering, but not before Saint could read it.

"This is a free pass to the End of All Things." She paused. "Wait...what the hell?"

Somewhere, off in the distance, she could hear the Devil laughing. Suddenly weak and exhausted, Saint pressed her hand to her forehead. Her vision blurred as the world spun wildly, and she realized, too late, what had happened.

"Crap," she breathed and crumbled into the mud.

Chapter Twenty-Two

This was the end of all things.

The campaign was a success. Nonbelievers had been flushed out in every corner of the Earth, and destroyed with impunity. For too long, they had served man who showed no reciprocation of the Creator's love. But now there was no choice. They had wiped out the undeserving, the hedonists, the heathens, and the nonbelievers, on this, the final crusade. Their love was absolute and unyielding, as was the ending. This would be a new world order, and the angels would take their place in the warmth and divinity of His grace.

They only had to wait.

***

So this is how it was at the end of all things…

She stood staring at Hofburg Palace for close to a solid minute before she fully realized what happened. Once again in Vienna, she was shocked by the silence of the great city. A car alarm blared pointlessly in the distance, desperately trying to summon an owner that wouldn't, or couldn't come. The wind swept down off the massive buildings making lights shimmer in the rain, while skyscrapers loomed like silent giants in the mist. Broken and abused bodies littered silent streets like trash, while cars were tossed about like a child's play things. Several emergency vehicles, their lights still spinning, lined the street helplessly.

There was no one coming to their rescue.

And she knew it was a scene that had been

repeated the world over. It was gone. All of it. Everything. She looked down at the wet piece of parchment in her hand and read the text again. As she took in a slow breath, she understood.

Walking through the courtyard, the rain fell heavy on her head and shoulders. The Lance in her pocket weighed down her jacket, but reassured her. Looking up, she saw the dark shadows of angels converging amidst the heavy clouds, yet their song seemed distant in her mind. It was there, but surprisingly not affecting her the same way. Perhaps it was the Lance in her pocket, or the new confidence Master Quinn had instilled in her, but something was different. Still, it was a gift horse, and she wasn't about to look it in the mouth.

Climbing the palace stairs, Saint pushed open the massive doors and heard something that sounded like thunder rumble in the palace. Looking through the doors, she saw the pile of furniture that had been the makeshift barrier. Curiously, she peered inside expecting to see heavily armed guards with automatic weapons pointed at her...but there was no one.

Cautiously, she stepped inside and carefully traversed the fallen furniture. Two steps in, she stopped with a gasp. "Oh my God."

Much of the grand entrance, the connecting hallways, and the main stairs beyond were simply gone. Where they once had been, there was nothing more than a gaping crater in the Earth. She could see into the sublevels of the palace, and beyond. Below the sheer rock walls, an eerie blue light swallowed the darkness at the bottom of the pit. It was massive, in both diameter and depth.

Grabbing a chair from the floor, she tossed it over the edge and watched it tumble into the pit. Falling end over end awkwardly, the chair disappeared into the blue light, but continued to descend without a sound. Keeping a mental count, Saint finally heard a muted crash.

"That's a helluva long way down," she breathed, peering over the edge.

But she already knew she had to get across. Ben was on the other side. Scanning the opposite side of the pit, she saw the hallway leading to the infirmary mostly intact. But that didn't mean the infirmary was. Saint tried to judge the distance across the pit, but was never any good at that kind of thing. The best estimate to the other side she could come up with was "far."

But she had to.

Grabbing the furniture from the broken barricade, she hastily started tossing it aside. Once the path was clear, she opened the doors wide and stepped out into the rain. Walking slowly down the stairs, she peered into the heavy clouds again and found the shadows of angels, still circling. Her fingers tingled nervously as she watched. Reaching the bottom, Saint turned and stared up at the open doors.

This is not a good idea, she warned herself.

Reaching into her pocket, the Wraith wrapped her hand around the Holy Lance and pulled it free. With the gold sleeve resting in her palm, she felt the same buzz of electricity she had before. The words of her Master echoed in her ears as she stared at the doors. If there was anyone who could do this, it was Saint.

And she knew it.

Charging up the stairs, Saint hit a dead sprint before her mind had time to react. Reaching the top landing, Saint screamed and pushed harder and faster than she ever had before. With the edge rushing at her with incredible speed, she waited until the last possible moment. Vaulting off the edge, Saint launched herself into the great emptiness above the pit. Swinging her arms and legs to carry her momentum, she felt her body become weightless for a fraction of a second.

Roughly halfway across, she felt gravity start to drag her down. Panic gripped her as she fell. She was short, and she knew it. Sailing toward the edge, she threw her arms and legs forward for that last bit of thrust…but it wasn't enough.

Saint hit the edge hard with her midsection. She folded over and felt her chin smack against what was left of the tile floor, and her knees hit the concrete substructure. With the wind knocked out of her, stars twinkled before her eyes, but she didn't feel any pain. She started to slide into the pit. Clawing the floor, and the concrete below with her feet, her heart pounded in her ears and her lungs cried for breath. She was going to fall.

Drawing back the Spear with every remaining shred of her strength, she slammed it down. Tile shattered and launched into the air as the Lance broke through and dug deep into the concrete beneath.

Wrapping her hands around the gold sleeve, she

strained to pull herself up. Kicking a leg up on the lip, she used the leverage to twist her body out of the pit.

Rolling onto her back, she calmed herself and drew a breath into her lungs. Slowly exhaling, she turned her head and stared back across the pit with a smile. Pushing off the floor, the Wraith stood and ripped the Lance easily from the floor. She had to get to the infirmary.

Coming around the corner, she found the infirmary empty save for the few remaining patients lying helplessly in bed. She headed straight for Ben. The werewolf was out cold, but after everything that had happened, he deserved some rest. She almost didn't want to wake him, but this was too important. Saint wanted to make sure the antidote worked, and show Ben the Lance. Reaching out, she touched him gently on the shoulder and said his name.

The wolf started to stir. Opening his eyes, he blinked them rapidly and tried to focus on Saint. Ben licked his lips to generate some moisture.

"How do you feel?" Saint asked softly.

The wolf coughed. "Like I was hit by a bus." He took a breath. "But okay."

"Good," she said with a smile. She slid her fingers around his hand. "Thank you."

Ben cocked his head on the pillow. "For what?"

"Saving my life," Saint answered. "Again."

The wolf laughed. "It's what I do."

Saint nodded, understanding his motivation now. "I know." She looked around the empty infirmary. "What happened here?"

Ben glanced past her, taking in the scene for the

272

first time. "I have no idea," he answered honestly. "I must've been out cold."

She reached into her pocket and took the Spear into her hand. The familiar buzz of electricity surging up her flesh, she pulled the artifact free and handed it to Ben. "I think this is what you were after."

Ben looked from the Spear to Saint, then back again. Unsure if he was actually worthy to touch it, his movements were tentative and careful. Lifting it out of Saint's hands, he stared at the gold sleeve, his eyes wide. "It tingles."

Saint smiled. "I felt it too. I can't explain it."

Ben sat straight up in bed. "I can feel it all the way down in my chest." He stopped. "I feel fantastic."

Catching sight of his exposed back, Saint's eyes widened. Moving closer, she grabbed the hospital gown the nurses had slipped him into and pulled it down.

"Hey," Ben argued. "I'm flattered, but—"

"Shut up," Saint snapped, running her fingertips over his flesh. Several deep wounds, created by the angels during his escape, were healing before her eyes. With complete amazement, she watched the skin around the cuts close as if there was no wound there at all, no scabbing, and no scar tissue. "Amazing."

She knew in that moment it was the Spear.

"What happened?" Ben asked nervously.

"Your wounds," Saint said, moving around to Ben's throat and chest. His bruises were completely healed as well. "They're gone."

The wolf's eyes fell on the Spear in his hands. "This is the Lance Michael told me about?"

Saint nodded. "The Holy Lance. It's supposedly the instrument that killed Jesus on the cross."

Ben nodded. "I have no doubt. I feel," his eyes met Saint's, "incredible." Tossing the covers back, Ben slipped his legs over the edge of the bed. He started pulling tubes away, and reached for his IV.

"Wait," Saint said, stopping him.

"I'm fine," Ben protested and pushed her hand away. "Trust me."

"Okay." Saint smiled, happy to see her werewolf protector healthy again. Saint turned to find the same physician who had treated Ben, and told him about the Lance. He smiled. "How are you doing?"

He pulled off his glasses and cleaned them on his lab coat. "I've had better days." He looked past Saint to Ben. "Well, you're looking well."

Ben smiled. "Yes, thank you."

The doctor pulled his lab coat back and reached into the back pocket of his pants. "I think I have something that belongs to you," he said, producing Saint's scythe.

Accepting the weapon, Saint cradled it for a moment and enjoyed the perfect vibration in her hands. "Thank you," Saint said, slipping the hilt onto her belt. "What happened here?"

"The angels returned," the doctor said quietly. "They killed everyone, and tore the palace apart. They created that massive hole in the entrance."

Saint nodded. "How did you escape?"

The doctor lowered his eyes. "I hid."

"There's no shame in that," Ben commented. "You're a healer, not a warrior."

"I know," the doctor stuttered, "but it still didn't feel right. The angels took everyone, except the few patients here in bed. They didn't seem interested in them for some reason."

Saint understood. The bodies were for Metatron's plan. Lucky for Ben, the archangel didn't want damaged goods. "Take a look at this," she said, lifting the Spear from Ben's hands and then handing it to the doctor.

Taking the Spear, the doctor studied it. "Is this really the Holy Lance?"

Saint nodded.

"Why would you willingly give this to me?" the doctor asked curiously.

"Because I trust you. And you know, no matter how fast you ran, or where you hid, Ben and I would find you." Saint smiled, flashing her fangs.

The doctor laughed uncomfortably. "Good point."

Saint turned back to Ben. "You still okay?"

The wolf smiled. "Yeah. It's weird though. I have this building sense of jealousy toward the doctor, because I want the Spear back."

"Don't you go all Gollum on me," Saint warned. "I'll kick your ass."

"But it's the precious…" Ben said with a scratchy, angry voice. His face was deadly serious then, as if a shadow cleared, the wolf smiled and laughed. "Teasing."

Saint punched her werewolf protector in the

shoulder. "Not funny. Come on," she smiled, "we have work to do."

***

Her eyes flashed gold and she screamed at the top of her lungs. Despite her best efforts, Kat was about to give birth.

The cocoon squealed angrily, while Metatron remained silent. Electricity skittered like sheet lightning over the hive causing the human/angel hybrids to moan, screech, and convulse. The blue light that filtered through the walls had gradually shifted toward white over the past few minutes, and the jolts to the hybrids had become more frequent. Hundreds of angels had begun filtering into the hive, gathering around Kat. They watched silently, as Metatron did, waiting.

They knew, as did Kat, the baby was about to arrive.

One final contraction gripped Kat's entire body. Gritting her teeth so hard she could actually hear the enamel cracking, her body arched painfully. Pain surged from her abdomen and down her legs, as the baby was dropped through the birth canal. Stars sparkled before her eyes as the pain became overwhelming. Then a strange emptiness overcame her, and her body finally relaxed.

Suddenly warm and slightly dazed, she knew her body was in shock…and that she had just given birth.

Lifting her head, she searched for any sign of her baby. Looking over the cocoon's skin, she saw a rounded bulge forming near the bottom. The cocoon squealed again as its skin started to stretch. The bulge took on the shape of a human head and shoulders, but much larger than a baby's should be. The skin stretched further, becoming almost translucent. She could make out dark eyes, and a mouth open in a silent scream. Horrified, Kat clawed and scratched trying to break free of the cocoon, but the tendrils held her in place.

With a thunderous snap, the cocoon's skin finally gave way.

And Kat looked at her child with horrified eyes.

Across the hive, cocoons started to open releasing the hybrids. As they hit the floor, the new beings struggled to their feet and slowly joined the angels around Metatron. It was time. Each lifted their hands in praise.

Their Savior had arrived.

Chapter Twenty-Three

Specter stumbled, weak and exhausted.

Landing on his hands, he felt a twinge of pain shoot up his arms. Grunting in agony, he felt as though flames were erupting from the wounds where his wings had been. Clawing ahead despite the pain, he fixed on a column of white light bleeding into the blue. He crawled quietly to the edge and stopped.

The Wraith nervously wrapped his fingers over the lip of the passage. Holding his breath, he pulled his eyes toward the edge. He gritted his teeth. In the massive chamber below, he saw hundreds and hundreds of angels surrounding Metatron at the bottom. Two angels were restraining Kat, while a solitary figure, unlike the others, stood watching. To make matters worse, the cocoons on the floor, walls, and ceiling were all empty.

It appeared Metatron's machinations had come to fruition.

Pushing back from the edge, Specter rolled onto his side and stared blankly into the blue light. He didn't know what to do. If he dove into the chamber below, he would most certainly be ripped to shreds by the angels, but he couldn't leave Kat down there. He had to do something—

A screech interrupted his thoughts.

Snapping his eyes up, Specter rolled to his left narrowly avoiding the slashing claws of an angel.

Throwing a jab across his body, Specter's fist connected lazily with the angel's jaw. Tossing another more focused punch, the Wraith snapped the angel's head back. Grabbing the creature's head and lunging forward, Specter delivered a solid head butt and felt the bridge of its nose crack beneath his forehead. Dark ooze splattered on Specter's flesh as the angel's broken nose bled. Rolling onto his back, Specter brought his legs up and kicked the creature hard in the sternum, knocking it away.

Using the momentum to carry him forward, Specter rolled onto his knees, but tumbled messily forward. He was utterly spent as every muscle in his body quivered. Lifting his head, Specter saw the angel's claws flash in the blue light. Pain sizzled across his cheek as flesh was raked angrily away. Stars sparkled before his eyes as he felt another blow to the side of his head. Crumbling, he felt another hit, and then another. He lifted his hands defensively, but it was too late. Specter felt another hit connect with his cheek and was swallowed by darkness.

***

Pinned in place by two powerful angels, Kat could only watch events unfold before her.

The cocoon that held her appeared dead, or seriously wounded, and she could see the deep gouges she had created in its colorful, oyster-like flesh. Tendrils were snapped and bleeding some kind of dark goo and only shreds of the skin that had held her in place remained. But it did not matter. It had served its purpose.

Stepping around the outer rim, Metatron circled the newborn, who already stood over six feet in height. Sizing it up, the archangel seemed pleased, despite his masked facial features. The Voice gazed at the newborn's musculature, still wet and glistening from birth. "Nephilim," Metatron breathed proudly.

She wanted desperately to look away, but couldn't. Kat was transfixed by the Nephilim. From its ash-colored flesh, coal-black eyes, and mouth full of razor-sharp teeth, it looked like a great white shark had sprouted legs and walked onto the shore. Long, stringy black hair fell from its head down around its grotesquely humanoid face, while horrid yellow claws sprouted from the Nephilim's fingertips. If nothing else, this being was the perfect engine of destruction.

Hatred burned in her guts, but there was a part of Kat that wanted to take the Nephilim into her arms and cradle it to her flesh. It was still hers…even though it disgusted her.

Reaching out slowly, Metatron lifted his fingers toward the Nephilim.

The newborn winced, unsure what to expect.

"Don't be alarmed," The Voice soothed. "I won't hurt you."

Eyeing the archangel warily, the Nephilim held his ground. His lips peeled back defensively, displaying his mouthful of weapons.

Metatron touched his fingertips lightly to the newborn's face, and ran them down its cheek. "You are beautiful. You will usher in a new age and we will finally take our place in His grace."

All the angels and hybrids crowded in closer, hoping to get a good look at their Savior. With raised hands, a song of praise started and quickly washed through the crowd. Its notes were long, drawn-out, low, and resonated off the sides of the hive.

Metatron nodded approvingly. "Sing! Sing proudly!" The Voice turned to the Nephilim. "Do you hear them?"

The Nephilim stood transfixed by the sound, its eyes wide with an emotion that could be called fear. It looked from Metatron to the crowd, then back again.

"They sing of joy!" Metatron laughed heartily, and placed his hands on the newborn's shoulders.

Something wasn't right. Kat watched her child warily.

The Nephilim's eyes darted over the crowd as the song's volume grew rapidly. Gnashing its teeth, it looked like a caged animal desperately trying to find a way out. It tried to slip from beneath Metatron's touch, but there was nowhere to go. It was become increasingly frantic by the moment.

Struggling against the angels, Kat tried desperately to break free.

"They sing for you!" Metatron pressed his hand gently to the Nephilim's face.

The Nephilim whined then snapped. Lashing forward, the newborn bit down onto Metatron's hand and shook. Ripping his hand away, the archangel found he was missing three fingers. The Voice screamed and fell back into Kat's cocoon, cradling his bloody, damaged limb.

Swallowing the stolen digits, the Nephilim licked his lips, settled his eyes on Metatron, then attacked.

281

Conrad, Stark, and Thomas hit the ground with a smack. Rolling onto his back, Conrad groaned and slowly sat up. His eyes were assaulted by the bluish-white light that seemed to be radiating from every surface. Standing, the High Wraith's eyes worked frantically over his surroundings trying to get some kind of bearing. The rounded, sloping terrain appeared organic, but biomechanical at the same time. Certain he was inside the body of some gigantic alien creature, Conrad drew the scythe from his belt.

Rolling onto his knees, Thomas lifted to his feet. His eyes burned into the back of his former Master, his hatred almost palpable. Stumbling back, he felt weak and powerless for the first time in his life. Always gifted, even when he was a boy, Thomas had never been merely human. It was Conrad who brought Thomas to the Academy, taken Kat away from him, and then tried to kill him. Conrad had now taken everything Thomas had left: his identity. And he hated the High Wraith for it. Nothing mattered anymore. He would see Conrad dead. Thomas turned and disappeared into the darkness of the hive.

Conrad activated his scythe as a woman's scream echoed through the passages. Looking to Stark, he suddenly remembered the third person in his group. Spinning slowly, he searched guardedly. He knew to never underestimate an enemy, but it bothered him to use that term. "Where's Thomas?"

"Hard to tell," Stark said, sniffing the air. "There are a lot of weird scents in this place."

"Well that's just great." Conrad sighed.

Conrad stared at Thomas' scythe in his hands. He had given the dual bladed weapon to his apprentice, after having it specially designed. Unlike most others, Thomas' scythe wasn't merely silver, but prominently featured a glossy black design that wound up from the hilt and extended to the tips of the blades. It was a work of art, crafted by the finest Wraith weaponmaster Conrad knew. But like Thomas, it was a beautifully crafted weapon more often used as a blunt instrument.

Stark stood, but nearly tumbled on the uneven, ridged floor. "What the bloody hell is this place?"

Conrad remembered the words on the paper the Devil had given him, and felt a shiver run down his body. Could this really be...? As he looked over the horrible surroundings, he had no doubt. Conrad drew in a breath. "The end of all things."

Stark didn't appreciate the Wraith's flair for the dramatic, especially now. He rolled his eyes and shook his head. "What now?"

Conrad stared into the passage before them, unable to see the bottom in the blue light. Deactivating the scythe and slipping it back on his belt, he placed his hand on the wall for support and started down the treacherous passage. "Into the pit." He glanced over his shoulder.

"You're such a drama queen. Can't you say anything normal?" the werewolf asked in frustration, and started to follow.

Conrad smiled. "Where's the fun in that?"

Chapter Twenty-Four

Saint, Ben, and the doctor stood on the edge of the pit inside Hofburg Palace. Each couldn't help but imagine falling and being crushed horribly on the bottom, but that was exactly what they were considering.

"This is where the angels went?" Saint asked, remembering nearly being swallowed by the pit earlier.

The doctor nodded nervously and adjusted the glasses on his nose. "Everyone they didn't kill, they took down there."

Ben snorted and hocked up a snot rocket. Spitting over the edge, he watched the phlegm until it disappeared into the blue haze. "That's a hell of a long way down."

"And that was utterly disgusting," Saint added.

Ben smiled sheepishly. "Sorry."

Still considering the pit, Saint held the Spear tightly in her hand. As it buzzed and vibrated up her arm, she heard a little voice in the back of her head urging her forward. She had to go. "I think this will work."

"You're risking your life on a theory," Ben pointed out. "There is no doubt that you'll be dead if you jump."

"That's the plan," Saint confirmed.

"What if you drop it?" the doctor asked. "There are no second chances."

"I won't," Saint said sternly.

"More importantly," Ben breathed, "what if this

284

doesn't work like you think it will?"

"Well, I don't see an elevator, so my options are sort of limited." Saint lifted the Spear and held it gently in her palms. She knew, just knew, that this would work. "I have to get down there. No choice."

The doctor reached into his lab coat and produced two slim, black, two-way radios. "Here," he said, handing one to Ben and the other to Saint. "I'm not sure if these will even reach or not," he paused, "but it's something."

Saint slid the radio into her jacket and nodded at the doctor appreciatively. Looking to Ben, she took a long, slow breath. She wanted to put her hands on him, and be taken into his embrace. Saint desperately wanted to feel his lips on hers...and she realized she had fallen in love with her protector. But she didn't say, or do, anything. With a nod, she turned and stepped to the edge of the pit.

Ben quickly reached out and grabbed her shoulder. "Saint, wait."

She wanted to hear him say, I Love you. She turned, looked into his eyes, and waited.

"Why do you have to do this?" Ben asked.

He didn't say it. But neither did she. Taking another breath, she nodded, "Just have to."

"Michael came to me," the wolf protested. "I should be the one to go."

"I helped create this mess," Saint replied. "I have to help undo the damage."

"I can't talk you out of this, can I?" Ben asked finally.

Saint considered the question, but already knew the answer. "No."

Ben held her for a moment longer, his eyes glassy. He wanted to say something, but couldn't find the words. In that moment, his heart ached. "Be careful."

"I will," Saint said. She turned back to the pit. Not waiting for any more words, Saint opened her arms and dove off.

Ben lurched forward, his initial urge to grab for her. Dropping to his knees on the edge, he watched Saint sail into the pit, her hair and leather trench whipping beautifully behind her. Cradling the black radio in his hand, he snapped the volume knob on and watched Saint disappear into the blue haze. Ben waited.

A muted thump echoed up the pit's walls.

The werewolf's heart raced wildly. He glanced up to the doctor, then back to the pit. Lifting the radio slowly, he keyed the talk button with his thumb. "Saint?"

Releasing the button, he heard static over the tinny speaker.

Ben keyed the radio again. "Saint? Are you okay?"

The werewolf felt helpless, and angry. As he closed his eyes, he pressed the back of his hand to his forehead. He pictured her lying at the bottom, broken and dying, with the Spear just beyond her reach. And there was nothing he could do.

"Saint," Ben said, keying the radio again. "Please say something…Saint?"

Static.

***

Slowly rising as it wiped its lips, the Nephilim

286

gazed with satisfaction over the sea of broken bodies it had wrought. Feathers flitted to the ground like horrible snowflakes over the corpses of angels and hybrids. Black blood dripped from its claws, and was splattered angrily on its chest and face. The newborn let its glittering black eyes settle on the two surviving souls. Crouching down, the Nephilim studied them, unsure why they had been spared.

Sniffing the air, the Nephilim took in their scents. Both were very different, yet similar. The same smell coursed through their veins, but the newborn didn't know exactly what it was. There was something familiar about these two, unlike the others he had destroyed. They were the same, but exact opposites. And he was part of them, and they of him.

The creature's visage horrified her, but she felt connected to it. It was her child after all, despite what Metatron claimed. "What is it?" Kat breathed.

"Nephilim," Metatron answered, its bloody hand wrapped in its robes. "It is perfect."

"Is that why it bit your fingers off?" Kat asked pointedly.

"It was merely frightened," Metatron rationalized, "and reacted badly. I hold no ill will."

"Then go give it a kiss," Kat suggested.

The Nephilim hissed at the two and lifted onto the balls of his feet. Its body was thin, but muscled, and its bone structure was clearly visible beneath its gray flesh. Dark veins created a terrible patchwork web through its skin, and seemed to pulse with a horrid purple hue.

"You are beautiful," Metatron said to the

newborn. "They," he gestured to the dead angels and hybrids, "were not worthy of your presence. You are everything we are not."

The Nephilim cocked its head like a dog trying to understand English. It started to bob like a bird.

"What the hell does that mean?" Kat spat out.

"Unlike the hybrids I created here," Metatron explained, "the Nephilim is the perfect genesis of angel and human. And it has one thing you and I will never have."

"What's that?"

Metatron considered the result of thousands of years of careful planning and manipulation. It seemed odd that its time had finally arrived, yet here it stood in all of its splendor. It was almost more than he could have hoped for. The Voice turned to Kat. "A soul, my dear vampire. The Nephilim has a human soul."

Kat was utterly shocked at the answer. "That thing has a soul," she paused and worked it through, "and I don't?"

"Vampires lost their souls long ago," Metatron replied. "To this day, the vampire virus carries with it a curse, and angels were never given a soul. It was something the Creator gifted to the talking monkeys. But all that has changed now."

"Is that what all this is about?" Kat asked. "Petty jealousy?"

"It is much more," Metatron replied, "but it is beyond the comprehension of your monkey brain."

"Bull," Kat spat out. "You're jealous of humans, so you created an angel with a soul to piss off daddy."

Metatron was shocked at the simplicity and rawness of Kat's statement, and moreover, how she had taken his entire plan and stripped it to the ugly core. What had he done?

The Nephilim glared at Metatron and Kat. Opening its shark-like mouth, a long, purple tongue slithered out and lapped the blood off its face.

"What is it going to do with us?" Kat asked quietly.

Metatron unwrapped his damaged hand and examined the cleanly severed digits. Black blood still spurted from the wound, and he quickly re-wrapped it in his cloak. "I wish I knew, child," the archangel breathed.

But somewhere, deep in the back of his ancient brain, The Voice knew it didn't matter. His plan was fulfilled, and the Nephilim lived again. The Voice recalled His anger and rage the last time this had happened, and the measures taken to wipe Eden clean. Surely this time would be no different.

Metatron had just killed the entire human race.

***

Specter opened his eyes and pain rampaged through his brain. Face down, he rolled onto his side and touched his hand to his cheek tenderly. The angel had done a number on him.

The angel…

Sitting up in shock, his pain instantly doubled and he wished he hadn't done that. Closing his eyes tightly and gritting his teeth, each throb of pain felt like his brain was about to explode from his skull. As it started to recede, Specter opened his eyes slowly.

He was in the same place, but there was no sign of his attacker. Had it left him for dead?

No, something wasn't right.

Rubbing his face, his hands felt cool against his skin. As the pain started to dull, he glanced to his right and found the passage leading into the hive. Watching the bluish-white light, he saw a lone feather waft up on some unseen current. Leaning over carefully, he felt pain explode into his head again. Fighting it back, he reached out with a shaking hand and plucked the feather from the air.

Sitting up, he stared at the long, white feather. Flipping it over in his hand, he saw it was splattered with black blood.

Specter held still as a sound met his ears. It was coming from the passage behind, and sounded very much like multiple footfalls. Dropping the feather, the Wraith was quickly on his feet. He pressed himself against the passage wall, not wanting to be caught off-guard again, and waited.

From the darkness, he saw two figures emerge. One was roughly his size and build, while the other was massive. They didn't look like angels... Specter spotted the silver glimmer of a familiar weapon, and felt an immediate wave of relief wash through him. He smiled. The cavalry had arrived.

Specter stepped away from the wall and waited.

"Hold there."

"I'm Marcus Specter," the wraith explained. "I was—"

"Marcus?"

Specter squinted his eyes in the darkness, and was hit by a spark of recognition. "Conrad?"

The two Wraith met in the passage, sized each other up, shook hands, then embraced.

"Damn good to see you, Conrad," Specter said quickly. Falling back slightly, he pressed his hand to his head again.

"You look like hell," Conrad said, deactivating his scythe and sliding it on his belt. He reached out and grabbed Specter as he wobbled, and looked as though he was about to fall. "Sit down."

Specter nodded, and with Conrad and Stark's help, slid down to the floor of the passage. Leaning forward, the Wraith pressed the meaty mound of his palms into his temples.

Conrad spotted the bloody stumps on Specter's back, and was hit with confusion and a streak of revulsion. "What the hell happened to you?"

"Metatron took me," Specter answered, "and tried to make me into one of his angels, but I refused."

"My God," Conrad breathed. "Those were wings?" he asked, pointing to Specter's back.

"I tore them off," Specter said without missing a beat.

"We need to get you out of here," Conrad said quickly. "You need medical attention."

"It's too late for that," Specter said, shaking his head. "I'm dying, old friend."

"No," Conrad argued. "Stark and I—"

"Stop," Specter barked. He paused, waiting to see if the younger Wraith followed his order. "You two have work to do. A pregnant vampire is down there." Specter pointed to the hive.

Conrad furrowed his brow. "Kat."

"Yes," Specter said with surprise, but realized he shouldn't be. Conrad was very resourceful, and always seemed to end up in the middle of things. He had a definite knack for that. "I promised to get her out of here, but it doesn't look like I'm going to be able to do that." He paused and let his head fall back against the passage. "Help her."

"That's why we're here," Conrad said, sliding his hand behind Specter's neck. "Stay with me, Marcus."

"I'm so tired..." Specter muttered and closed his eyes.

"Marcus?" Conrad said, but the older Wraith was unresponsive.

"The artifact," Stark offered, "did you bring it? It could heal him."

Conrad quickly checked his pockets, but then clearly remembered setting it on the floor as he took the paper out. "No," he breathed, and mentally scolded himself.

"We need to get him medical attention," Stark said, "So that means we need to get to work."

Conrad patted Marcus on the shoulder. "Quite right." He looked back at his friend. "Stay with us, Marcus. You fight, dammit."

Specter didn't reply.

Conrad cursed under his breath and pressed his fingers to Specter's throat again. Conrad sighed and looked up at Stark. "He's gone."

The wolf placed his hand on Conrad's shoulder. "I'm sorry."

Conrad nodded and turned back to Specter. "He was a good man, and a good friend."

Stark moved to the passage and dropped to his knees. "Holy hell."

"What?" Conrad asked, moving to his side. Staring inside, he felt a deep sense of confusion. "They're all dead." He scanned over the hundreds of angel corpses littering the floor, then spotted Kat in the center. "There she is."

"Who's with her?" Stark asked about the other two figures. "Looks like an angel and," he paused, "I don't know what the hell that other thing is."

Conrad's eyes settled on the dark gray creature. He couldn't make out many details at this height, but was filled with dread as he looked. "I don't have any idea."

"There's only two. We can take them," Stark said.

"We need a plan. Something killed all of those angels," Conrad said warily. "We can't just charge…"

Conrad's words died in his throat as the gray creature turned and locked its eyes on him. Opening its mouth, it screeched horribly.

"Bloody hell," the High Wraith moaned.

Chapter Twenty-Five

The sound of static woke her.

She groaned in agony. Bloodied and broken, her body was twisted in a weird angle...but she was alive. Saint could hear the two-way radio hissing in her pocket, but she had no immediate desire to reach for it. Every breath hurt, and every heartbeat ached as she slipped in and out of consciousness.

Turning her head painfully, Saint looked at her arm. Broken in three places, it looked like a serpent prepared to strike. In her hand, barely balancing on the tip of her fingers, sat the Spear. Saint couldn't remember the impact, but from the pain running rampant over her body, it was obvious she didn't land well. Without the Spear, she would certainly be dead.

She tried to move her fingers, but found them unresponsive. The multiple breaks between them and her brain probably had something to do with that. Saint knew she had to get a better hold of the Spear, or she could still die. Her body had taken a brutal amount of damage.

Rolling onto her side, Saint gasped then cried out. It felt as if every pain receptor in her body lit up like a Christmas tree. The sensation was overwhelming and she was gripped by the immediate urge to vomit. Fighting it back, she slung her arm over and reached for the Spear. Her fingers inched along the floor like spider legs, moving ever closer to the artifact. She could almost reach it. Agony welled up in her throat and burst from her mouth in the form of a bone-rattling scream.

With one final push, she rolled onto her broken arm and grabbed the Spear with the other.

Lurching forward, she vomited...

Then stopped.

Sitting up, Saint felt an immediate sense of release erupt in her mind. Holding the Spear to her chest, she looked at her broken arm. She watched, amazed as it popped, cracked, and then straightened. Furrowing her brow, she lifted the arm and wiggled her fingers normally. Running her fingers over the wet bloody spots on her pants, she felt no wounds. There was no pain. She uttered a silent thank you to the Spear.

Saint stood with a laugh. Lifting her eyes, the laughter immediately died. She felt a shiver run down her back as she was certain she had fallen into Hell.

Unwilling to blink, Saint reached into her jacket and grabbed the two-way radio. As she keyed the mic, she hoped it would work at this distance. She lifted her eyes up, but only saw a blue haze above. "Ben? Can you hear me?"

Static.

Slipping the Spear into her pocket, she checked the settings on the radio, despite having no idea what she was doing. Twisting knobs and pressing buttons, she keyed the mic again. "Ben? Is this damned thing working?"

Still nothing but static.

Frustrated, Saint dropped the radio back into her pocket. Looking over the pit, she saw passages leading off in all directions and cursed under her breath. There was no more time. She had to go to work.

Dropping to her knees, she pulled her scythe and activated it. Laying it on the ground, she took the Spear and carefully placed it on the tip. Amazed at how well the two locked together, Saint knew she still needed something to secure the Spear. She tore off the bottom of her shirt and wound it around the Spear and scythe, tying it as best she could. It wasn't perfect, but it would work.

Lifting her gaze to the blue haze, she imagined Ben somewhere above looking down on her. She wondered if he knew how much she needed him right now.

She let her eyes fall back to the pit. Holding her makeshift spear out like a dowsing rod, she spun slowly, but the sensation in her hands didn't change.

"Oh well." She sighed. "Had to give it a shot. The damned thing can do everything else."

Choosing a passage at random, Saint set off into the hive.

***

"She needs me," Ben argued, marching forward.

The doctor shook his head and moved between the wolf and the pit. "I'm not going to let you do this. You will die."

"I can't just leave her down there alone," Ben argued. He tried to step around the doctor, but the smaller man was persistent. "Get out of my way."

"No," the doctor protested, despite a quiver of fear in his voice. "You're not doing this."

Ben knew the doctor was right. If Saint was

hurt, or incapacitated, there was a good chance Ben would plunge to his death. Stepping back, the werewolf leaned against what was left of the grand staircase's banister. "Fine."

The doctor breathed a sigh of relief. Ben was much taller, and almost double in width. Even if the doctor wanted to, there was no way he could have stopped Ben. He patted the wolf on the shoulder and chose a spot on the banister next to him.

"Now what?" Ben asked.

"We wait," the doctor answered.

The answer didn't satisfy Ben. "There has to be a way down. I can't just leave her down there."

"You love her," the doctor said.

Unsure if it was a question or a statement, Ben stared at the doctor. "I am her protector, not that it's any of your business."

"And," the doctor drew out the word, "you love her."

Ben huffed. "What does that have to do with anything?"

"Everything!" The doctor smiled. "There is no force in the known universe that can stop a man in love. Love will find a way."

Ben cocked his head and stared at the doctor. Dressed in a slender blue suit, red tie, with red Chucks, and wild, messy, brown hair, he didn't look like a physician at all. "Who are you?"

"Just a doctor," he replied. "Let's find a way to get you down there." The doctor turned and headed back toward the infirmary. From there, they had access to the rest of the palace.

Ben smiled and followed. "Good man. Thank

you."

The doctor nodded and returned the smile.

***

The Wraith turned vampire turned human wandered aimlessly through the blue lit passages. His mind swam with schemes of revenge, but he felt small and weak. Anger blossomed in his heart like a nuclear furnace, threatening to consume his entire being to sustain itself. He had been here too many times before, and even his rage felt empty and pointless now. It had made him driven, but unfocused, and as a result, Thomas became sloppy...and lost everything.

Again.

But Kat was alive...that counted for something, didn't it?

Every night, for as long as he could recall, his dreams were filled with the mysterious blond woman, and each time he lost her. But fate had dealt him a different hand. She was real, and instead of dying in his arms, he saved her that night only to find out she was a vampire. He had promised to love Kat until the stars grew cold, only to have her taken away by his Master and closest friend...but she hadn't been.

Thomas stopped. He had fought, and died, for no reason. Conrad hadn't killed her. He was telling the truth.

He had been played the fool.

Thomas had come up wanting. Never satisfied with what he had, his eyes were always on the horizon, looking for the next big step in his life. He was a Wraith, but he wanted more power. He found

298

the woman of his dreams, but he wanted her to be something more. His arrogance had cost him his very life, and still that wasn't enough. So he turned to Bane and his Vampire Master for the power to wage revenge. Even death wasn't enough to quell his selfish desires.

The truth cut through him like a blade.

Stumbling through the passage, he looked at the numerous, empty indentations on the wall. Tubes and flesh hung free, lifeless, in the quiet. Whatever this place was, it seemed that it had fulfilled its purpose, much as Thomas had. He realized in the grand scheme of things, he was only a tool. His entire life he had been used for someone else's purposes. This life was not his own, nor would it ever be.

Once, he was a hero…

Stopping, he leaned against the passage wall. Lost in his thoughts, Thomas slowly slid down to the floor and hung his head.

***

"We're too high," Stark said. "It can't get up here."

Conrad shook his head. "I don't think…"

The Nephilim, its eyes fixed on the two intruders, squatted down then leapt straight up in an incredible display of strength and power.

Conrad and Stark stumbled back from the passage as the creature sailed through and landed on the balls of its feet. Throwing its arms out and extending the talons from its fingertips, the Nephilim shrieked angrily.

Leaning forward, Stark roared at the top of his

lungs as his flesh ripped and exploded off his muscular frame. Unleashing the wolf inside, his eyes snapped to red and he growled at the Nephilim. Hunching down, the werewolf dug his claws into the passage floor, poised to strike.

Rocking back, Conrad threw off his coat and spun the dual-bladed scythe. Settling into a defensive position, he centered himself and prepared for battle. Knowing full well this thing had just wiped out several hundred angels, he was convinced their odds weren't very promising.

Stark launched at the Nephilim, bringing his claws to bear. Snatching the werewolf out of the air, the Nephilim tossed the beast away with little effort. Stark hit the passage and skidded. Finally righting himself, he shook his head and snarled. He charged back toward the Nephilim.

Using the distraction, Conrad struck quickly, bringing his scythe across then up. His blade opened two deep wounds in the Nephilim's chest that immediately spilled black blood. Not even pausing, the Nephilim attacked. As it swiped out with its claws, Conrad leaned back barely avoiding them. Swinging his scythe over and up, he knocked the Nephilim's hand away, and threw himself forward. Conrad pressed his attack, moving with speed and agility well beyond a human's. His scythe spun around him like a whirling tornado, cutting and slicing the Nephilim again and again. A spray of black blood filled the air around them. Bringing the scythe around his body, Conrad snapped the blade straight up and swung with all of his strength.

The Wraith watched the blade slice into the

Nephilim's chin, and erupt from the top of the creature's head. Lodged in place, Conrad let go of his scythe and stepped back.

That should have been the killing blow.

The Nephilim tried to open its mouth, but found it was pinned shut. Wrapping its fingers around the scythe, it ripped the blade free with a shriek. Blood spilling from its mouth, the Nephilim tossed the weapon down and locked its black eyes angrily on Conrad.

"Damn," Conrad breathed, his weapon well out of reach.

The Nephilim lurched forward.

But Stark pounced.

Slamming the creature to the floor, the werewolf landed on the Nephilim's back with a crunch. Not giving the creature a chance to react, or retaliate, Stark started savagely clawing and biting. Grabbing a mouthful of flesh, Stark ripped it away and felt a warm font of blood on his tongue.

Getting its hands and feet down, the Nephilim pushed off the floor and slammed it and Stark into the roof of the passage. The wolf yelped as its body was smashed by the force. Reaching up, the Nephilim dug its talons into the ceiling and grabbed Stark with its feet. Swinging him down, the Nephilim let go of the wolf. Careening off the lip awkwardly, Stark clawed wildly trying to hold on, but slipped into the hive below.

Without hesitation, the Nephilim was on Conrad. Throwing his arm up defensively, the creature latched on and bit down with his shark-like teeth. The High Wraith winced as he felt the teeth pop through his flesh and slice easily into the muscles. The force of the bite was incredible. Throwing a punch across his body, Conrad connected solidly with the Nephilim's eye but the creature refused to release. Wrapping its arms and legs around the Wraith, the Nephilim started to shake its head like a dog with a toy.

Conrad roared as he felt flesh and muscles tearing away from bone. He punched the Nephilim again and again to no effect. Spinning, Conrad charged and slammed the creature against the passage wall with every bit of his strength. Pinning him in place, Conrad pressed his hand to the creature's head and dug his thumb into its black eye. He felt the membrane burst, and the eye spewed a brown, gelatinous substance down the Nephilim's face.

Finally, the creature shrieked and released. Kicking Conrad away, the Nephilim slapped its hands over the damaged eye and crumbled to the floor.

Conrad searched the passage quickly and spotted his discarded scythe. Holding his injured limb to his body, he dove over the writhing creature and snatched the silver weapon with his remaining good hand. Rolling and spinning, the Wraith came up to his feet and charged.

Broadsiding the Nephilim, Conrad knocked it back and swung his scythe. Lodging it in the creature's shoulder, the Wraith twisted and felt bone shatter and muscle pop. Kicking the Nephilim in the chest, Conrad ripped his weapon free, spun it in his hand, and drew it quickly across his body. The blade sliced cleanly through the Nephilim's throat. Sputtering and clenching its bloody neck, the creature crumbled to the floor.

With a sigh, Conrad deactivated his weapon and watched the Nephilim writhe, trying to draw breath. A hiss of air expelling from the neck wound, the creature jerked and finally fell still.

Conrad turned to the passage leading into the hive. Leaning over, he could see Stark lying motionless on the floor far below.

Behind him, the Nephilim moved.

Chapter Twenty-Six

Kat and Metatron stared at the apparently dead werewolf that had fallen from the ceiling, not noticing the two men walk casually into the hive.

"Metatron! Good to see you!"

Metatron lifted his head and instantly recognized both. To see them together was strange, but in this setting it was just weird. Each was dressed in a perfectly tailored black suit, one with a blood-red tie, the other, midnight blue. The archangel stood, hiding his damaged hand.

Lucifer adjusted his suit and extended his hand. "How long has it been? Millennia?"

Metatron refused to shake the Devil's hand. Turning to the other man, he wanted to drop to his knees and beg for forgiveness, but he didn't. "Michael," The Voice finally said with a nod.

Michael returned the nod, his face stoic.

Lucifer looked at his outstretched hand, shrugged and let it fall to his side. "Wow." Glancing around the hive at the corpses of angels, the Devil smiled. "Somebody had fun."

Metatron started to retort, but one glance from Michael silenced him.

"What did you think you were doing, Metatron?" Michael asked softly.

The Voice, for the first time in its entire existence, had no words.

"When was the last time you spoke with Him?" Michael asked. "Or more importantly, for Him?"

Metatron looked from Michael to Lucifer, and

then to Kat. He suddenly felt like a child who was being disciplined. He pulled back his hood, revealing his perfect angelic features, and curly brown hair. Looking up at Michael with his beautiful blue eyes, a tear rolled down the archangel's cheek. "It has been so long." He sighed. "We came first. We should be loved best, not the talking monkeys."

"Now you're singing my song." Lucifer laughed and started to dance playfully over the corpses about his feet.

"You," Michael continued, trying to ignore the Devil, "of all people, should know better. You fought at my side during the first War of Heaven. You saw what jealousy did to the mighty."

"Hey," Lucifer barked, "I rule a whole dimension now. Not that big of a demotion in my opinion."

Michael shot Lucifer a quick, angry glare.

Standing behind Metatron, Lucifer flipped Michael the bird before placing his hands on the archangel's shoulders. Lifting his hand, Lucifer started to run his fingers playfully through Metatron's hair.

"What's going to happen?" Kat asked.

Michael stared at her. "Ah, the half-breed. And where is your bouncing, baby boy?"

"Half-breed?" Kat said spitefully.

"She belongs to me," Lucifer hissed possessively.

Michael rolled his eyes, as though listening to an overexuberant little brother, and adjusted the expensive leather trench that hung off his shoulders hiding his wings. "The world is about to end," he said, finally answering Kat's question. "Father is wiping the slate clean and starting again because of Metatron's interference."

"What?" Kat stood and faced down the archangel. "One angel goes rogue, and the whole Earth is destroyed?"

"This one rogue angel," Michael shifted his eyes to Metatron, "has manipulated the evolution of three species over the course of thousands of years, and forever changed the natural order of things."

Kat sucked in a forced breath out of shock. "Well, when you put it that way." She paused and turned to Lucifer. "And what does 'she belongs to me' mean?"

Lucifer only smiled devilishly.

Michael opened his leather trench exposing the sword hanging at his side. Wrapping his hand around the beautifully ornamented gold hilt, he drew the weapon and pointed the blade at Metatron's throat.

"We vowed to no longer interfere, but you willingly disregarded our diktat. You have been judged by the Creator of All Things, and His indictment is," the archangel paused, considering his dear friend he had known since the beginning of time, "expulsion."

Metatron fell forward with a gasp, while the Devil laughed at the top of his lungs.

"Will you go willingly," Michael asked, "or no?" He held his sword at the ready.

Metatron considered his actions, and understood the judgment. All things considered, it seemed fair and just to him. The Creator had the power to erase him completely from existence. To allow him to live showed His love and compassion for all things, even jealous angels. He lifted his beautiful face to Michael and smiled. "I will go."

Michael returned the smile. "It was good to see you again. I'm sorry it had to end this way."

"I'm not," Metatron said softly. "If it is any consolation, I do regret my actions. Thank Father for me, will you?"

Sheathing his sword, Michael nodded. He shifted his attention to the Devil. "He's all yours." Turning, he started to walk out of the hive, but stopped. The archangel glanced over his shoulder. "Oh, and, Luc?"

The nickname sounded like fingernails on a chalkboard to the Devil. "What?" he asked through gritted teeth.

"Stay out of trouble," Michael said, then laughed and vanished.

"Does anyone else think he's a pompous jerk?" the Devil asked to everyone, and no one. He looked up and smiled. "Ah, the final player in our little production has arrived."

Walking slowly into the hive, carefully avoiding the corpses, Saint had her eyes locked on Metatron, Lucifer, and Kat. She held the Spear at the ready.

"Good to see you again, Saint!" The Devil waved exuberantly.

Saint stopped well short of the two angels, and stared warily at the Devil. "Looks like I missed the party."

"Oh no." The Devil laughed and pointed up to the ceiling. "You're just in time!"

Saint snapped her head up to the passage directly overhead. She could see the shadows of two figures wrestling just beyond the opening.

"Have fun with your new toy, and new friend," Lucifer said knowingly. "Remember to share."

Turning back at the strange comment, she found the Devil and Metatron gone. Saint quickly rushed to Kat's side and dropped to her knees. "I'm so sorry I lost you," she breathed. "Are you okay?"

Kat nodded.

Saint looked down at Kat's stomach expectantly, then saw the dried blood on her legs. "And the baby? Where's your baby?"

Lifting her hand, Kat pointed to the ceiling the way the Devil just had as tears fell from her eyes and rolled down her cheeks. "You're about to meet him."

Again she looked up at the passageway, but this time Saint saw a dark gray creature and another person screaming toward her.

Chapter Twenty-Seven

"There was a story circulating among the help a few days ago of an angel sighting right here in the palace," the doctor said as he walked. "Of course, at the time, I completely dismissed it, but now I wish I hadn't."

Ben followed the doctor closely through the massive palace hallways briskly. He wasn't entirely sure what to make of the doctor yet, but he had to get to Saint...anyway he could. "What does the sighting have to do with anything?"

"There wasn't always a big hole in the center of the palace," the doctor reasoned, "but the angels still had to get in and out, right?"

"Makes sense," Ben followed.

"So maybe the servants really did see an angel," he concluded. His sneakers squeaking on the marble floors, the doctor slowed to a stop. "It was around here."

Just north of the Schatzkammer, the two stood in a huge hallway decorated with massive paintings that stretched toward the arched ceiling. Columns, part of the Roman design, were spaced evenly through the hall. They waited, hoping the answer, and the entrance, would present itself.

Ben scanned over the paintings. They seemed especially gothic, but not out of the ordinary. The architecture appeared intact, as nothing was broken or appeared damaged. "I don't get it. What am I looking for?"

"If we knew that," the doctor replied, "we

wouldn't be searching. See if you can find something out of the ordinary," he paused, "besides yourself."

Ben shrugged off the dig at his preternatural heritage, but then realized the doctor had given him the answer. Ben wasn't ordinary. He could sense, see, and smell things normal humans could not with his heightened werewolf senses.

Stepping into the middle of the hall, Ben closed his eyes and let go. Sniffing the air, he focused and tried to separate the myriad smells of the palace. He knew what angels smelled like, but his nose was being overpowered. There had been an angel here, but he could tell little more. Clearing his nose with a quick breath, he instead focused his ears. Listening to the tiny sounds of life, Ben heard how they impacted and changed the sonic palette of the hall. The high ceilings and marble caused massive reverberations in this place, but there was a dead spot on the right side of the hall. Ben cocked his head slightly and snapped his fingers. He listened to the click echo off the walls, but die oddly to his right. Ben turned. It wasn't the paintings, because they were on both sides...

He opened his eyes and marched straight forward. Stopping before the wall, he lifted his hands and pressed his fingertips gently to it. He couldn't detect any seams, but there was definitely a void behind the section of wall. Licking his lips, the wolf took a deep whiff. It smelled of angels. "It's here."

The doctor turned and looked at Ben curiously. "How do you know?"

310

"I just do," Ben answered without taking his eyes off the wall. "Does it look like it opens?"

The doctor adjusted his glasses and inspected the wall. "It doesn't appear to."

"Okay," Ben breathed, "we'll have to do this the hard way. Stand back." Backing away from the wall, Ben pressed himself against the opposite side.

"What are you doing?"

Ben only grinned.

Throwing his head back, he howled and ripped free of his flesh. His body popped, contorted, and transfigured itself. Leaning forward into a three-point stance, Ben snarled and gnashed his massive fangs. As his eyes snapped to red, the werewolf snorted like a bull preparing to charge. Launching like a rocket, Ben careened across the hallway, dropped his shoulder, and hit the section of wall at full force. The section imploded beneath the power of the wolf, sending him skittering down a blue-lit passage into the hive.

***

Grabbing Kat, Saint dove forward just missing the Nephilim as it slammed to the floor. Rolling over the corpses of dead angels, Saint tumbled to her feet and lifted her scythe. Quickly checking to see that the Lance of Destiny was still held tightly in place, she targeted the gray creature and dropped into a defensive pose.

Then her mouth fell agape.

Beneath the Nephilim's feet, his arm mutilated as though by a wild animal, and blood spilling from his mouth, was Conrad. The High Wraith brought his eyes up and saw Saint and Kat. He did his best

311

to draw breath. "Run."

But she would not. Saint looked at the Lance, and then to Conrad. All she had to do was slay the Nephilim, then bring Conrad back to life. Easy, right?

Saint looked at the Nephilim. It was a grotesque beast, made all the worse by the black blood that spilled from numerous wounds on its body. One of its black eyes was punctured, leaving a dark brown trail of sludge down its face. Its jagged, shark teeth were stained blood-red, and its right arm hung limp at its side, the wound in its shoulder clearly visible.

She knew in that moment Conrad had fought hard, but it hadn't been enough. She felt a tremor of self-doubt. If one of the best warriors in the Order had fallen to this creature, what chance did she have?

Saint looked over her shoulder at Kat. "That came out of you?"

Kat nodded. "That's my boy."

Saint looked back to the Nephilim and drew a breath in. "Are you sure?"

The Nephilim charged.

Saint jabbed with the Lance, but the Nephilim dodged the clumsy attack and launched straight into her body. Knocking her to the ground amidst the corpses, the newborn threw its head back, opened its horrific mouth, and dove forward. Saint shrieked as the Nephilim's teeth sliced into her chest, just below her collarbone. After bringing her scythe up, she slammed it hard into the Nephilim's throat as a font of blood erupted from her chest.

The newborn reared back again, gagging and

clasping its throat. Kicking it hard in the stomach, she knocked the Nephilim off of her and rolled to her feet. Saint jabbed the Lance down hard, but the newborn rolled out of the way. Throwing its arm around the shaft, the Nephilim ripped the weapon from Saint's hands and sneered.

Lurching up, the Nephilim brought its claws across Saint's midsection, tearing open her flesh. Stumbling back, Saint yelped as the creature's claws ripped across her face. Warm blood spilled into her eye, partially blinding her. Luckily dodging the Nephilim's next attack, Saint threw several quick jabs into the newborn's midsection. Pushing forward, she dropped below the creature's next swing, and came straight up with her fist, connecting hard with its chin.

Watching chunks of teeth fly from the Nephilim's mouth, Saint grabbed a handful of the creature's black hair and delivered the most vicious head butt she could. Stars sparkled before her eyes, but she felt the Nephilim's skull crack. Letting go, she shifted her feet quickly and threw all her force into a right hook that snapped the Nephilim's head back. The newborn stumbled back and collapsed over an angel's corpse.

"Saint!"

She turned to see Kat holding her scythe.

Kat tossed the weapon to the Wraith, her gold eyes flashing. "Kill that thing."

Saint caught the weapon, nodded, and turned—

To find the Nephilim, mere inches away, sneering horribly.

There was no time to react.

313

Gagging, Saint felt blood well up her throat and dribble over her lips. Dropping the Lance, she looked down to find the Nephilim's hand buried to the wrist in her chest. Pain radiated out in all directions, and consumed her mind. As the Nephilim ripped its hand free, she gasped and crumbled to the floor. Lifting her hands to the wound, she felt warm blood spill like water down her chest. She knew she was about to die.

The Nephilim smiled, lifted its clawed hand and prepared the deathblow.

"No!" Kat screamed, rushing to Saint's side.

Dropping down next to her protector and friend, she wrapped her arms around Saint. "Don't do this," she pleaded with her offspring.

To Kat's amazement, the Nephilim stopped and looked at her with a spark of recognition. Its expression softened and it slowly lowered its hand.

"That's good," Kat said softly, cradling Saint. "You don't have to do this."

The Nephilim cocked its head trying to comprehend. Squatting down, it bobbed anxiously.

Saint moaned, holding her hands over the wound. "The Lance," she whispered, "use the Lance."

Kat, trying to soothe her friend, brushed Saint's hair back softly. Her eyes fell on Saint's scythe and the battered spearhead at the tip. She turned her attention back to the Nephilim. Even though she felt a maternal connection to the creature, she knew it couldn't be allowed to survive. This both saddened and angered her. Hoping this child would be her living memory of Thomas, it had instead been

314

perverted into something truly horrible.

She just missed Thomas so much...

Lifting her eyes to the Nephilim, she saw a dark figure standing near the newborn. Her heart pounded loudly in her ears, and she refused to blink in case she was hallucinating. It wasn't possible. He was dead, right?

It was him...she knew it. He was every bit as she remembered him from a year ago, and just as breathtaking. He looked powerful, but sadness sat deeply on his face. She couldn't shake the feeling she was looking at a ghost.

"Thomas," Kat breathed as tears streamed down her face.

"Kat," Thomas said softly.

The Nephilim spun and faced Thomas. Screeching angrily, it threw out its arms and opened its talons.

"No!" Kat shouted at her child. "Stop it!"

Thomas held up a hand to Kat and patted the air.

Starting to circle, the Nephilim shrieked again. It locked its eyes on Thomas and prepared to attack.

Scooting from behind Saint, Kat stood. She looked from the dead werewolf to Conrad, and then to Saint. This was it...the end of all things. Grabbing Saint's scythe from the floor, she knew what she had to do.

"Get ready!" she shouted to Thomas.

"I can't do this," Thomas argued. "I just found you again."

"No choice." Kat tossed the weapon to Thomas, and lunged for the Nephilim. Wrapping her arms around its torso, she held it with all of her preternatural strength. "Now!"

Dropping the scythe down like a lance, Thomas charged toward his child. The tip of the Lance of Destiny sliced cleanly into the Nephilim's chest, and straight through. Thomas held his position, keeping the Lance lodged inside the newborn.

The Nephilim screamed at the top of its lungs as its flesh darkened, and began caving in around the wound. Dropping to its knees, the creature writhed in agony. Dark veins ripped up its body and burst open, as its skin cracked, peeled, and flaked away. Its good eye sank back into its skull, leaving only a horrid opening. Blue flame engulfed the Nephilim, charring its flesh.

But Thomas realized, too late, that the fire wasn't emanating from the Nephilim. He let go of the Lance as his heart sank. "No..."

Pushing the dying Nephilim out of the way, he saw Kat's body turn ashen gray as she burned. He saw a dark, bloody spot on her chest. The Lance had gone all the way through the Nephilim and into her.

She smiled softly as if to say, It's okay.

Thomas wouldn't lose her again.

"I love you," he whispered.

Dropping to his knees, Thomas wrapped his arms around Kat and the fire immediately spread to his body. Understanding, Kat returned the embrace and buried her face in her lover's chest. Embers from their flesh flitted up around the two as they held each other. They both knew where they were going, but it didn't matter. Everything that mattered was right here, right now, in each other's arms.

316

For right now, they had each other until the stars grew cold.

Chapter Twenty-Eight

Saint watched the two lovers disintegrate in unholy blue flame. Embers flitted up as the ashes crackled and popped. As the fire slowly died, Saint was saddened to see her two friends gone, but relieved to be released from her burden.

Rolling forward, the Wraith cringed as pain shot up her body. She let her head fall to the floor and took a breath. She could feel blood gurgling in her lungs with each breath, her heart weakening with every beat. Lifting up, she crawled through the ashes and embers toward the writhing newborn. She used every ounce of her remaining willpower to pull herself up. Her face throbbed, blood had completely covered her eye, blinding her, and her chest was a throbbing mass of pain.

Lifting on top of the Nephilim, she straddled it and wrapped her hands around her scythe. The familiar buzz of the Lance raced up her arms and collected in her chest. She started to feel better.

Saint looked down at the creature. Kat and Thomas had started this, it was time to finish it.

The newborn's flesh around the Lance was black and decayed as it died. Ripping her scythe free of the Nephilim, she stared at the creature's bloody face. This was what she had given up her status in the Order for? This was what she had been on the run protecting for the past year? Anger swelled in her brain. She had given up so much, only to find that she, like everyone else connected with the Nephilim, had been used. It stretched all the way back to the creator, Gwyn ap Nudd. She understood in that moment that the entire Gwyliad Wriaeth had been created to bring about the Nephilim.

It was all a lie.

The Nephilim turned to face her and whimpered.

Saint had no mercy for the creature. As she stood, she dropped her curved blade next to the Nephilim's throat, and yanked. Its body jerked and seized, but quickly stopped when its head rolled free.

It was over.

Deactivating her scythe, Saint pulled the Lance free and held it in her hand. Little by little, she felt better.

Sliding the scythe hilt into her pocket, Saint walked carefully through the corpses and dropped down next to Conrad. The Nephilim left a massive, bloody bite wound in the High Wraith's back. Rolling him over, Saint pressed her fingertips to his throat. There was a pulse, but it was barely detectable. Laying the Holy Lance on his chest, she held her hand over it and waited.

Saint had known this man since she was a child, but had only truly learned who he was since the destruction of the Academy. Conrad Verge was what every Wraith should aspire to be: strong, courageous, vigilant, and proud of who and what he was. She often wished she possessed his strength, and clarity of thought. It seemed that, no matter the situation, Conrad knew the correct course of action. He was powerful, utterly brilliant, and a hero in every sense of the word.

She truly admired him.

Conrad's eyes fluttered then he slowly opened them. They seemed glazed and distant for a moment, but they suddenly dilated and he shot up. "Kat!"

Saint patted her friend on the shoulder. "It's okay, Conrad," she soothed, "It's over now."

The High Wraith leaned forward with a groan. He pressed his hand to his forehead. "I feel like I've been hit by a bulldozer." He breathed out slowly. "What happened?"

"Thomas and Kat gave their lives to stop the Nephilim," Saint answered quietly, her eyes watching the ashes that flitted over the hive.

"Thomas?" Conrad asked, as a deep sadness overtook him. He remembered fighting with his former student and friend, and the venomous hatred Thomas spewed at him.

"He died a hero," Saint said, seeing the turmoil on Conrad's face. She could have elaborated, but there was no need. Those four words were far better than any lengthy explanation ever could be. "How are you feeling?"

Conrad nodded. "Okay, thanks. What did you do?"

Saint held up the Holy Lance for a moment then replaced it on Conrad's leg. "Believe in the power of miracles."

To his amazement, Conrad watched the scratches on Saint's face healing before his eyes. And that was all he needed to know. "Thank you, Emily."

Saint nodded.

Conrad's eyes swept slowly over the hive, but stopped on a familiar dark form. Crawling quickly, the Wraith placed his hands on the wolf's head. "He's still in werewolf form," Conrad muttered positively.

Against his better judgment, he leaned forward and pressed his head to Stark's side. There nothing more dangerous than a wounded werewolf. Known to attack wildly out of pain, Conrad was risking his life. He closed his eyes and listened and found the rhythmic beat of the wolf's heart. Stark's breath was slow and labored. The wolf was barely holding on.

"Does that thing work on werewolves?" Conrad asked Saint.

"It did once," she acknowledged. Tossing the Lance to Conrad, Saint smiled. "It healed Ben."

Conrad snatched the Lance out of the air and nodded. Turning, the High Wraith pressed it gently to the wolf's side. "Wake up, Stark," he breathed.

The wolf whimpered, and Conrad felt his heart race. The thick, black hair started to fall away revealing human flesh beneath. As the wolf's eyes shifted from red back to brown, Stark moaned. "I feel like I've been run over by a bus."

"I thought it was more like a bulldozer," Conrad commented.

Stark turned his head and looked at Conrad. "Why didn't you let me go?"

"You would rather I'd let you die?" Conrad shook his head and extended his hand to Stark. "You don't get off that easy. We still have work to do."

Stark hesitated, but grabbed Conrad's hand. Sitting up, he nodded at the High Wraith. "Thank you."

"We're even now," Conrad added.

"Like hell," Stark barked. "I've saved your butt three times now!"

"Yes," Conrad agreed, "but I just brought you back from the brink of death. I think that's a triple word score."

Saint snickered. Her eyes lifted to see a familiar form walking tentatively into the hive. She took a step toward the figure, and then her pace quickened. She slowed for a moment, unsure if she would be rebuked or not. Saint thought of Kat and Thomas holding each other in death, and her fear didn't matter anymore. Racing as fast her legs would carry her, Saint charged. Leaping forward, she threw herself into his arms. "Ben."

Ben struggled for a moment to keep his balance, but wrapped his arms around Saint. "What are you—?"

"Shut up," Saint ordered and pressed her hand gently to his face. Lifting up, she pressed her lips to his and kissed him passionately. To her delight, he returned the gesture. After a moment, she pulled away and pressed her forehead to his. "Ben," she breathed, "I don't want to waste another moment of my life."

Ben closed his eyes and smiled. He had been waiting to hear that for a long, long time. Lifting his hand, he caressed Saint's cheek.

She kissed him again, and then looked into his

big, beautiful, soulful eyes. "What took you so long?"

"I had to find a way in," Ben protested. "I didn't have the holy hand grenade like you did."

Saint laughed as she hadn't in a long time. It felt good. Her hand slipped into his and they laced their fingers together. There was something perfect and calming about that simple gesture. She lifted her eyes to his. "There's another way in?"

Ben nodded. "I can show you the way."

Smiling, Saint turned to find Stark and Conrad standing behind them with cheesy grins on their faces. Their expression said everything without uttering a word. "All right, knock it off, you two." Saint laughed again.

Ben nodded stoically to Stark, and then to Conrad.

Stark returned the gesture of respect.

"Let's get out of here," Saint said after a moment.

Conrad put his arm around Saint. "That's the best idea I've heard in days."

Chapter Twenty-Nine

Walking out of the palace, the four looked at the majestic red and orange sunrise painted across the eastern sky. They stood in silence for a long time, simply watching the sun lift beyond the horizon, enjoying the beauty of it all. It wasn't the first sunrise any of them had seen, but they couldn't recall another before it. It was a new world...for all of them. The deceit had been washed away, leaving them cleansed and free, some of the four for the first time.

As the sun rose high into the blue sky, the four sat on the palace stairs as Saint recounted her meeting with Lucifer. She explained the truth behind the creation of the Prophecy, the Order, Thomas and Kat's relationship, and Metatron's involvement. Each listened, understanding how one man's nefarious plan of jealousy had in some way affected them all. A melancholy silence fell over the four as they processed the truth.

"I've been living a lie," Conrad blurted out.

"We all have," Saint countered, "but that doesn't make what we fought for any less valid. Yes, Metatron manipulated the Order, and the prophecy, but we were still doing the right thing. We were still fighting for those who couldn't."

Conrad nodded, but her words didn't soothe him as much as he would have liked. He could see the ripples of Metatron's jealousy in every corner of his life.

"How do you think the Chancellor will react to

this?" Saint asked.

"Chancellor Alexander," Conrad paused uncomfortably, "is dead."

Saint's eyes widened in shock.

"He was killed when the angels attacked the Academy," Conrad lied, then shot Stark a knowing glance. "There was nothing we could do."

"So the Order is gone," Saint said quietly.

"No," Conrad disagreed, "you said it yourself. We were always fighting for the right thing, despite why or how the Order was actually created." He put his hand on Saint's shoulder. "We just have to find a way to move forward." He turned and looked at Stark. "We all do."

"At least it stopped raining," Ben remarked finally.

The four fell into an awkward silence again. It was over, but they had all been affected so significantly by the manipulation that it felt as though a piece of each was missing.

"What now?" Saint asked the question on all of their minds.

Conrad took a long breath then looked at Saint. "Rebuild the Order. We can learn from our past. We may have been a mistake, but this is our chance to wipe the slate clean of the old and begin again." It seemed strange to say that now, especially after having fought to uphold the old ways, but he knew it was the only way the Order would survive.

"Find any remnant members of our clan," Stark said in turn. "They have to be out there, somewhere."

Saint slipped her arm around Ben's waist. "I

think Ben and I are going to take a vacation."

"Really?" Ben asked, unaware of any plans.

"I'd like to explore America," Saint continued, "and Ben." She laughed, her blue eyes sparkling in the morning light. "I mean, if that's okay with you?"

"I'm in!" Ben smiled and hugged Saint. He turned and looked to his clansman and extended his hand. "I know I left the clan, but we still have each other, Stark. You're not alone."

Stark shook Ben's hand with a smile. "Thank you. That means a lot."

Ben considered Stark for a moment. This wasn't the werewolf he knew from before. Stark was a changed man. Ben was proud of him.

"Listen," Conrad said slowly to Stark, "you can come with me, if you want. I could use the help."

"Rebuild the Order?" Stark scoffed. "Okay."

Conrad smiled, laughed, and patted Stark on the back. "Good man."

"Come on," Saint breathed, "let's go home."

Turning, the four heroes walked into the sunrise, leaving the angels, and the past, to the silence.

And this was how it was at the beginning of all things.

THE END

www.ingramcontent.com/pod-product-compliance
Lightning Source LLC
Chambersburg PA
CBHW010830250626
47157CB00010B/3234